A Mother Abducted . . .
and Accused

She felt panic. "Please. Why do you hate me so? If I'm Katy's mother, then I'm part of her, so I can't possibly be all bad."

Giving her shoulder a push, he headed Margot toward and down the stairs. "A mother who would beat her own child is always first to ask why people say she's not a good mother."

"Beat her?" Margot had reached the basement floor and felt the chill from the concrete walls. "I don't beat her. Never! Honestly, I—"

"Shut up."

He pushed aside an old metal storage locker to reveal a heavy steel door. He turned a key in the lock and pushed the door open. Striking like a snake, he grasped her wrist. In one quick movement, he shoved Margot into a black space.

She screamed, but the door shut in her face, leaving her in total darkness . . .

NO HARM INTENDED

GLORIA DYAL

DIAMOND BOOKS, NEW YORK

This book is dedicated with love to my family: Jim, Jeffrey, and Jimmy; my mother, Marjorie Bolin; and most especially to the memory of my father, Roy Bolin.

Special thanks go to my editor, Melinda Metz, for her insight and sensitivity, and to my agent, Henry Dunow, for his faith and unfailing good counsel.

This book is a Diamond original edition,
and has never been previously published.

NO HARM INTENDED

A Diamond Book / published by arrangement with
the author

PRINTING HISTORY
Diamond edition / July 1992

ISBN: 1-55773-737-1

Diamond Books are published by The Berkley Publishing Group,
200 Madison Avenue, New York, New York 10016.
The name ''DIAMOND'' and its logo are trademarks
belonging to Charter Communications, Inc.

PRINTED IN THE UNITED STATES OF AMERICA

10 9 8 7 6 5 4 3 2 1

It is a wise father that knows his own child.
—WILLIAM SHAKESPEARE,
The Merchant of Venice

1 . . .

THE MUSIC WAS really loud. That's the way she liked it, Katy thought, smiling. But mostly Katy was happy because Mama trusted her—trusted her to ride on the merry-go-round alone, to show how grown up she was.

The metal pole had become warm and a little slippery. "Hold on every minute. Don't let go. And sit up straight," Mama had said. So Katy clutched the merry-go-round horse's pole tightly, enjoying the loud music, the hard, warm wood of the horse she rode and the sugar-sweet scent of the air that brushed her cheek. She wore her favorite blouse—the one with the yellow giraffe with a yellow yarn mane. And on her feet, tucked firmly into the stirrups, she wore her best white shoes. Mama had told her she could not wear them to the carnival, but when Katy said, "They're almost too tight and I haven't weared them out yet," Mama had smiled and answered, "You've got a good point there, honey." Katy just loved it when Mama treated her like a grown-up.

The only thing that spoiled the perfect ride was the little boy who sat atop the horse next to Katy's. He cried and cried even though his mother was standing right next to him holding him around the waist. Katy looked at him with five-and-a-half-year-old disdain. He looked pretty big to be such a crybaby. But she couldn't help feeling a little sorry for him. "He could sit on my horse with me if he's afraid," called Katy to the boy's mother. After all, she reasoned, it wasn't really his fault if he was scared. The woman smiled, but shook her head no.

The merry-go-round began to slow; Katy's horse hardly

moved at all. When it stopped completely, it was in the highest position. Katy blinked as bright sunlight streamed through the carousel's woven canopy. She squinted her eyes. "Here, I'll help you down," said a man who'd been standing nearby. He must be the father of one of these other kids, she thought, as she placed her hand in his.

"Thank you for helping me," she said in a whisper. "I don't want Mama to think I can't get off by myself."

"I know exactly what you mean," he answered, still holding her hand as they walked across the shaky wooden floor of the merry-go-round. His hand felt hard, like dried-out wood. Katy caught a glimpse of her mother's face in the crowd near the exit. But there were so many people getting off that Mama disappeared from sight.

As she walked, Katy realized that she had lost her shoe. She started to turn back toward the horse, but the man yanked her in the opposite direction.

"Hey," she said, angry at his rough treatment. "You let go!"

The man leaned over and spoke loudly, directly into Katy's face. "I told you, that was your last ride. And I meant it." His eyebrows were pulled down and he looked angry. His words didn't make any sense.

Suddenly she felt fear. All the dangers she had ever been warned about seemed to spin around in her head, like that house in *The Wizard of Oz*. She had done it. She'd talked to a stranger! She'd let the stranger touch her! With a rush of shame and terror, Katy felt herself wet her pants. "Mama," she cried weakly.

Then Katy remembered what her mother had always told her. "If you can't find me, just holler. Don't worry about bothering anyone. Just call out 'Mama' as loud as you can."

"Mama," she shouted. She yanked her arm, freeing her hand. "Mama!" Katy pushed against the people who filled the area between her and the place where she'd last seen her mother, all the while yelling "Mama."

Then pain suddenly quieted her. She felt fingers like sharp sticks digging into her shoulders. Tears blurred her vision.

Katy felt herself twisted around and pulled roughly away from the crowd—away from her mother.

Again, she began to wail, but not quite so loud, as fear threatened to close her throat. "Mama, Mama—"

They were passing near the carnival man who took the tickets. Katy looked up at him, hoping he had some power to help. "Please, mister, help me. My mama is waiting—"

Katy's words were squashed from her along with her breath as the man picked her up and squeezed too tight. They could not move for a minute as people poured out of a sideshow nearby. "Look what you did," grumbled her captor, holding out a damp hand. "It's all that lemonade. I told you—"

The carnival man had started letting more people onto the ride, but he stepped aside to let the man holding Katy pass through. He smiled at Katy and said, "Don't you worry, little miss. It happens to everybody sometimes." And to the man he said, "There's a john down past the Tilt-a-Whirl if you want to try to clean her up."

With that, something snapped inside Katy. The carnival man didn't understand. He wasn't going to help her. "MAMA!" she screamed. She twisted in the man's arms, punching with her fists and kicking. She felt the edge of the fence that surrounded the merry-go-round, and she hooked one arm over the top of it. She felt a tug, then a tear, as the yarn mane of her giraffe blouse caught on something, then tore away.

The man's bony fingers hurt her as he carried Katy even farther from the place where her mother had been and down the congested path, then out to the parking lot, where he pushed her into the back seat of a car and squashed a bad-smelling cloth over her face so that she could hardly breathe. As the world went to gray, then black, Katy wondered why no one had tried to help her. Why had so many people just smiled at her in that funny way grown-ups often smiled when some kid was acting bad?

2...

AS THE MERRY-GO-ROUND began to slow down, Margot stood near the exit from the ride. Even if Katy had been frightened by being on the horse alone, Margot knew her daughter would never admit it. The child's hold on her independence had been deliberate and tenacious since the day she was born. Even as a toddler, she hadn't just babbled the random "no's" of the terrible two's. She had gone along quietly with all the house rules until she got fed up and decided that her independence was threatened beyond reason. Then she'd stomp her foot, sit down and practice an infuriating toddler version of the sit-down strike.

Occasionally, as the old carousel wheezed along its circular path, Margot caught a glimpse of her daughter. But each time, her view was sharply cut off by a man who stood near Katy. He gazed down fondly at a child on the bench in front of him, a tiny toddler who sat with her mother. The man looked familiar—maybe one of the parents of a child in Katy's preschool, Margot thought. The scene was precious, reminding Margot of herself, riding on a bench hugging Katy just a few short years ago. Katy was three or three-and-a-half before she mustered the courage to mount one of the immense horses. To a child so small, the carved and painted beasts must have looked like mountains with scary faces.

Again, the merry-go-round brought Katy into view, then she was instantly erased by the tall man. He didn't really look like anyone she knew, Margot decided. He was just another redhead. She always noticed carrot-tops because of Katy's sunshine red mop of hair.

Margot slapped at a fly that buzzed around her ear. She wished that she and Katy could have come on a weekday when it wasn't such a mob scene. But this Saturday was her only chance to bring Katy to the carnival. Margot had been tied up all week at the station with her talk show and had worked late nearly every night. And the little traveling carnival by Station Square would be perched on the edge of the Allegheny only for the rest of the day. There was no telling if there would be another carnival through before the summer ended. Already the nights were getting cooler and the sun was setting earlier as August passed the midpoint. Margot was jostled by one hot, overheated reveler after another.

The merry-go-round halted, and Margot watched the motley crew of sweaty children and parents climbing off the worn wooden platform. Feeling just a tinge of worry, Margot scanned the group. Katy must be at the back of the bunch, she thought. Already, there was a frenzied scramble of people from the other side of the circle as new riders began to hurry around, looking for the best horses, the best seats for the adult chaperons. ''Katy,'' called Margot, aware of a hint of panic in her voice.

''Mama,'' she heard in reply. Yes, Katy had answered her. But her voice sounded far away, muffled. And scared. *Idiot*, Margot thought—what an imagination. Forcing herself to appear calm, Margot climbed onto the jouncing platform of the merry-go-round. A small boy ran full speed into the side of her leg. ''Hey, move,'' said the little barbarian as he shoved Margot rudely aside.

Margot looked around, trying to find Katy among the people scrambling on or off the carousel.

Katy was not there! No!

All the former passengers had gotten off the ride. The music was grinding slowly into life and the platform began to move. The pole Margot grasped rose slowly up. "Katy," she shouted. A tall fat man standing next to her glared down at her and pointedly rubbed his ear as if she'd deafened him. "Katy!" she cried even louder.

"Jeez," grumbled the man as he stepped away from Margot. The platform was picking up speed, the music blaring from the speaker just above Margot's ear. She looked around wildly. Katy wasn't there. Her heart kicked in her chest. She jumped off the merry-go-round, twisted sideways, and fell to her knees in the gravel.

Margot felt a hand under her arm and allowed a man to help her up. "Are you okay?" he asked.

"Please, my daughter, Katy. She was on the merry-go-round." She paused, frowning, then said, "Her giraffe blouse. That's it." She could see the man's confusion and tried again.

"I can't find my daughter. She had a blouse with a giraffe on it. She's only five. Have you seen her?"

"No, ma'am. But you look familiar. You're not that one that's always advertising that new show, are you?"

Something clicked. As if the world had suddenly transformed itself into a movie screen, Margot saw her surroundings with sharp clarity. This man could be of no help. As women have always done, she turned to another mother for assistance. She reached out and touched the arm of a young woman toting a sleeping infant in a denim carrier. "Please, my daughter and I have gotten separated. She's five years old, has straight red hair and she's wearing a yellow blouse with a yarn giraffe on it. Would you help me look?"

"Sure," said the young mother, unconsciously hugging her baby closer to her chest. "What's her name?"

"Katy," said Margot. Then once more she yelled, "Katy, where are you?"

"Mama," came a voice. Margot spun around, but it was some other child speaking.

Plunging into the crowd in the direction of the merry-go-round entrance, still calling Katy's name, Margot focused on two other women, each with a grubby toddler in tow. "Have you seen a lost little girl with a giraffe on her blouse?"

The women looked at each other, then shook their heads no. One said, "We'll keep an eye out for her."

Margot finally worked her way over to the entrance to the merry-go-round. A man stood there taking tickets. "My daughter just got off the merry-go-round, and now I can't find her. Do you have security people here who can help?"

"Hah," replied the gatekeeper with a rueful smile. "We hardly got enough people to watch the rides today, what with this summer flu going around."

"Did you see her get off? She's five years old, has red hair and she's wearing a giraffe blouse."

"No way. This is where you get on. I don't see 'em getting off. You'd need— Wait a minute. Did the little girl's blouse have some kind of string on it?"

"Yes. Exactly. It has a yellow yarn mane. You saw her?" Margot felt a little hope.

"Yeah. Her dad took her out this way. Hate to tell you this, ma'am, but she wet her pants. I guess he musta took her off to the john." He pointed down the midway. "There's a toilet 'bout halfway between here and the parking lot."

Margot stood very still. Her father? It could not be. Since the separation, Katy had needed a great deal of reassurance from her parents, and Joseph had been dependable about remembering to tell Katy whenever he planned to be out of town. He had called a few days ago to tell Katy and Margot that he'd be away for the long weekend doing research.

"Where can I find a policeman?" An icy certainty came over Margot. Katy had been abducted. Katy was no longer at the carnival. Margot could search the grounds all day and night and she wouldn't find her daughter here.

The ticket taker was guiding more children onto the merry-go-round, trying to keep several rowdy kids from trampling the little ones. Margot grasped the carnival worker's shoulders roughly and waited until she'd established firm eye contact.

"The man who took my daughter was *not* her father. Do you understand me? *Not her father!* Her father is out of town. Something is very wrong here. Now, I need your help to find her. I need you to turn this damned merry-go-round off and go find a policeman. Tell him that I'm heading for the parking lot. My daughter's name is Katy, she has red hair, she's five years old and she's wearing a yellow blouse with a giraffe made of yarn on it." For an instant, Margot was aware that if she weren't holding on so tightly to the carnival worker, she would surely fall down. "Now!"

Her tone of voice must have gotten through to him, because the man fiddled with some levers and controls that stopped the merry-go-round.

"I can't just up and leave, ya know." He glanced around, then shouted in the direction of a carnival worker who was making his way down the midway lugging a couple of full garbage bags. "Hey, Bruce, will ya put them bags down and watch this for a minute. We got a 'mergency here."

He turned to Margot and pushed her gently away from the carousel. "You go ahead and look for your little girl, ma'am. I'll see if I can find somebody for you."

Satisfied that something had been set in motion, Margot ran toward the parking lot, pushing people aside as she went. The crowd grew thinner as she neared the lot. She skidded on the gravel; a hot cloud of gray dust fumed up around her feet. She stood still, with no idea of where to look. "Katy, where are you? Katy? Kateee!"

Then Margot listened. Voices, hundreds of them. But the voices were all behind her. There was not a soul to be seen in the lot. "Oh, God, help me," she cried as she ran toward the driveway that led out of the lot. She reached the exit and stood still, wheezing as her breath came painfully from a chest constricted with exertion and cold terror. Gone. Whoever had taken Katy was gone. Long gone.

A pain surprisingly like a labor pain passed through Margot's belly as she turned back toward the carnival, where she saw a policeman coming toward her, with the fat merry-go-round tender hurrying along beside him.

3 . . .

THE MUMBLE AND hum of voices behind her reminded Margot of a cocktail party that wasn't quite getting off the ground. She wasn't sure why the several police officers were in her house, but they all seemed very busy. She huddled in the old loveseat in the front hall, waiting. Waiting for what? Part of her just wanted to believe that the nightmare would stop, that Katy would fly up the dozens of front steps and burst through the front door with a grin on her face.

Margot squeezed her eyes shut and tried to imagine that all of this was a gigantic mistake, that Joseph had indeed taken Katy. Of course, Margot couldn't figure why Joseph might have just *happened* to be at the carnival. Unless he'd spoken with someone who knew Margot's schedule . . .

"Mrs. DesMarais?" A gentle hand touched her shoulder, and Margot abandoned her fruitless guesswork.

"Yes. Sorry, I was just thinking," she said to the detective.

"We've got a definite confirmation from your husband's employer. He has not been to work at his lab today."

"I know that already. He's away working on a research project. I told you—"

"Please, ma'am. I know you can't accept that he might have taken your daughter, but believe me, it happens all the time. A parent never shows much attachment to the kid until the marriage breaks up. Then bingo, they want custody. It's—"

The doorbell rang, and Margot gratefully escaped from the detective's lecture to answer it.

When she opened the door, there, huffing and puffing from the long climb up the front stairs, were her parents. "Darling," said her mother, planting a kiss on Margot's cheek. Her mother's fur held the sweet odor of old perfume and face powder. "What can we say?"

Her father gave her a bear hug, and Margot buried her face in the soft Shetland wool scarf that hung against his lapels. "Honey, how can we help?" he asked, his long face mournful, worry lines permanently set between his eyebrows.

Again feeling that odd sensation that she was at some weird cocktail party, Margot introduced her parents to the detective, then to Mick, her producer, and to Beth, Margot's best friend and the head researcher for her talk show. When Margot phoned them, they both had left their Saturday activities to come to her house. Mick had said that Margot could use part of her show on Tuesday in whatever way she thought best to appeal to the kidnapper or to do anything else she thought might help. Beth had already outlined a plan to do some fast research into patterns in child kidnappings. Thank God for Beth. Margot suspected it was mainly loyalty operating, but Beth had joined Margot in trying to convince the police to search for someone other than Margot's ex-husband.

"Pleased to meet you," said Margot's mother to Mick and Beth. Please, Mama, help me, thought Margot, the plea reverberating in her head, as it had when she was a child. Mama can make it right. And it used to be true. But ever since the day that they had learned the truth about Katy's biological father, Margot's parents, especially her mother, seemed to have turned away from Margot—not completely, just a quarter turn that left them unable to make eye contact, unable to connect.

"You got a minute, Mrs. DesMarais?" asked the detective. Margot nodded, and he led the way into the kitchen.

"Now, you remember what I told you before. If anyone phones, don't worry about how long they stay on or what

they say. We're recording *and* tracing all your calls. This
new technology is great in a case like this.'' As he
completed his instructions, Margot listened carefully.

When the detective was finished, Margot leaned down
and stared at the phone. How many movies had she seen
where the anxious parents waited for the fateful call? And
she'd always sympathized, thinking that kidnapping must
be one of the most unbearable of all the ''don't-have-any-
facts'' situations. And here she was, waiting for a call
herself. And she was the only one who believed there might
be a call coming—the only one who wasn't merely waiting
for a repentant Joseph to show up or phone.

And yet Margot was very surprised to realize that she
wanted Joseph to show up—but not because she suspected
that he'd abducted Katy. After years of depending on each
other in crises, she'd come to trust Joseph, to trust his
judgment. Strange, they'd always been at their best when
the other one needed some kind of critical help.

A crash and the sound of shattering glass broke into
Margot's private thoughts. She turned to see her mother
standing by the kitchen sink, the glass coffee carafe in
smithereens at her feet, and her hands in the air, fingers
spread in horror like a child's.

''Why . . . why I'm so sorry, dear,'' she whispered. ''It
just slipped . . . oh, my, your coffee pot, how horrible . . .''

''No, Mom,'' said Margot, reaching out, but finding
herself unable to move her feet. It had been too many years
since they'd been close, since they'd opened up to each
other. ''It's okay, it's just an old—''

''No dear, it's not okay. I am so sorry.'' She stood there
unable to go on as tears streaked through her face powder.

At last, some hard, sour thing broke in Margot. She
embraced her mother. The two women clung to each other,
murmuring the same words together like a lullaby, ''Oh,
Katy, where, where . . . oh, Katy, where, where—''

Later that evening, after all the friends and relatives,
neighbors and police had cleared out, Margot found herself

alone. As she wandered through the rooms of her first floor, mindlessly gathering dirty cups and the remains of the doughnuts that her neighbor across the street had brought over, the silence was painful. It wasn't really silence, but a drumming inside Margot's head, her pulse loud. The emptiness followed her from room to room, demanding to be filled. But her tired mind offered no help. She couldn't think of a single thing to do to find Katy. There was no one to help, no one to call—simply no one.

Leaving all the lamps burning, Margot climbed the stairs, so weary that she half-pulled herself up by the banister. After switching on all the lights upstairs, Margot found herself sitting on Katy's bed, unaware of how she'd gotten there. Her hands seemed to be operating on their own; they were folding Katy's clothes, the small knit shirts rumpled from being piled together in the laundry basket since early that morning. As she smoothed out a lavender cotton pajama top, Margot recalled Katy's nightmare that had awakened them both in the dark hours before dawn only this morning. "No, no, no. Daddy, Daddy," had been the piercing cry from Katy's room. Margot had hurried in to comfort Katy. In the moonlight, she could see Katy thrashing among her blankets where she'd fallen on the floor. Gently, Margot gathered up her daughter, whispering, "It's okay, honey. Mama's here."

"Daddy was leaving me." She gulped for air. "He said he would never come back. And he took my puppy with him. He was mad at me 'cuz I was so bad. I'm scared, Mama."

"Daddy will always be nearby. And I'll always be here, too. We both love you very much."

"But he was so mad."

"Everybody has bad dreams sometimes, baby. But that's all they are—just dreams. They're not real." As she continued speaking softly, Margot tucked Katy in. Then with a smile, she asked, "And by the way, young lady, since when do you have a puppy?"

Katy smiled sheepishly. After months of pestering, she'd finally gotten a promise from Margot to at least consider getting a puppy. "I guess I have one in my dreams. He was really cute, Mama, just little, and white, and really fat."

"Well, when we go to get a puppy, we'll be sure to look for one that's very fat," said Margot.

Katy had clutched her mother's fingers, her grasp relaxing as her eyes closed and the rest of her body went limp.

Now Margot lay down on Katy's small bed, remembering the feel of her daughter's soft skin and her sweet smell. Margot didn't start to cry until the thought struck her that she'd been right here holding Katy in her arms less than a day ago.

4...

"IT WASN'T HER father, I'm sure of it," she said for what seemed the hundredth time. The police officer was looking directly at Margot, but she suspected that his mind was far away. "It's true we've argued about custody, but he wouldn't do something like this."

"When Doc Haver gets here, maybe he can explain it to you, ma'am. Nobody knows about what somebody else is gonna do until it happens. A kid's a powerful draw, and lots of fathers—and moms, too—just decide to forget about the court and take the kid. They figure they got the right."

Margot shivered. The room in the police station was barren and cold, with air conditioning blasting out from hidden vents. It was less than twenty-four hours since Katy had disappeared. Margot had driven down to the police headquarters in the hope that she could help somehow. All the personnel involved in the investigation seemed hurried and concerned, but they were clearly not thrilled with Margot's theories.

The police officer took out a stick of chewing gum from his pocket. "Gum, ma'am?"

"No, no thanks," said Margot, distracted by the question. "I'm trying to tell you that our situation is different. It's just not the same as most people's." Even as she spoke, Margot realized how lame her words must sound to the detective. He had no way of knowing what she meant by "different."

Margot sighed and tried again. "Even if you were right, Joseph couldn't possibly have taken her. I've told you, he's out of town and has been since Thursday."

"Tell you what," said the officer, pushing his wad of gum into his cheek, "I'll go see if they're having any luck in digging up your ex."

"Please, can't you just go out and question more people at the carnival? I heard Katy scream. Katy screamed. She wouldn't scream if Joseph took her. She loves him. She trusts him. She wouldn't scream. Katy would—" Margot broke off suddenly, hearing her own voice growing more shrill with each word. Hysteria threatened to overcome her as she got up and followed the officer, who had quietly walked away from her. Rage pounded in her temples; he was ignoring her. He plunked some coins into a soda machine, then turned and wordlessly offered her a can of Diet Pepsi.

"Here, now. I can understand your feelings, Mrs. Des-Marais. I got kids of my own." He popped the top of the can and gently led Margot back to her chair.

She gripped the vinyl arms of the chair and bit her tongue. She felt as if she'd entered another dimension. On her show, she'd interviewed people who complained about slow and inaccurate police investigations. She'd thought she understood their frustration, but realized now that she hadn't. This experience fell into that category of things-you-couldn't-understand-unless-you-went-through-them-yourself. It was like the kind of nightmare that wouldn't let go even when you woke up.

Already the police were treating her assertions that Joseph was not the abductor as the ravings of an understandably disturbed woman. They must perceive her as cold and sarcastic, but Margot was afraid that if she let go, if she let the tears flow, they'd be even less inclined to listen to her.

"I just can't spend any more time here doing nothing," Margot said, standing up, gathering her purse and sweater.

"Ma'am, please wait."

"There is no reason for me to stay here."

The officer followed her out of the room and down the

hall, talking, talking, talking, but Margot couldn't listen. She couldn't let him stop her.

She punched the elevator "Down" button and concentrated on the indicator lights that showed its slow progress from the top floor. Just as she was considering using the stairs, a short, gray-haired pug of a man approached her. "Please, Mrs. DesMarais, may I have a word with you. I'm Captain Lewis. Perhaps I can convince you that we're doing everything possible to locate your daughter. It would help if you would stay here and assist us in our investigation."

The elevator doors parted and Margot stepped in. The captain reached inside and held his finger firmly on the "Open Door" button. Margot was vaguely aware that there were several people waiting for the elevator to proceed.

"Look, you're not Barney Miller and I'm not some mindless character actor. My real-life daughter is missing, and you are looking in the wrong place!"

With that, she roughly pushed his finger off the button and pressed the "Close Door" circle. She could see a look of resignation on the captain's face as he stepped back, saying something unintelligible to the other policeman who leaned against a nearby doorjamb.

As she hurried to her car and maneuvered through traffic, she was aware of only two sensations: the painful dryness of her throat and mouth, and the broken-record replay of Katy's small scream.

The police were wrong—they insisted that she'd imagined her child's cry for help, that she'd simply inserted it into the situation. Over and over again they'd said it: "You argued with your ex over custody, ma'am. It was only a week ago that you swore you'd never give her up. He swore he'd take your child from you. He may even have been afraid that *you'd* take Katy out of state. People get desperate; they do surprising things." Their arguments had been endless, like a self-repeating loop, all based on the assumption that Katy had been snatched by her father.

"But why," she'd cried, "would he make it such a public

mess? Why not simply take her away on a day when he had visitation rights? That way, at least he'd have a twenty-four-hour head start.''

''Because, ma'am,'' they answered patiently, as if she were an adolescent or perhaps slightly hard of hearing, ''because lots of guys get this stupid, dramatic idea that if they make it look like a kidnapping, the police won't figure that they got the kid tucked away somewhere, usually with some girl friend who'd do anything for the guy.''

''No! No. I don't know who you're talking about, but you're not talking about Joseph and me. We're separated, but we're not that kind of people.''

They rolled their eyes at that, as if they thought her the ultimate snob on top of being the ultimate idiot.

''If she were nearby, she'd call me. She knows her phone number, and she knows how to dial.''

They just shook their heads.

5...

"PLEASE, DEAR. BE reasonable. The police will bring her back. They've assured me that they've alerted the West Virginia authorities. There isn't anything you can do there."

Margot's father, Gregory Newhouse, looked down at his wife, who was standing like a sentry at the front door. "You're wrong, Emily. I can reach Margot before the authorities do. I can bring her back before they accuse her of abducting her own child. That's what I can do." Impatiently, he pushed his wife aside and was immediately sorry for his harshness. His frustration with this whole business was mounting, and he felt so helpless.

"But how will you find her?" Emily asked.

"She told you she was going to look for that carnival, right? How hard can it be to find a carnival?"

"Greg, dear, please don't go. The police will find her," Emily insisted again.

"That's right. And they'll start questioning her all over again. Even if she's able to convince them that she's just trying to help find Katy, I don't want her to be alone right now."

"But they only suspect Margot *because* she left town," said Emily. She twisted her hands together. "I simply don't understand it; they never told her she couldn't leave town. How absurd to think that our daughter could have abducted Katy—her own child! If they only knew how honest—"

"Slow down, Emily. I don't really think the police believe Margot took Katy. But I also don't think they like it when they lose control of an investigation. They don't want key people wandering away and making inquiries on their own.''

Gregory was checking his wallet to make sure he had his credit cards in case he needed them. He wasn't listening to Emily.

''Please, Gregory,'' said Emily. ''Margot's a grown woman. She—''

''If she'd told me she was going, I could have stopped her, or gone with her, or—''

''She's always been so headstrong and independent. But she'll—''

''Gotta go,'' said Gregory, taking his wife in his arms. She always smelled like flowers to him. ''I'll call you later,'' he said in a softer tone. ''I'll go crazy if I just sit here and do nothing.'' He kissed her cheek, noting its coolness. When Emily was sick, she always had a below-normal temperature. He wondered now if Katy's disappearance would make his wife ill. He hurried out the door, feeling fear for every member of his family beating in his chest. The fear, coupled with a lack of sleep, was causing his blood to crash and roar through his heart like a river undammed. It was only when he reached the expressway and was speeding southwest toward the hills of West Virginia that he felt an easing of the pain around his heart and the pressure at his temples. Absently, he reached into his pocket for his medication and swallowed the pill dry.

Sometimes it's the mother who grabs the kid and hides it. If she's not sure of getting custody, you know, it's one way she sees to make things go her own way.

The words of the police detective drummed in Gregory's ears as he drove. How could they think his daughter would steal her own child? If these people weren't so hardened by their jobs, they'd see that Margot wasn't acting—that she couldn't possibly have done anything that would hurt Katy.

A screech of tires brought Gregory out of his ruminations. He swerved into the breakdown lane to avoid a collision and was momentarily grateful for the diversion. Whenever his thoughts turned to Katy, the center of all this trouble, he became so full of conflicting emotions that he wanted to break something, anything. And he had to admit that the strongest of his emotions was guilt. Guilt for all the grief he'd caused Margot by opposing the artificial insemination. Guilt for secretly believing that Katy was not his true granddaughter. Guilt for not realizing the extent of his love for the child. He understood now that it was a different love than the one he felt for Margot—not greater, but more passionate, more vulnerable because he did not see his granddaughter every day, because he saw only the best of her, because he indulged Katy, assuming no need to teach or to correct her. A selfish love, he could see now.

As he entered West Virginia, the day seemed to grow unnaturally dark. It was like the flip side of that sensation of riding in an airplane on a cloudy day, seeing the bright sun on the clouds—the very clouds that caused patches of darkness for the people underneath them. As he turned onto a two-lane road, he felt the presence of the sun somewhere above him, but it could not quite make it into the shrouded darkness.

At an intersection, Gregory slowed to read the road signs. The highway numbers seemed wrong, so he pulled into a driveway to consult his map. The buzz and hum of insects in the brush was the only sound. A rusted, abandoned mobile home loomed above him on the hill overlooking the road. At one time it must have provided someone—maybe a family—with a beautiful view of the rugged countryside; now it sat forlorn, somehow threatening, in its decay. At last he figured out where he'd gone wrong, and he backed out of the dusty driveway, reversing his direction on the dim road.

It was nearly nine in the evening when Gregory saw the pinkish glow of the carnival's lights at the edge of the tiny town where Margot had tracked it by phone. His Mercedes looked out of place as he parked it—an overdressed British lord among the muddy pickups and wagons of the locals.

The din of calliopes and flashes of multicolored lights

gave Gregory the impression of chaos, not celebration, as he walked the perimeter of the carnival. A mutter of thunder and sheets of heat lightning mingled with the carnival noises and lights as if an integral part of the traveling entertainment.

The vehicles of the workers were parked at one edge of the carnival—mostly RVs and a few converted vans. Many had the names and specialties of the owners on small signs on their doors. The biggest RV, an old, battered Winnebago, was parked closest to all the activity, and the sign read "Manager." Scratched beneath the word was a handwritten note reading, "of the people, animals, and those that may qualify as both." The inscription was literate, almost poetic, and Gregory was ashamed of his sudden awareness that he had assumed carnival people to be less than intelligent.

There was no answer to his knock, although a dim, reddish light glowed in a back window. Gregory felt vaguely threatened standing there by the door of the RV. He turned and headed for the lights and noise, and felt oddly comforted when a barker, a plump fellow with bad skin, shouted out, "Hey, mister. Looks like you're on your way to meet some important lady. Why not take a shot at winning her this nice, fat piggy?" The man's voice was loud, hoarse and pleasant. He brandished a hot-pink plush pig in the air as Gregory walked past the shooting gallery, waving a quick good-bye to the man and his piggy.

Workers were still setting up a few of the rides. Gregory was amazed at how quickly the carnival could be relocated. The noise of the merry-go-round grew in intensity as Gregory headed straight for it. From the looks of him, the operator appeared to be the one who'd been working when Katy was kidnapped.

Gregory had seen the man's photo in Margot's files. In her extreme need to do something active, Margot had gone and photographed most of the carnival workers while they were packing up before heading to West Virginia. A few people had refused to let her snap them, and one man had informed her calmly that if she pointed the camera in his direction, he would take it from her and eat it for lunch. Margot had almost smiled when she'd told her father that the man was the sword swallower and there might possibly have been some truth in his warning. But still, she had made a point to confirm that the swallower had been doing a show at the time that Katy had been abducted.

Gregory waited near the entrance to the merry-go-round. As soon as the horses came to a halt, and the pink-cheeked, sweaty children tumbled off, Gregory approached the man. When Margot's father introduced himself, the fellow looked down at his shoes. "Hey, mister, if I could do that day over again, don't you think I would?" He rubbed a grimy, work-scarred hand across his chin. Gregory felt sorry for him.

It took only a few moments to discover that Margot had been there earlier on this hot day and that she had questioned every carnival employee again. The man thought that Margot then had left the carnival. The only clue to her whereabouts came from a woman who ran the funhouse. With one skinny arm around Gregory's shoulders, the funhouse lady had led him aside, behind the canvas tent where things seemed quieter. "Now, look, I'm a mother myself. Got four kids. 'Course, they're all grown and out on their own, if you can believe it." She paused, but when Gregory made no response, she went on. "Your little girl looked about as miserable as a body can be. I could tell this thing about her kid being snatched is driving her loony. Asked me where she could find a motel. Guess she's planning to hang around a while. You should make her get a good night's sleep. And if I was you, I'd try to get her to give it up. There's no way one young girl like her is gonna find a kid that somebody's trying to hide. She looked like she'd fall over in a strong wind."

By the time Gregory was back in his car, the sun had set. He followed the hilly road in the direction of the nearest motel. The funhouse lady's words rang in his ears. *If I was you, I'd try to get her to give it up.*

It was late when Gregory pulled past the neon "NO" under the Ma-and-Pa motel vacancy sign. He'd nearly missed the place because it seemed to have been carved out of the mountainside. He rang the night bell and was greeted by a yawning woman in a plaid bathrobe. She said that Margot had been there earlier in the evening. "I told her I saw her on TV and I knew about what happened and all. And how we didn't have any vacancies." The woman leaned across the counter and spoke more quietly, confidentially. "You know, I don't do this with just everybody now, but I told her she could spend the night with my husband and me if she don't mind sleeping on the sofa. No charge, her being somebody and all. But she said no."

"I appreciate your being kind to my daughter. I wonder if you might know—"

"Where she went? You bet I do. I sent her on down to Scotty's." She pulled out a map and unfolded it next to the cash register. She pointed out the route to the other motel and patiently described landmarks that could be seen in the night. "You know most of the people around here are either asleep or up to no good by this time of night," she said, winking. "Just be sure you don't miss that turnoff to the Widow's Road or you'll find yourself back in Pennsylvania before you see any signs of life at all."

Just as he was about to leave, the woman placed her hand firmly, in a motherly fashion, on Gregory's arm. "You feeling okay?" she asked. "You don't look a whole lot better than your daughter did."

"I'm fine, ma'am. And thanks for your help." But Gregory didn't feel fine. He'd left the rest of his medication at home, and he was feeling the lack of it now. He tried to ignore the thudding pressure in his temples as he climbed in his car and followed the winding roads in search of Scotty's Motel. The heat lightning continued and made a monster movie set of the outcroppings of rugged rock and twisted trees. He had the sensation that the map on the seat beside him had no relationship at all to the road he was traveling. After fifteen or twenty minutes had passed, Gregory was sure that he'd missed the Widow's Road turn that the woman had warned him about. He was supposed to have turned after only three miles. An attempt to backtrack led him to forks in the road which required decisions that he didn't remember having made going in the other direction. The roads were empty of traffic, empty of any sign of habitation, any businesses.

Then ahead, outlined in his headlights, he saw a friendly, familiar green sign. He pulled into the roadside rest area, gliding quietly past trucks, cars and campers full of sleeping travelers.

Feeling an overwhelming weight on his heart, both physical and emotional, Gregory parked his car, then reached into his backseat and pulled out his leather liquor case. He poured a full two ounces of gin into one of the little silver tumblers and sat back to let the alcohol do the job of the medication he'd forgotten to bring. He was just wondering if he'd ever find this Scotty's Motel when a sudden flash of lightning illuminated the vehicles on either side of him. A truck loomed over the driver's side, but the car on his right looked familiar. A yellow Saab. Margot drove a yellow Saab. Quickly, Gregory removed his flashlight from the glove compartment and pointed the beam into the next car. Incredibly, her head resting against the doorjamb, there was Margot.

Gregory got out and walked around to her car. "Margot, honey, it's Dad," he said softly, hoping she could hear him through the slightly open window. When she didn't move, an unreasoning panic filled him, and he rapped hard on the glass.

They'd lost little Katy—or *maybe* they had. And now, why didn't Margot respond? Gregory banged again. Margot jerked upright, staring wild-eyed before seeing who was outside her car. Dazed, she rolled down her window and whispered, "Daddy?"

"Open the door," he said. Margot swung open the door and sprang out of the car and into her father's arms. She trembled in the darkness, clinging to him tightly.

"I couldn't find anything, Daddy." Gregory was vaguely aware that she was calling him *Daddy*, a word she'd replaced with *Dad* on her thirteenth birthday." Somehow, he found it comforting. "I talked with everyone at the carnival," she said. "It didn't do a bit of good. Katy is still—" She gulped and then stood placidly, not crying, no longer shaking, simply defeated.

"I'm sorry, honey. Maybe tomorrow we'll hear something." His words sounded empty, meaningless. "Maybe tomorrow," had always been his antidote for smashed dreams. *If you keep trying, if you don't give up, things will work out eventually*, he'd always told her. *Maybe not the way you expect, maybe in surprising ways, but if you keep trying, something good will happen.* And in his mind, like annoying feedback from bad speakers, were the funhouse woman's words. *If I was you, I'd try to get her to give it up.*

As Gregory sought some way to comfort his only child, rain began to fall—first in a gentle sprinkle, then in fat, wet, cold drops. The two ducked into Gregory's car. Abandoning his attempt to offer verbal comfort, he poured his daughter a drink, then covered her with a hand-crocheted afghan that his wife kept folded on the backseat. When they finally spoke again, it didn't take long to discover that they'd landed in this spot, not entirely by coincidence, but by both missing the elusive turnoff to Widow's Road. With the motel owner's warning that there was no civilization to be found if they missed the turn, they had both sought rest at the roadside stop. The torrent of summer rain surged across the roadside rest area, hitting the darkened windshields of the vehicles trapped in this encampment. The West Virginia back roads were obviously too convoluted for nonlocals, so father and daughter decided that they would be wise to simply spend the night there, in the rest area, in the Mercedes, together.

At last the night passed. With dawn, the rain slowed, and Gregory could hear the sound of engines roaring to life, mingled with the soft troubled breathing of his daughter. He had seen no point in waking her to tell her that he wasn't feeling well. Besides, he'd dozed off for a while, and he felt somewhat better.

Margot stirred and woke, instant recognition of their situation coming into her tired eyes. Then, as they both yawned and stretched, the semi on the driver's side of Gregory's car pulled slowly backward. Like a curtain rising at the theater, it slid away to reveal a surprise. There, in what Gregory had taken to be a no-service rest area, was a restaurant. A brightly lit, welcoming, faith-restoring restaurant. "It's a miracle," cried Margot. They looked at each other and smiled, then they laughed. They laughed until their sides ached and they were gasping for breath.

Then, all at once, as if on cue, they stopped laughing. Each took a deep breath. "What now, Dad?"

"I don't know, honey. But whatever we do, we can't give up. Let's go eat."

6 . . .

MARGOT AND HER father hurried through the misty rain and entered a wonderfully warm, bright, cozy restaurant. First they each went to wash up. In the women's room, Margot cleaned her face with a steamy hot paper towel, rinsed her mouth and combed out her hair. When she rejoined her father, they ordered breakfast.

"Just some toast and tea, please," said her father quietly. Margot said nothing, but studied his face. For as long as she could remember, he'd eaten mammoth breakfasts. Since his high blood pressure had been diagnosed, he'd been very good about the change of diet. He'd cut down on bacon and eggs and butter, but he still ate huge amounts of cereal, fruit and whole-grain bread.

Margot told her father more about her visit to the carnival. She hadn't found out anything new or useful. "At least you tried, honey," he said. It helped so much to have him wanting to help—even though there appeared to be nothing either of them could do. Katy was still missing. There was nowhere to go but back to Pittsburgh.

When their breakfast arrived, they ate quietly, each lost in thought. As they left the restaurant, her father stumbled against Margot, and she caught his arm. He pointed to a puddle and said, "Oil on the pavement, I guess."

"You feeling okay, Dad?"

"I'm fine. I just don't sleep as well in a Mercedes as I do on a Sealy."

His attempt at a joke did little to allay Margot's worries. But when she tried to convince her father that they should stay together on the highway, he reacted testily. "The minute you try to follow someone on the highway, you meet up with hundreds of jerks all trying to split you up." He passed a hand across his brow as he unlocked his car door. "I'll just see you later this afternoon." He gave Margot a quick peck on her cheek, climbed into his car and was off before Margot even had her seatbelt on.

As Margot crossed into Pennsylvania, she was painfully aware that she was heading toward an empty house. When she neared the Fort Pitt tunnel leading into Pittsburgh, traffic began to slow. Margot followed along, her apprehension growing. Just before the entrance to the tunnel, she suddenly wrenched her wheel to the left. She pulled behind the emergency vehicles stacked up behind a dark green Mercedes. She was sure it was her father's car. It didn't look as if there'd been an accident. Just as Margot jumped from her car she saw them. Three paramedics clustered around a man lying on a stretcher. With one desperate thought that maybe it was someone else, she looked inside the car. She recognized the afghan and knew the car was her father's.

She hurried over. "Daddy. I'm here," she cried as she neared. He was conscious, and his eyes met hers for an instant, then closed again in an ashen face.

Margot rode in the ambulance with her father to Allegheny General Hospital. She stayed in a corner, out of the way of the paramedics who had worked every mile of the short trip. They monitored his vital signs, and one of them started an IV. After her father was taken to an examining room, she quickly phoned her mother and delivered the news as gently as possible. Then Margot set to pacing the hall.

By noon, his doctor said that Margot's father was out of immediate danger, but he asked that only her mother go in to stay by his side. "I want absolute peace and quiet for him right now. Don't mention anything that might upset him, because his condition is—"

Doctor Carter stopped in midsentence and looked at Margot. "I'm sorry, dear. I've been hearing all about your Katy in the news. Probably that has something to do with your father's condition right now.'' At Margot's increased look of distress, he hurried to add, ''I'm not telling you this to make you feel bad. I just want you to handle things carefully. If you can give your dad any hope, tell him anything positive—now don't lie—but let him know that things are looking up. That would help.''

''I understand,'' was all Margot could choke out. As soon as possible, she went in search of a taxi so she could retrieve her car. It seemed as if she'd been away from home forever. And after the fiasco of her ''investigation'' in West Virginia, she felt foolish and helpless. She had a strong need to get back home and try to think of a new strategy. And her normally optimistic nature was battling to assert itself, telling her that maybe there'd be some word of Katy when she got home. But it was hard to be optimistic—nearly impossible—when her family seemed to be under siege and all the enemies were as substantial as a whisper.

7...

"OKAY, LITTLE MOTHER. Okay, little Barrel." Billy crooned in a sing-song voice to the cat as it labored to deliver its kittens. It was a huge cat of no particular breed. It was so big that most people mistook it for a dog on first sight. Billy, in fact, had thought it was a dog the first time he'd seen it, limping across his front lawn from the highway where it had apparently been dumped. *This cat looks like a kraut barrel*, he'd thought, laughing aloud over his beer. "Poor Little Barrel," he said, and the name had stuck.

Billy found the process of giving birth fascinating, but also painful to watch. He left Little Barrel in her carton behind the washing machine and went back into the kitchen.

The weekend of drinking had left him shaking and sweating, but he'd managed to forget for a few days. Now, with a deep sigh of resignation, he turned on the Channel 4 morning news. Billy had become more and more of a pessimist since he'd lost his job, but now he tried hard to be hopeful as he waited for the ads to be over.

His hopes were soon crushed. "No word yet on the whereabouts of five-year-old Katy DesMarais. She was abducted on Saturday while at a carnival with her mother, talk-show hostess Margot DesMarais. Police have—"

Billy switched off the set and stared out of his kitchen window toward the garage. He glanced down to see his left hand cradling a bottle of whiskey, unaware of having reached for it. But it was too late. He'd stopped drinking last night when Little Barrel went into labor. He didn't want to miss the birth of the kittens. And now he was too sober to ignore what he had to do. He slipped on a pair of old Nike's and headed out to the garage.

Little Barrel yowled when the screen door slammed shut behind him. He turned back for a moment, thinking maybe he should soothe her. But he knew it had nothing to do with him. The cat had its problem to face alone, and Billy had his own.

Billy had little doubt of what he'd find in the yellowing files stored in his garage. When he'd seen that woman's face on TV Saturday night, then the photo of the little girl, he'd known.

Margot DesMarais was one of "his." And the little girl was one of "his," too—from the good days, before everything fell apart. Most of his clients had faded back into obscurity where they'd come from, but this one had become famous, at least in his home town of Pittsburgh. She'd been only a production assistant when she and her husband had applied to the sperm bank Billy managed. He'd checked his records when Margot had first appeared as a reporter on the evening news, and he had followed her career ever since. Early this year she'd gotten her own daytime talk show. Billy had read articles about her. Because of her charm and compassion, they said, teamed with an ability to cut to the heart of matters, her show had taken off like a rocket. It was rumored that it might be syndicated nationally.

Billy stood for a minute on his small back porch. It was cluttered with parts from his '81 BMW. Each time he went at it, tried to make it run again, he ended up with more pieces that didn't seem to fit back in. He sometimes wondered if someone was playing a practical joke on him, buying old parts and adding them to the collection just for a laugh.

He walked slowly through the dusty yard, hesitant to check what he suspected. He had a very bad feeling about this kidnapping. He was pretty sure he'd screwed up again.

In the back corner of the garage, he moved a moldy

director's chair and a box of old *Geographic*s away from the front of some sturdy metal file cabinets. The one on the right was locked, the key long gone, but the one with the drawer labeled "A to D" was unlocked. He pulled out the file marked "DesMarais" and opened it.

Shit! he thought. No doubt at all. The papers in the file were neatly stacked, all edges precisely lined up. Billy shook his head. Setting the DesMarais file atop the box of magazines, he took several other folders out of the drawer. The contents were all in disarray, papers jumbled, some folded, some wrinkled from having been shoved in carelessly. Billy had never put anything away neatly in his life. Someone had definitely been looking through Margot Des-Marais's file.

Billy unfolded the director's chair and sat down. He heard the screams of his cat as she labored. Strangely, he recalled that it had been the day Little Barrel had first wandered across the road into his yard that the guy had tricked Billy. Billy had been so stupidly grateful for a little company and a lot of free booze that the guy had easily played out his sick game with Billy's willing help.

Billy recalled now that he had just put down a plate of tuna on the porch when the tall, well-dressed man had come walking up to him. Because almost no one but local residents ever traveled his road, the man looked out of place in his clean suit and tie and his hair neat in spite of the brisk breeze.

"Pardon me. My car's broken down. I wonder if I could use your phone to call for a tow."

"I'd be glad to let you use my phone if it was still connected," said Billy. "But Ma Bell gets pissed when she doesn't get paid. 'Course, I'm not too bad as a mechanic if you could use a hand. You think she's overheated?"

"Doesn't seem to be. It's just back down the road a bit. I have some tools in the trunk."

When they got to the Volvo, Billy had to stifle a laugh at the guy's "tools." From the spotless carpeted trunk, he took a neat canvas roll that opened to reveal a baby wrench, a tire gauge and a can opener.

Fortunately, Billy didn't need any tools. He got the car started easily. The car was new and so well built it seemed strange that the starter had just popped off in the middle of nowhere for no reason. "Can I pay you something for your time?" asked the fellow.

Billy almost said "yes." He could sure use the money. But at the last second his pride stopped him. "Hell no," he said. "I wasn't doing anything anyway. Glad to be of help."

"Well, maybe a drink then. Could I offer you a drink?" The guy pulled a paper bag from his backseat and opened it. Billy's eyes widened when he saw the contents. It held two quart bottles of bourbon. And not the cheap stuff, either. He could see another matching bag still on the seat.

"Hey, thanks. That'd be great. But I don't want to keep you. You must have been headed somewhere—"

"No. I'm all done with work for the day. I was just taking a shortcut back to Pittsburgh, but I got off track somehow."

They sat on the front porch the rest of the afternoon and into the evening. Billy vaguely remembered opening a can of chili and sharing it with the guy. By the time the sun set, they'd finished off most of the two quarts. Billy was feeling a happy buzz and had to admit it was nice to have someone to talk to for a change. Sometimes Billy got sick of the sound of his own voice. But with this guy, and this guy's liquor, and the evening warm and comfortable, Billy felt good.

The guy didn't talk much about himself, but he seemed to be awfully interested in Billy. At one point, like most people, he asked about Billy's name.

"What'd you say your last name was?"

"Kid."

"So that makes you—"

"Billy the Kid. Right." He glanced at the guy. Wanted to see if he needed another shot, but his glass was still close to full. "When I was born," Billy began, "my dad was out of town. And there weren't any relatives who lived close to help my mom, so she was all alone in the hospital. I guess she must of been groggy when the woman came to get the name for the birth certificate, so maybe she wasn't speaking real clearly. See, I was supposed to be 'Maximilian Kid.' Maximilian was my mom's father's name. But the woman heard it wrong and put down 'William Kid.' By the time the birth certificate came in the mail, Mom figured it was too late to change it. She was real timid and never liked to deal with anything like that. And my dad wouldn't do it. Said he never liked that old son of a bitch Max anyway. So Billy the Kid I stayed." Billy finished off his drink and poured another.

"That's a great story. To the Kid," the fellow said and raised his glass. Seemed strange the guy would make a toast and not drink.

And the guy was even more interested in Billy's old job as director of a sperm bank. He'd laughed at first and made some crude jokes about it, but then he apologized and listened as Billy told him what it was really all about. Maybe it was the booze, but Billy nearly cried when he started to talk about his hopes for his work. He'd screened everyone so carefully, trying to make sure that couples who came to him would get not just healthy babies, but smart kids with good looks, and talents, and athletic bodies. He'd had to change the subject then or get maudlin about how he'd screwed it up, how his mistakes had allowed some wretched babies to be born with defects—serious defects.

Billy recalled how he and Rick—that's what the man had said to call him—had wandered out to the garage, and how Rick had laughed until he almost lost his chili when he saw the sperm storage canisters still sitting out there all covered with dust. "You mean there's no regulations? This stuff can just sit around out here like old newspapers?"

"Well, it's not viable anymore, of course. The sperm is dead," Billy said, feeling a bit defensive. He'd never been sure why he hadn't gotten rid of the tanks that had once held dry ice and healthy frozen little sperm. Maybe he had some kind of affection for the potential babies. Maybe he was just punishing himself, keeping them as a reminder of what a loser he was.

He'd passed out, and when he woke up, the guy was gone, and Billy had the hangover of the century.

Now, feeling sick dread, Billy looked through the Des-Marais file. There it was—everything the guy needed to know—her address, phone number, information on the successful donor sperm. Grader. The successful donor sperm had come from Richard Grader. And that kidnapped girl was Grader's daughter!

This is too crazy, Billy thought suddenly. I'm not responsible for the troubles of the whole world. I'm just guessing, based on one file folder being neat. With that, he pulled open the drawer holding the Grader file. Slowly, he opened it and stared. Same thing. Papers neatly arranged. He opened other files. All sloppy. All with papers jammed in helter-skelter. Billy had never let anyone else into his files. He'd guarded them as if they were his children. Of all the donor and recipient folders he checked, only two were neat. And only two had any relationship to the woman whose daughter had been kidnapped. The guy who had gotten him drunk—not that it was difficult to do, everyone knew that was the reason for the mess his life was in—what did Grader look like? Billy remembered how cleancut Grader had been—tall, slim, lean; short red hair, green eyes. Having spent all that time trying to match donors with prospective parents, Billy noticed things like skin, hair and eye color. He looked at the description of Grader in the file. Yeah. Grader had the woman's kid all right.

He wondered how much trouble he would get in if he told what he suspected. Maybe he was wrong and should just keep quiet and not cause trouble. He returned to the house and poured himself another shot of bourbon, then checked on Little Barrel. She gazed at him and at his glass. He restrained the urge to apologize. After all she was only a cat.

But when he looked more closely at the tiny black kitten Little Barrel was cleaning, he felt his heart sink. He hoped there were more coming. And Billy wondered how long it would be before the mother cat realized her first kitten was dead.

8...

RICK HAD ALWAYS believed that if a man wanted something bad enough, he should have it. Oh, not in a fantastic, Aladdin's lamp sort of a way, but in a normal way. He believed that every man had a right to a home and a family. At least every man who was willing to work for it—willing to struggle and sacrifice and even face danger.

Rick paced back and forth, annoyed that Sonya's plane was late, annoyed at other people who got in his way as he moved restlessly from one end of the lounge to the other.

At last her plane landed, and Sonya appeared at the door, her eyes scanning the crowd for Rick. When she spotted him, she smiled—a good sign. He stood still while she edged her way to him through the fumbling, bumping crowd.

She stood on tiptoe to kiss him—a short, quick peck—then she brushed the hair back from his forehead. "You need a haircut," she said, puzzlement in her voice. "You need a haircut," she said again, as she took Rick's arm and followed him to the baggage checkout.

"I've been busy," was all Rick offered by way of explanation.

After they'd gotten to their car and onto the highway, Rick was silent until they reached the Franklin Park exit. Franklin Park was one of Pittsburgh's better suburbs, and it usually gave Rick a satisfied feeling to drive through it, but today he gave it no thought.

"I have something to tell you," Rick said. "But first I want to hear about your folks. How are they?"

"Oh, God, I don't know." Sonya fumbled about in her

purse, pulling out her plane ticket stubs, some Kleenex and other clutter, piling it all on the seat between her and Rick. "Daddy's a lot worse. Last Friday, Mom and I went shopping and when we came back, we found Daddy in the kitchen with all four burners on the stove turned on high. He said he was going to sharpen the knives." Sonya's voice caught, and she coughed twice before continuing. "He had a burn on his right hand and a gash on his left, and he didn't even feel either one."

"I'm sorry to hear—"

"Daddy was bleeding all over the stove and didn't seem to be aware of it." She began to cry freely. "He seemed so proud of himself, with all the carving knives lined up on the counter."

"What did—"

"Mom admitted that she couldn't handle him alone anymore." She paused again, but Rick waited. He was getting tired of being interrupted.

He turned onto their street and parked the car. After he'd gotten Sonya's bags upstairs, he came down to the kitchen. She had poured two glasses of Scotch, and she handed one to Rick.

They each drank deeply before making eye contact. "So," he asked his wife, "are you back to stay?"

"Yes. I'll try."

"No more rules, no more ultimatums?"

"Not if you say you'll try."

It was at that moment that Sonya set her glass on the counter and glanced into the dining room. She stared directly at the table—at the three place settings. "Oh, Rick," she said, her voice beaten and quivering. "You promised you wouldn't keep—"

"Wait. Just look and you'll see there's a difference." He touched her upper arm lightly and led her into the blue-and-white papered dining room. Rick could sense the tension in her body and knew why it was there. Even though Evan had died nearly two years ago, Rick had insisted that a place be set for him at the dinner table every night and that Evan's plastic clown plate and cup be put through the dishwasher along with Sonya's and Rick's soiled dishes.

He handed her the bright china plate from the table. She took it from his hand, looking confused as she examined it. It was clearly a child's plate, but it was not Evan's. The picture was of two curly-headed little girls in a Victorian rose garden. Around the rim were hand-painted tiny pink rosebuds.

"All right. There's a difference. This is not Evan's plate. So—?" Her face muscles tightened, her lips looked thin and stretched.

"Do you remember back when you were pregnant, how you used to dream that you'd had a little girl? You'd wake up crying because you were so happy?"

"I remember."

"Well, I have something to tell you. It's a surprise. Maybe even a shock at first, but I think you'll say I did the right thing after I explain."

Sonya slumped into a chair, still clutching the little dinner plate.

"I'm warning you, Rick. I promised no more talk about counseling, no more ultimatums. But this looks like a giant step backward. You have to admit—"

"Wait. Okay? Will you just wait one damned minute before you start lecturing me?"

Rick circled the dining room table, moving quickly to keep his anger down. What he really wanted to do was change into his sweats and run—run until his heart hammered, then settled down to the calming, rhythmic rush that drowned out the angry voices in his head.

He stopped pacing abruptly and sat down facing Sonya. Rick took her left hand in his right and kissed her fingertips, then nuzzled her palm. She moaned slightly and tried to pull away, but the effort was halfhearted, and Rick held on. With her free hand, she tugged lightly at the hair at the back of his head.

In a hushed voice, Rick said the words he'd been rehearsing all day. "There's no way I can make this easier on you. Sonya—I have a daughter."

A subtle, well-known shifting of her eyebrows was the only sign that his words had registered.

He plunged ahead. "It happened before you and I met. I never asked her to marry me. The bitch never even told me she was pregnant." Rick paused, trying to gauge Sonya's response.

"The bitch—" she said through her teeth.

Rick couldn't tell if Sonya was offering some woman's-lib defense or if she was confirming his assessment of the child's mother.

"I've known about the little girl for a while now, but I didn't want to upset you, so I never said anything."

"You didn't want to upset me?" she cried, as if she'd just been slapped hard. Sonya was gasping. He watched her hurtle her body upward, knocking the chair to the polished hardwood floor. "You have a daughter, and you never told me because I might be upset?" She held the small china plate in front of her, looking for all the world like a hostess offering hor d'oeuvres. Then, suddenly she crumpled to the floor.

Rick knelt and tried to take her in his arms, but she slumped down farther, her face in her hands.

"Too much. It's too much," she cried. "First Mama and Daddy. Now this." She sat up and looked at Rick. "I can't take it, Rick. It's too much."

Now he held her, his arms wrapped tightly around her as she sat weeping, the china plate resting in her lap, her hands clutching weakly at Rick's arms, her lips seeking his in a familiar way—a way that meant she needed his strength as much as she ever had.

"I know," he murmured. "I know. But don't cry. I have a daughter. And that means you have a daughter, too. A child. Your own child, Sonya. It's not over, after all. Don't cry."

Rick didn't know how long they sat like that. But when Sonya finally disentangled herself from his arms, the sun had nearly set and the dining room was full of deep shadows. He rather enjoyed the cavelike feel of it, as the furniture outlines blurred and only the brass of the chandelier stood out, etched like gold, reflecting the setting sun. But, of course, it couldn't last. *Of course, she had to start with the questions*, he thought, as Sonya sniffled, then spoke.

"Where is she?"

"The girl, or her mother?" he asked.

The question seemed to fluster her. She frowned, then pulled herself up off the floor and settled heavily into a chair. Rick picked up the overturned chair and sat down facing her. When he reached for her hand, she pulled away, as if she hadn't only moments before been cuddled in his arms.

"I was asking about the girl. But I suppose you'd better tell me about the mother, too."

Rick hated the way her voice sounded—all flat and drained of emotion. He'd planned this as a happy moment, a big moment. Sonya was threatening to ruin it. But he couldn't wait any longer to tell her. "Like the comedians always say, there's some good news and some bad—"

"Oh, God! Please don't tease me. I can't handle it tonight. I really can't."

"Okay. I was just trying to make it easier for you." He reached for her hand again, and this time she let him take it. "The upsetting thing is that the mother has been abusing the child. The girl's name is Katherine, by the way." He watched Sonya's face. Still no response. Her eyes like gray stones. He plunged ahead. "I've suspected for a while that something was wrong."

"You mean you've been seeing the girl all this time?"

"No. Not in the sense of visitation, if that's what you mean. But I knew where she lived, and I'd drive by sometimes and watch Katherine playing. Even from the car,

I could see the bruises. Not just the normal skinned knees, but black eyes and—'' He hesitated and took a deep breath, really into his lie now, savoring the details he'd worked out so carefully; almost believing it himself.

"How old is she?"

I've done it! She's buying it, Rick thought.

"She's almost six. Actually, she's very tiny, so she looks more like a four-year-old."

"You don't suppose her mother—" Sonya paused and swallowed, her eyes wide, the pupils huge in the semi-gloom.

"It's hard to tell if she's been feeding her properly or not. I haven't had anything to do with the mother, but—'' Now Rick paused for effect. "With all the men I've seen coming and going from the house where they live, it's possible that sometimes she just hasn't been fed. Or maybe she's just naturally thin."

"Oh, Rick. The poor thing!"

Part of him felt sorry for her. It really was a lot to lay on her after all the troubles they'd been through. And he knew how deep Sonya's depression had been since Evan's death in spite of the visits to the shrink and all the medications he'd prescribed. And now Sonya's parents were coming apart at the seams. But still, he had to get her involved fast. And she had a predictably tender heart.

Rick watched her now as she held the china plate, running her fingertips over the raised rosebuds along the edge.

"Honey, look at me for a minute."

"Huh," was all she said, but Sonya looked up at him.

"A little while ago, I found absolute proof that the mother has been beating the little girl. So I did the only thing I could do. I took her."

"You what?"

"I grabbed her, abducted her, saved her, call it whatever you want."

The room was almost completely dark now. He could no longer read her thoughts from her eyes.

"When? What? I mean—" She stopped, swallowed hard, then started again. "If you've taken the girl, then where is she?"

"Here."

"Here where?"

"The little girl is right here."

"Enough!" Sonya stood up abruptly, her posture defensive and aggressive at the same time. "Here could mean here in Pittsburgh, here in the county, here in Pennsylvania, here on the damned planet, or here in the house, for God's sake." She took a deep breath, then spoke more slowly, pronouncing each syllable with exaggerated force. "Precisely where is the child?"

"You got it right on the last guess. Here in the house."

Rick stood up and hugged her. His embrace was not returned.

"In the house?"

"Just upstairs. That's what I've been wanting to tell you all evening, but I didn't want to upset you. I wanted it to be a happy moment for us."

Rick walked into the kitchen and switched on the muted light over the stove. He opened the refrigerator and produced a magnum of champagne. He opened it, then with a flourish he poured two glasses and handed one to his wife, who had followed him quietly into the kitchen. He raised his glass and said, "To our daughter."

Sonya's hand went limply to her side, and the glass shattered at their feet in a delicate fountain of crystal and liquid.

She glared at Rick. "Show her to me."

"Would you like me to pour you another glass of champagne? Maybe it'll help your nerves."

"Show her to me."

"Follow me. Quietly."

With that, Rick set down his glass and headed for the front hall stairs. Sonya followed him, and their feet made only a whisper as they went up the carpeted stairs and down the hall. At the second door, he stopped and turned the wheel of a combination lock hanging on a sturdy hatch. He turned the doorknob and softly stepped into the bedroom. The shades were drawn. The only illumination came from a Garfield nightlight plugged into the outlet beneath the window. As Rick did each time he entered, he stopped for a moment and savored the scent of the child—that sweet mixture of sweat and clean hair and somehow an earthiness.

Sonya brushed past him and went to stand by the bed where little Katherine slept. She reached out her hand toward the girl's hair, but did not touch it. She turned her face toward Rick, her eyes full of questions. He only smiled and nodded, much like a proud new father gazing at a newborn through the nursery glass wall.

Then Sonya turned back to the child and knelt next to the bed. This time she did touch the damp, matted hair, running her fingers gently down the girl's neck, feeling the pulse there. With her other hand, she wiped away tears that were flowing down her own cheeks.

Rick moved closer and knelt by his wife. "Isn't she beautiful?" he asked.

With her hand still lightly stroking Katherine's back, she turned to Rick. "What have you done? Why doesn't she wake up?"

"She's just sleeping very soundly. Don't worry, honey, she's all right."

"How could you? From her mother. Oh, Rick, what have you done?"

The pain in her eyes was huge, and he began to feel the anger coming back. Why did she always have to spoil things?

"What I have done," he whispered in the warm room, "is gotten you a child. You thought we'd never have another child; you thought we'd lost everything when we lost Evan. And now it's all going to be okay. We have a child, our own child."

"Forget all that for now. I want to know what's wrong

with her. Why doesn't she wake up? And who's been with her all this time? While you were picking me up at the airport? And while we were downstairs with the champagne?''

But then Katherine stirred in her sleep. She flailed weakly about, clutching at air with her small hands, then turning her head so that she faced them with her eyes still closed. Even in the dimly lit room there was no mistaking the ugly bruise on her right temple.

''Oh, my God! What happened to her?''

''I told you. The mother.''

With her fingertips, Sonya tried to smooth away the frown on the child's forehead. ''Poor baby,'' she whispered.

Katherine, her eyes still closed tight in sleep, reached out and grasped Sonya's hand. She held it to her cheek and the frown vanished. Katherine looked peaceful.

For a long while the three people remained in the warm, dark bedroom, the sound of their breathing mingling in a restful way. Rick watched Sonya and the girl, aware that some sort of bonding was taking place.

His legs began to tingle. He had been afraid to move, afraid to disturb the pair. Just when he thought he'd have no choice but to break the spell, Sonya stood up and motioned for him to follow her into the hall. He did so, closing the door behind him. He followed her to their bedroom, where she turned on all the lights and opened the windows.

Then Sonya turned to face him. In that maddeningly self-assured tone of voice that she'd been using all evening, she said, ''I have a thousand questions, but let's start with her health. You tell me now why the child is sleeping so soundly. What's wrong with her?''

''She's fine. She's sleeping because I gave her some of that Benadryl we used to give Evan when he couldn't sleep through the teething pain. If you'll think back, you'll remember that Dr. Morris said there was no harm in using it once in a while.''

''You drugged her?''

"Come off it. She's not drugged, just sleeping. The stuff's sold over the counter."

"And who was watching her while you were getting me from the airport?"

"Will you think a minute, please. That's why I gave her the Benadryl."

"You left her alone? Are you insane?"

"Damn it, Sonya. Don't get so dramatic." He paced the room, stopping long enough to close the windows. He didn't want the nosy neighbors eavesdropping on their argument. "This is an unusual situation, and it calls for unusual measures. It's not every day my daughter needs rescuing."

"Okay. Let's talk about that rescue. You said you had proof that the mother was abusing her. What proof?"

Rick gritted his teeth and glared at Sonya for a minute before answering. "You saw the proof yourself. That bruise on her temple didn't come from a loving pat."

"Granted, she has a bruise. But how do you know the mother did it?"

Pretending weariness, Rick slumped into an armchair. "It's a long story. A long, sad story, and I don't think I can tell it all if you're going to act like a B-movie district attorney." He rubbed his eyes, then rested his hands in his lap.

It worked like a charm. Already Sonya was coming over to him, sitting on the thick white rug beside his chair, her body language softened, her eyes full of concern. "I'm sorry. It's just the shock. I mean, a little girl—right here in our house—in Evan's room. And to hear you have a daughter— I'll need some time to adjust. But there isn't any time, is there?"

"No, there's no time. You're right. In fact, that's the part of the story that needs more telling. Katherine's mother is a celebrity. Oh, she's only known in Pittsburgh, but since she's on TV every day, there's been a lot on the news about Katherine disappearing." Rick massaged the back of Sonya's neck as he explained. Now that he had her attention and she'd calmed down a little, it would be easier to tell his story.

"On TV? Who—?"

"That talk show in the morning. You know, 'Pittsburgh Today.'"

"Not Margot DesMarais?"

"Right."

"Beating her child. Oh, Rick. I can hardly believe it. She seems so nice. Well, that's stupid I guess; everyone seems nice most of the time. But still, Margot DesMarais!"

"I know, I know. I've been through it all myself. When we get Katherine away from here where she'll be safe, we can talk about it more, maybe figure out a way to straighten things out. But meantime, we have no time to waste."

"What are you saying? You're not making any sense."

"I'm saying we have to get Katherine out of Pittsburgh. Every cop in the city is looking for her, not to mention the morning talk-show buffs who think Margot's some kind of saint."

"You're kidding, right?"

"No, I'm dead serious. I'm afraid for Katherine's life."

"You have to give her back. I mean I feel for her, and maybe we can help somehow, but not this way. Now you're the one who's being melodramatic. A bruise on her head is bad, but it doesn't mean her mother's out to kill her. Think of what you're saying."

"There's no way we can help that little girl if we give her back now." He bounded from his chair, and gripping Sonya's arm, he pulled her to her feet and out the door. When she pulled back, he tightened his grip. "Quiet," he said, then dragged her into Evan's old room, where Katherine still slumbered. He rolled the girl onto her back and pulled back the cotton blanket.

"Can you see how thin she is?" His voice was quiet, but he could not keep the anger out. He was not used to Sonya talking back so much. It enraged him to have to wheedle like this, but even he knew how dangerous it was to leave a child alone in a house, how risky it had been this evening to leave Katherine with no one to guard her. He needed Sonya's cooperation now, and her new sassiness was screwing up his plans. He hadn't expected to have to do so much convincing, so much arguing.

"And look at this." He pulled up the hem of Katherine's blouse, revealing the bruises on her ribcage. He certainly hadn't intended to harm Katherine, but she'd been amazingly strong in her struggles. "A mother who would do that to her own child—?"

Tears welled in Sonya's eyes. He could see she was hurting for the girl. A small moan escaped her lips, and she swallowed hard before she spoke. "Did you see the mother do this?" When Rick didn't answer at once, she hurried on. "I mean she could have fallen off a skateboard or tripped and gone down the stairs. Remember all the bruises Evan had when he went down my mother's basement stairs. And he was still in his balloon walker when he reached the bottom."

"In other words you don't believe me?" Rick's voice came loud to his own ears, and Katherine stirred in her sleep, tugging at the edge of the blanket. *Can't lose control now*, he thought. He got up and motioned for Sonya to follow him.

He led her back to their bedroom where they sat together on the loveseat. "You look tired, love. I'm sorry to lay all this on you after the mess with your parents," said Rick. He reached over to his left and switched on the radio, tuning it to a station playing classical music.

"It's not that I don't believe you, Rick," she said. "But I know how emotional you get when it comes to children. And to discover that you have a daughter— Oh, God, she *is* a beautiful child. And how she looks like you. Even more than Evan did, and I never thought that could be possible." Her voice shook, but she swallowed and continued. "I'm not saying I don't believe you. I just need to know more about it. I'm scared, can you understand that? I mean—

kidnapping. That's one of the biggest crimes possible. You could go to jail. So could I. And that won't help Katherine.''

"But don't you see? Sonya, it's not kidnapping. That's the beauty of it. Because she's my daughter, it's only child snatching.''

"What's the difference?'' Sonya demanded.

"All the difference in the world, hon. Now's one time you should be glad you're married to an attorney. I've done my research, and even with the updated laws the penalties for snatching your own child just aren't that big a deal.''

Rick held his breath, expecting her to point out that he'd never married the child's mother. He was prepared to carry his lie one step further and say he'd been married for a few months to Margot DesMarais, but was relieved when he saw Sonya's eyes fog over again. She was shaking, and tears covered her cheeks. "She's so beautiful,'' Sonya said. "I'm just trying to understand how a mother could do that to her own child.''

Sonya moved to sit on the corner of the bed. She plucked at a loose thread in the down comforter. "I've read it in the papers and seen it on talk shows a hundred times, but I've never *really* seen anything like this before.''

While Sonya talked, Rick went quietly to the closet behind her and opened the door. From the top shelf, he brought down two large suitcases and a couple of overnight bags. He paid little attention to Sonya's words as she droned on, trying to sort out her feelings. But he caught the word "police'' in her ramblings.

"What?'' he demanded.

"The police, honey. I can understand why you took her, in the heat of the moment and all. I mean, if I'd been there and seen that woman hurting Katherine, I'd probably have done the same thing myself.'' Now she stood up to face him. "But it's still illegal. You can't just keep her. You'll get caught. I don't care what you say about the legalities. We're just not people with good luck. We'll end up in jail.''

"Her mother has been beating her. I'm her father, and I have a responsibility to protect her."

"But that's going to be hard to prove, since you never married Katherine's mother." Again, Rick held his breath, prepared to expand on his lie.

A moment later he was pleased he'd hesitated. She was off on a new track, one he was ready for.

"Once they see Katherine's injuries," Sonya said, "the authorities will take her away and find a good home for her." As if she had just come out of a trance, Sonya glanced down at the luggage piled on the bed. "Why have you got all the suitcases out of the closet?"

"Never mind that now. I want you to answer one question for me. Honestly."

"Okay."

"On all those talk shows, and in all those newspaper articles about child abuse, what do they say usually happens when the abuse is discovered? Now think a minute and answer honestly."

Sonya shook her head, then gazed down at her hands. Absently, she rubbed her palm with her fingertips. "The child is sent back to the home."

"Exactly. Right back to the abuser. And will you just answer one more question?"

"Rick, please, let's—"

"One more question, Sonya. When a child dies from child abuse, is it ever a surprise to anyone?"

"What?"

"Do they ever say, 'Hey, we had no idea this child was in danger'? Do they?"

"Well, what can we do?" Her voice had taken on its old whine. While it would have driven Rick crazy a few weeks ago, before Sonya left for Detroit, he heard it now with relief. He needed her cooperation, and that new assertive behavior she'd started up with, that attitude that she could control her own life—well, that had promised nothing but trouble.

"There's only one thing we can do. We have to get Katherine away from here, to someplace safe until things calm down." Now Rick began packing in earnest, throwing his sportsclothes and toiletries into the bags. When he was done with his own things, he dumped the contents of Sonya's bags onto the chair and turned to where she sat, watching everything as if she'd gone totally brainless. "Come on, quit moping and get busy. Pack some pants and shirts—warm clothes, things for the woods."

"But where are we going?"

The wording of her question told Rick that she had given in. She hadn't asked, "Where do you want to go?" or "What are you planning?" No, she was getting back to normal. She would follow him now, just as she always had.

"We're going somewhere safe. I don't think it's too late to help Katherine. She's young enough to recover from the abuse. But first, we all need to spend some time together. In a safe place. A happy place."

As he talked, Rick helped Sonya pack. She acted dazed, and he tried to be understanding. To come home and find this "instant family" must be a shock. He felt tender toward her, almost the way he'd felt when she was pregnant with Evan. He hoped she'd be a good mother to Katherine—just as good a mother as she'd been to Evan—except for that one time, that one time when she had failed as a mother—that one awful time when she'd let Evan get hurt—when she'd let Evan die.

9...

SONYA CONTINUED TO worry about the child as they drove through the warm, dark Pennsylvania hills. She'd asked Rick where they were headed, but he was evasive, and she didn't pursue it.

Just as she'd always done when Evan was little and feeling tired, Sonya rode in the backseat of the car, the child's head cradled in her lap. Only now the child was Katherine, a total stranger to her—a little girl in trouble.

"We'll be there in about half an hour," Rick said. He didn't take his eyes off the winding road, so all that Sonya could see was the back of his head. She still couldn't get over how badly he needed a haircut. His hairline was a ragged fringe against the dim lights from the dashboard. "How is she doing?" he asked.

Sonya detected some worry in his voice. It had been many hours now that the girl had been sleeping. He was vague in his answers about so many things tonight. And he was especially vague about how much medicine he'd given her to make her sleep.

"She's fine," answered Sonya. Of course, she was not at all sure about that. But somehow she didn't feel like sharing her worries with Rick. The hair against the back of Katherine's neck was soaked with sweat and her hands felt clammy. Maybe it was merely the warmth of the night. It *was* very humid. Sonya clearly remembered Evan being the same way. On her last visit to his room before going to bed herself each night, she had often debated about whether to cover him with a blanket. The night would grow cooler, but he'd always seemed so overheated in his sleep. On the other hand, Katherine's forehead felt warm and dry. The conflicting signals worried Sonya. But she didn't want to say anything just now.

Rick was in such a state over this. Obviously they'd have to call the police at some point—she knew he wasn't thinking clearly. First chance, Sonya would phone their own lawyer. Maybe he could reason with Rick without the emotions that Sonya knew were muddling her own arguments.

Rick's heart was in the right place. She would join him in doing everything they could to make sure Katherine wasn't abused in the future. And on the long ride, Sonya even spent some time thinking about what might happen in a custody battle. From what she'd heard of this sort of case, the father would have almost no chance of gaining custody. Things looked especially grim since Rick had never married the woman who was Katherine's mother—unless, of course, she had listed Rick as the father on the birth certificate. She'd heard that some women did that to try to get child support. But Rick had never sent out any money for child support—at least not as far as she knew. *No,* she thought. *I can't think about that now, can't add the possibility that he's been hiding something that important to my list of worries right now.*

As they continued to drive through the deep forest, in what seemed like an endless circle, Sonya tried to make sense of things in her mind. She recalled that Rick had mentioned something about "proof" that Katherine had been abused. Maybe, just maybe, they had a chance—

Sonya opened her eyes, aware that she'd almost fallen asleep and had allowed herself for a moment to accept Rick's dream of an instant family. She had begun to consider the tantalizing possibility of having a child again. As always, when she was exhausted she had begun to slip into a fantasy world—a world with more pleasure in it than her real one. It was one of Rick's biggest complaints about her. He'd gone into a rage once when he discovered that she had a lottery ticket in her purse. "This is what you do with my money?" he'd roared. "Blow it on some stupid fantasy game?"

"But it's only once a week—"

"Once a week! You mean you've bought these before?" With that he stomped out of the house and hadn't come home until the next morning.

And when he did come home, he wasn't less angry, just less noisy. "And how much did we win in last night's lottery? Can I quit my job now and buy a yacht?" Then he went to change clothes. She was used to his sarcasm, but it still stung.

The subject of lottery tickets never came up again, but Sonya sometimes felt a twinge of anger when she passed the lottery booth at the grocery store without indulging in her weekly purchase of hope. Not that money was the answer to her troubles, but she knew how much Rick wanted money, and she'd always hoped to surprise him with a big win. She had often imagined the look of pleasure on his face when she told him they were rich. There didn't seem to be much she could do that would please him anymore.

"Mama."

Sonya felt a sickening panic in her throat as she realized that the child was beginning to wake up. "Rick. She's waking up. What should I do?" she asked in a desperate voice. It was only now that she realized that she didn't know anything about how long Rick had had the child, what he'd told her, what Katherine's response had been.

Katherine lifted her head slightly from Sonya's lap. "Mama, the milk is all gone. Thirsty, thirsty—" Katherine moaned the last two words before dropping her head down and drifting off into her stupor again. Of course, her mouth would be dry from the antihistamine. Also, she might be running a fever, but Sonya couldn't be sure.

"I told her that I was a close friend of the family and that her parents wanted me to take care of her for a while," Rick said, glancing briefly over his shoulder. "You can tell her that you're my wife and that you remember her when she was a little baby. She seems to like to talk about babies.''

"Could you tell me—'' Sonya cleared her throat and tried again, aware of how much Rick hated any form of questioning. "I mean did you pick her up from a playground, or—''

"Be quiet. She may hear us. This is something we can talk about later. Besides, we're here.''

The car vibrated slightly as they left the road and traveled up a steep gravel driveway. After a minute or two, Rick pulled the car up in front of a building. By the moonlight, Sonya could see that it was a rustic log cabin with a modern addition of angled glass and stone. There were no other cars in sight and no lights inside. The night was very quiet. An owl hooted dismally nearby, and the trees surrounding the house rustled slightly in the breeze. No other signs of life could be seen or heard.

Having been born and raised in the noisy chaos of Detroit, Sonya had always experienced the solitude of the country more as a threat than a comfort. And this midnight ride on the rural back roads of western Pennsylvania, on top of the disastrous trip to visit her parents, left Sonya near tears. But she knew herself well enough to know that if she succumbed, she'd be helpless to stop for a long time. And this little girl needed her now. She was certain that Rick would be of no use if Katherine was ill. Rick had always been a good father to Evan, but he'd been helpless when their son was sick. She recalled coming home one time to find Rick offering Evan some baby aspirin to try to stop him from vomiting.

With a huge effort, she spoke clearly now. "We can't stay here. I didn't want to worry you, but Katherine may be sick. I think we'd better go back home, or at least stay in a motel near a city. If she needs to see a doctor, we shouldn't be out in the middle of nowhere.''

The whole time that Sonya was talking, Rick was busy gathering Katherine gently in his arms and lifting her slowly from the car. "We're not in the middle of nowhere. And there's a phone if we need to call for help." With that, he walked up several stairs to the porch. Sonya followed him, and he handed her his key ring. "It's the large one next to our house key."

Too tired to argue further, Sonya unlocked the door and stepped inside, full of uneasiness at what her submission might mean. With one final thought that she'd try to reason with Rick tomorrow, she switched on the light and prepared to care for the child.

"Mama? No!"

Sonya dropped the key and turned to see the child twist violently in Rick's arms, her eyes full of fear as she saw who held her. He set her on her feet, and she stared wildly around the room. Her eyes lit on Sonya's face. The child shook her hands in the air as if trying to dry them, then bolted toward Sonya, grabbing her leg and clutching tightly.

"It's all right, Katherine. Don't be afraid," she said, kneeling by the girl.

Katherine threw herself into Sonya's arms and squeezed. In quick, darting movements, she glanced over her shoulder at Rick, then buried her face in Sonya's neck.

The child was shaking violently. The contrast between this frightened child and the sleeping infant she had seemed to be only a few minutes earlier made Sonya shake, too. She glanced about her and saw a leather sectional sofa through an archway. Lifting Katherine in her arms, she made her way over to the couch and sat down. Katherine clung to her as if they'd each been molded especially to fit the other.

"Please, baby. It's all right. Rick won't hurt you. No one is going to hurt you."

She looked up to see Rick, perched nervously on the edge of an ottoman. Katherine lifted her head to peek in his direction, then dove back into the protection of Sonya's shoulder.

Sonya tasted the bittersweet joy of holding Katherine like this, remembering how unbelievably good it felt to be able to offer comfort to a child. She felt the power, the ecstasy of the gift of comfort. Sonya held on tight to the little girl, amazed at the emotions she felt awakening in her, emotions she thought had died when Evan died. And she wanted them to stop. She realized now that she had tried to kill those passions. She knew now that she had been trying to feel nothing—not pain, not relief, not even love. She had been trying to kill herself.

Sonya didn't know or care how long they'd been sitting like that, the tired, anxious trio of people seeming to be waiting for something to happen to tell them what to do next. But at last Katherine broke the spell. Suddenly her grip on Sonya loosened, and she sat back. When Katherine glanced around her, the hunted look was gone. Her eyes held only a sadness, a loneliness that tore at Sonya's heart.

No one spoke as Katherine got up from Sonya's lap and wandered around the room, touching the leather sofa and chair, the rough stone of the fireplace, the solid oak of the old cabin door, and finally stopping to examine the polished brass lock that held it shut.

The girl, her peaked face looking frail, almost aged, turned and looked at Rick. She swallowed, the sound clearly audible in the quiet nighttime of the cabin. "Please, can I go home to my mother?"

"I told you before, Katherine, your mother is sick and can't take care of you right now." Sonya glared at Rick, hardly believing her ears. What an awful lie.

"When will she be better?"

"I don't know. But she wanted me to tell you not to worry. You'll be safe with me and Aunt Sonya until she gets well."

Aunt Sonya! He'd told her they were relatives?

"Could I go to the hospital and see her? Maybe it would help her to get better."

"No, Katherine," Rick said firmly. "The hospital has rules that I can't change. You're too young to visit."

The girl hung her head and tugged at a strand of hair.

Sonya stood up and held out her arms to Katherine. But now, instead of seeking comfort from Sonya, she retreated, bumping against a table and sending an abstract marble representation of the Madonna and child crashing to the floor. Sonya stood still, stunned by the pain of the sudden rejection—amazed at the power this little stranger had already assumed in her life. She had merely refused to come to Sonya, and Sonya felt herself crumbling.

"I'm sorry," said Katherine, stooping to pick up the unbroken sculpture.

"Damn it, girl," boomed Rick. "That's an irreplaceable piece of art."

Sonya was released from her spell of hurt by the look in Katherine's eye. "It was an accident," she said. She knelt and wrapped her arms around Katherine's shoulders. The child was quivering all over again. "She's tired and scared."

Sonya gently tilted the girl's face up and wiped away a tear that ran down one cheek. "He's just crabby from the long ride. Why don't we find out where you're going to sleep tonight?" Her tone was firm; she hoped Rick would understand that this child needed some kindness.

"Could I have—" Katherine's voice was so quiet that Sonya missed the last few words.

"What, dear?"

"Could I have something to eat?"

"Oh, Katherine, you're hungry," Sonya cried, feeling an unreasoning happiness flood through her. "Of course you can have something to eat." She looked up at Rick. "She can, can't she? Is there food here?" She heard the contempt in her voice when she spoke the word "here," as if she were referring to a bat cave full of guano.

Rick glared at her for a moment before answering. "Of course there's food here. And there's more out in the car."

With that, he went out the door, leaving Sonya and Katherine alone. Sonya glanced around, then headed into the kitchen. This was in what she guessed was a very old part of the cabin. The logs were chinked with moss, and the room had the smell and feel of a place where a pioneer woman might have cooked venison for her family. But the room was crowded, the center dominated by a burnt-orange U-shaped counter with a Jenn-air range built into it. Glass-fronted cabinets held stemware and decorative serving trays. She didn't know whose house this was, but it was clearly a place meant for serious entertaining. She only hoped the owner would want the house back soon so she could get Rick home and bring him to his senses.

But for now Sonya accepted that the three of them would be spending the night in this wilderness, so she opened the refrigerator and cabinets, taking stock of what food was there. To her surprise, the refrigerator, although not full, did contain what looked like new packages of cheese, lunchmeat, and a large canned ham. Then Sonya noticed a bowl of fresh fruit sitting on a side table. She had assumed that they would be here alone, but maybe this food belonged to the cabin owners and maybe they would return tonight, or soon.

In an old-fashioned breadbox, Sonya found a loaf of whole wheat, and she set about making Swiss cheese sandwiches for everyone. Katherine perched on a stool at the counter and watched her silently.

When Rick came in, he had a smile on his face. "You won't believe what I just saw outside!" he exclaimed, as he set down a huge Coleman cooler.

"What?" Sonya's reply was quiet, forced.

"I saw a black bear and two cubs heading down to the creek." He grinned at Katherine, but she looked away.

"What happened?" asked Sonya. She couldn't understand his apparent happiness at seeing a wild animal so close to where they were supposed to sleep.

"What do you mean what happened? They went on down to the creek." The annoyance was back in his voice, and Sonya wondered why she hadn't just played along with him, pretending to be excited, too. She'd always been able to cope with Rick before, saying the things that kept him happy—or at least not in a rage. Lately she found herself talking back, irritating him without meaning to.

"There's milk and things in there," he said, pushing the cooler toward where Sonya stood slicing cheese.

She opened the Coleman and found it crammed with milk, lettuce, carrots and celery, a whole chicken and three small steaks. She washed some lettuce and added that to the sandwiches, then set a plate in front of Katherine.

"Could I please have a bowl of cereal?" Katherine's request was delivered in a tired voice.

Sonya realized that she'd never even asked Katherine if she liked Swiss cheese. Evan had always loved it, so she'd just assumed Katherine would, too.

Feeling shame at her assumption, Sonya searched the cabinets and soon found a box of Cheerios. "Do you like Cheerios?"

"Yes. With raisins, please."

"You want some raisins?"

"My mama always puts raisins in my Cheerios." Katherine's voice held a mixture of hurt, fear and defiance. There was a package of little boxes of raisins in the same cupboard with the cereal. Sonya opened a box and poured a few into Katherine's bowl. "Thank you."

Katherine ate a single spoonful, then just stared into the bowl the whole time. Rick carried his plate into the living area. But instead of eating, he set about lighting the fire. It had already been laid with kindling and perfectly arranged logs, so it took only a bit of fanning to get the blaze going. Sonya stared in amazement at everything. She felt as if she was watching a movie of a perfectly normal family relaxing and having a snack before heading off to bed.

"Are the owners coming tonight?" she asked. She wanted to explore the house, but felt like she'd be trespassing.

"No. We have the place to ourselves. Take a look around. It's not bad."

Sonya detected a note of pride in his voice, as if it were his cabin. She remembered sadly the days when he'd sat at the dinner table with her and Evan, talking about the country place he'd buy for them all if his law practice continued to grow. He'd been flush with success, generous with his money if not his time. Now she wondered if maybe he had bought the place. With their current finances in such a mess, she couldn't believe he'd show such bad judgment. She almost laughed out loud at that. He'd just stolen a child from its mother—talk about bad judgment!

As she wandered through the rooms, she felt more and more insecure. The only way he could buy real estate as trendy as this place would be if he raised money by selling their house in Franklin Park. Surely he wouldn't consider anything that wild.

No. Sonya decided that she was letting her fears get out of hand. She set about making arrangements for sleeping.

There were three bedrooms on the first floor. One had two mirrored walls and a king-size bed with a velvet quilt. The second was rather plain and utilitarian. The walls were painted ivory, but there were wallpaper books lying open on the bed. So someone had been planning to redo the room. But when Sonya touched the opened page—a deep hunter-green plaid—it was dry and brittle. The corner broke off with a sound of old leaves. She got the impression that the book had been lying there for a long time. She inspected other books. They were all yellowed with age, too.

Frowning, Sonya traveled down the hall to the third bedroom. She was delighted to see that this one was bright and airy. It had a huge four-poster bed that looked like it came straight from an illustration in a children's book. And when she turned back the bright red-and-white patchwork quilt, she found the sheets were clean. She had the odd notion that maybe she had indeed fallen into some warped fairy tale. This bed was "just right" for Katherine—the others were too big or too plain. Perhaps those bears that Rick had seen earlier—

"Silly!" she said out loud, aware of how far her mind had wandered. Exhaustion was making her giddy. Except for a fine film of dust, the room was clean, and when Sonya opened the window, a fresh breeze stirred the candy-striped curtains, freshening the air.

At the far end of the hall there was a bathroom with a pleasing combination of the old and the new. The shower and tub were of a molded material, the showerhead the kind that would provide several kinds of massage. In contrast to the modern new tub, the sink looked like something from an old, very elegant hotel. A two-foot-high gray-and-white marble backsplash was topped with an intricately shaped shelf which held an antique shaving mug and brass shaving utensils. The faucets were old brass, and the soap dish was supported by a hand-carved mermaid. A stained glass panel of gold and green had been fitted into the only window, but its beauty was marred by several holes. It looked as if someone might have tried to break in, since the damage was near the window's lock.

Sonya returned to the kitchen. Katherine had apparently eaten no more of her cereal; she was staring glassy-eyed at Rick's back, where he sat before the living room fire. Katherine's expression was unreadable. Sonya felt a flash of anger at Rick for ignoring the girl. But maybe he was just giving her some time alone to adjust. In any case, it was nearly midnight.

"Katherine, would you like to take a bath, or do you just want to go to bed now, dear?"

Katherine shuddered, apparently startled by Sonya's voice. "I don't know."

The child's voice was filled with sadness. Sonya regretted offering her a choice. Katherine was clearly worn out, in need of guidance.

Sonya eyed the suitcases, then went over to Rick. For some reason, it angered her that she had to talk to him right now. She wanted to give all of her attention to Katherine.

"Do you have pajamas for Katherine? Or could she just sleep in one of your undershirts?"

''In the blue leather bag,'' he said, without turning to face her.

When Sonya lifted the suitcase lid, her eyes opened wide. Not only was there a soft, pink nightgown in the bag, it was filled to bursting with clothes in Katherine's size. There were blouses, shorts, jeans, a lightweight jacket, socks, tennis shoes and a set of underwear. The clothing was all new, most of it still had the store tags on.

As Sonya searched for scissors to cut the labels off, she tried to account for the clothes. The clothes, and all the food, too—it all seemed so organized, so planned. If Rick had taken Katherine in a fit of emotion, after seeing her being abused, then how and when did he do all the shopping and arranging? And whose house was this, anyway?

Sonya glanced at Katherine. She was sitting quietly, tears running down her cheeks, falling unheeded into her cereal bowl. *Enough!* thought Sonya. Who could figure anything out under these circumstances.

She went to Katherine, took her hand and helped her down from the bar stool, then led her to the back bedroom where she helped Katherine change into the nightgown. She was unaware that she'd been humming until Katherine said, ''I like that song. My mama used to sing it to me when I was little.''

''So did mine,'' said Sonya. Dreamily, the woman and the girl gazed at each other. Then Katherine climbed into Sonya's lap and rested her head against Sonya's breast just over her heart. In another moment, they lay down, and Sonya pulled the quilt up to cover them both. *I wish we could keep you*, she thought as she drifted first into a half-sleep, where all she sensed was the warmth and solidity of the child, then slid deeper into a dark and silent slumber.   .

10...

MARGOT KNOCKED AND waited. At just after five-thirty A.M., it was quiet in the white-on-white, sterile hallway. She could almost hear the breathing of the sleeping high-rise occupants. She imagined she could hear Katy's laughter behind Joseph's door. The fantasy began to grow as she pictured the door being flung open, and Katy leaping into her arms the way she always did after spending a few days with her father. This, Margot's last hope, was so strong that she felt removed from herself, as if she hovered somewhere over her own body, her face distorted, as in a Fellini film.

Dimly Margot wondered if she were hallucinating. She'd had almost no sleep since Katy's disappearance. And at two o'clock this morning, she'd given in and swallowed the Valiums her doctor suggested she take.

How long have I been waiting, she wondered, and rapped at the door with her keys. Five tiny dents appeared in the perfectly enameled surface of the door; Margot realized she'd struck it too hard.

"Hold on a minute," she heard; then the door was wrenched open.

Joseph had a bath towel wrapped around him. His hair was dripping on the marble tile of the foyer. Margot felt embarrassed to have caught him so, awkward at the sight of him undressed, now that they were no longer living together.

"Sorry, Joe. I should have phoned first," she said, standing in the hall.

"That's okay. I'm just surprised the doorman let you up without—"

"Well, he knew me. I mean he knew my face. From being on TV so much the last few days. I mean more than normal. Because of Katy." Margot stepped around Joseph, careful not to touch him. She sat in the big leather chair and glanced around the living room. Her hallway fantasy of Katy, her own Katy jumping up and running into her arms popped like an overfilled balloon. She wasn't even sure why she'd come. "Please, go on and get dressed. I didn't mean to disturb you."

Joe closed the front door quietly and started down the hall. But he stopped and called out, "There's Ovaltine in the cabinet above the stove if you'd like some."

Margot bit her lip. She'd always joked that they were probably the only family in America in which everyone loved Ovaltine. They'd all started drinking it a few years ago when Katy had been recovering from tonsil surgery and ice-cold Ovaltine was the only food she'd take when she came home. Margot and Joseph had begun drinking it themselves just to get her to join in, and since then they'd all become addicted to the stuff. Now, Margot wondered if whoever had taken Katy would buy her Ovaltine. That was if— As she'd been doing ever since Saturday, Margot jumped up and tried to physically escape the thought, unwilling, completely unable, to face the rest of the "if" questions.

As she wandered around the room, the hem of her coat brushed against a tall stack of magazines piled neatly atop the brass and glass coffee table. They slid sideways, then began to slowly cascade over the edge to the floor. "Damn," she muttered and knelt to pick them up. Joseph came out, dressed in his jogging clothes and bent to help her.

"What can I do?" he asked.

"You can tell me if the police were right in the first place." Margot stood and looked down at Joseph. "Did you have anything to do with Katy's disappearance? Do you know where she is?"

"Are you crazy?" Joseph stood up quickly, leaving the magazines on the floor. "Did I kidnap my own daughter?"

Margot stood still, refusing to break eye contact with him. She had to know.

"Did you?"

"No! I did not." Joseph shook his head, turned and stomped away. He wheeled and headed back toward Margot, then away again.

"I can't believe you could ask me such a thing. Kidnap Katy!" Again, Joseph bent to retrieve the magazines. He threw them at the table top; they slid across and onto the floor again.

"And what about you?" asked Joseph. He paced briskly around the room. Margot had to twist and turn to keep him in sight.

"What do you mean, 'What about me'?" she said.

"Are the police checking you out? You have a big show. Who knows how many nut cases watch you every day? And who knows what's in their minds? Could be one of them didn't like how you covered a topic and decided to punish you. Have you thought of that? Have you?"

Margot was growing dizzier by the minute. Trying to watch Joe as he paced the perimeter of the room was like trying to watch Katy on the merry-go-round. Round and round and not going anywhere but still out of sight. Like watching TV when the cable connection is loose. Only glimpses.

"I've thought of that, Joe. And so have the police." He wasn't asking an unreasonable question. The guilt she felt at the possibility of her show as the cause of Katy's abduction leached any anger from her reply. "In fact, at the beginning I was just as much a suspect as you were. They apparently thought we were playing the game that starts with one parent demanding custody and then both parents hurrying to be the first to hide the child."

"But we'd never do that. Hey, we've had our problems, but no, not that." He sat down hard on the couch and just stared, helplessness in his eyes, his shoulders drooping, his hands open before him.

Margot noticed for the first time that his eyes were red-rimmed. *Like mine*, she thought. And his hands were shaking. *Like mine*. She sat down across from him.

"I'm sorry. I never really thought you took her," Margot said. "I told them that, but apparently it's the pet theory." Margot swallowed hard. "I didn't realize until just this minute that I secretly hoped you *had* taken her. Then at least I'd know she'd be treated well. Even if I didn't know where she was, that is."

"They said down at the police station that there's been no word, no clues at all. Is that true?"

"You don't believe them? What—? Do you know something you haven't told them? Tell me, if you do."

"Damn! You're reading things into my words again." He stood up and paced angrily over to the windows, his back to her. Margot stared at him, silhouetted against the floor-to-ceiling expanse, with Pittsburgh's steel and glass towers glowing coldly against a gray sky. A few drops of rain spattered against the glass; the sound was like tiny fingers patting damp skin.

I will not argue with him, she thought. *It's Katy that matters*.

"I'm sorry. I've been looking for clues everywhere, trying to figure this thing out. I just thought maybe you had a new angle on it, something—" Margot began to pick up the magazines again, thinking as she did so how bizarre it was that she and Joseph seemed to be locked into everyday actions, tidying, offering beverages, when these things no longer mattered.

Joseph turned and gazed at Margot, then came and knelt beside her. "Do you think she's all right?" he asked.

He looked, at the moment, no older than Katy. He was pleading with Margot for reassurance. She wanted to shout at him, to slap him, to demand that he grow up, face the realities. But she couldn't. She wanted reassurance, too. She slid off the chair onto the Berber rug. It felt like dry grass against her knees. "Oh, yes, I'm sure she is. She has to be." She reached out, and Joseph grabbed her. He wrapped his arms tightly around her and buried his face against her neck. "Of course she's all right," cried Margot, as they held each other, rocking slightly, clinging to each other.

Joseph joined her in what had become almost a prayer, more a plea than a statement. "She's all right. Katy is okay."

"We'll find her," said Margot. "Of course we'll find her."

And Margot was suddenly struck with a sense of déjà vu. She recalled the evening of Katy's abduction. She remembered clinging to her mother, seeking answers and comfort. And here she was three days later, still seeking answers, still finding nothing, still waiting for some hint that Katy was even alive.

"Okay," she said, disentangling herself from Joseph's warm arms. "If we're going to look, we have to get organized. It's time we count our assets."

Joseph cocked an eyebrow. "Sounds good to me. But I give. What are our assets?"

"Well," she said, "gimme a minute."

While Margot thought, Joe went to the kitchenette and got out the makings of two glasses of Ovaltine. He stirred them with a huge clatter and brought them into the living room. Before he sat down, he got a couple of legal pads and some pencils from his desk and set them on the coffee table.

"Assets?" he asked.

"I've been debating whether we should list the police investigation under assets or liabilities."

"I know what you mean." Joe took a long pull at his drink. "But aren't they just going by the book? You and I know that neither one of us snatched Katy, but they're right to suspect us."

"That's true. But it's wasting time."

Margot twisted the eraser end of her pencil in her curls. "At least they're following some other leads. I spoke with the captain late last night, and he said they're comparing what they have on Katy with those kidnappings in Ohio. So far they've been mostly in the western part of the state, but it's close enough geographically to consider a possibility."

"Did you tell him how Katy was conceived? About the sperm bank?"

"I did. I asked him to check it out in case there might be a connection. He managed to keep a straight face, but I could tell he thought I was a crackpot for even bringing it up."

"Well, it does seem far-fetched, but you never know. Did he agree to investigate that angle?"

"Sort of. He said he'd 'keep it in mind.'"

"That's how he put it? 'Keep it in mind'?"

"Uh huh. Not too promising."

"He didn't take down any information on it?"

"He made a few notes. But to be honest, I think he's still not too sure about us. I don't know what it would take to convince him that we don't have Katy hidden away somewhere, but—"

"Okay. How about the possibility that it might be one of your crazy fans?"

"You make it sound like my viewers are all psychopaths."

"Sorry. I didn't mean it that way. But have they checked to see if there's anything threatening or weird in your mail?"

"Yes. I talked with Mick, and he said the investigators will be at the station today going through every letter and every phone call in the log. They're checking all the way back to when I did the weather."

"And Katy's friends? Our neighbors?"

"All being canvassed."

"Anything else?"

"Not that I know of." Margot set down her empty glass and sighed.

"Why do you think they're not doing more with the information on the sperm bank?"

"Maybe the other leads are more promising?" said Margot, more as a question than a statement.

"Do you want to hear what I think?" asked Joe.

"Sure. Couldn't hurt."

"I think we should get out everything we have on the artificial insemination. All the paperwork we can find. And we should write down any names connected with it that we can remember. Then we talk with Dr. Barryman and get his records. I can start making some calls about that while you go down to the station and see about the fan mail."

"Couldn't hurt," said Margot. "And to be honest, I *have* gotten some off-the-wall letters. The kind of love letters that don't have much to do with love."

"If either one of us finds anything, we'll call or leave messages on the machines?" said Joe.

"Okay. Why don't you come over to my house tomorrow at ten," said Margot. It sounded odd saying that to Joseph when not that long ago it had been *their* house. "Beth is coming by with the research on kidnapping that she's doing. We can coordinate our efforts."

"Good. I'll be there. And Margot—"

"Yes?"

"We'll find her. She'll be all right."

"I know." Like doing their own research, Margot thought, it couldn't hurt to be positive. It was really all they could do for Katy at the moment.

11...

BETH CHECKED THE printouts one last time to make sure she hadn't missed anything. With a wry smile she recalled how she'd always described her attitude toward her research work for Margot's TV show. "Dead serious," Beth would say. "I'm dead serious about the research. If I screw up, then Margot screws up. Maybe it's only Pittsburgh viewers who would know, but it could also be the day the national network people decide to watch." Now "dead serious" held a new meaning for her, and she shivered inwardly. Katy was as close as family to her. Beth could barely stand to think about where the child might be at the moment or what might be happening to her.

"Hey, Beth," called a station go-fer as he passed by her office door. "Ms. DesMarais wants to see the notes ASAP."

Carefully, she stacked the notes together, then tucked them into a leather folder stamped with the distinctive blue-and-white "Pittsburgh Today" logo. She walked slowly down the hall, and with a soft tap on Margot's dressing room door, she entered. The sight of her friend broke her heart. There were no tears on Margot's face; she wasn't wringing her hands. She merely sat, her face a stone study of pain.

"I think I've found some useful stuff here," said Beth, trying to sound upbeat and positive.

Margot just held out her hand for the folder. Beth took a seat at the dressing table and watched as Candy continued blow-drying Margot's hair. The room was warm and stuffy, filled with the hum of the hair dryer.

Margot riffled through the pages, anxiety and exhaustion

evident in the shaking of her hands. She gestured impatiently at Candy, batting at the blow dryer. Candy immediately switched it off and asked, "Did I burn you?"

"No, I'm fine. But please, just tie it back or something. I haven't got time for hair today." Her words were brusque, and Candy looked more surprised than hurt.

"Sure. I've got a pretty blue satin—"

"That's fine," said Margot. As if to hurry Candy along, she pushed hastily at her hair, tucking it behind her ears.

With big eyes, Candy glanced at Beth, then shrugged and began fashioning a ponytail.

Beth pulled her chair closer to Margot's, and together they bent their heads over the notes.

"What's this?" asked Margot, indicating a page titled "Alternate Motives."

"Oh, crap, it's out of order. It's supposed to follow the page with the most common motives for kidnapping." While she reshuffled the pages, she explained, "An overwhelming percentage of kidnappings are really child snatchings."

A sound that could only be described as a hiss came from Margot's lips. "I really can't handle this today," said Margot, squeezing her temples.

"I know. I'm sorry. That's all I was going to say about it. The point is that all three of the psychiatrists agree that, except for child snatchings and straightforward ransom demands, the other motives are so diverse that you can't do much with them." Beth paused, wishing for the hundredth time that she'd found something more useful to offer.

"So what am I supposed to do? I've got a half hour to convince someone—we don't know who—who's grabbed my daughter—we don't know why—to say 'Oops, sorry,' and just give her back." She began pawing through the papers, sending a few sheets floating to the floor. "What good can it do?"

"I know," said Beth, placing her hand on Margot's shoulder. "I know how hard it is, but at least you have the

chance to go on TV. I'm sure whoever has Katy will be
watching, and—''

''But that's just it,'' said Margot. ''What if it's the fact
that I *am* on TV that made him take her? If I had never
gotten my own show, would Katy be at home right now?
Safe in her own room? Would she?''

Beth shook her head, then took Margot's hands in her
own. ''Okay, now look at me.'' Margot looked at the floor.

''I said look at me!''

Margot looked up.

''Don't fall apart now. You've been doing great so far.
Use this opportunity to help Katy. And, Margot, please,
please remember—guilt won't help. It's a waste of energy.''

''Guess you're right,'' said Margot in a weak voice.

''Damned straight, I'm right! Use your brains here, will
you? Can't you see that's your best weapon? You've got to
outsmart this guy. That's how you can help Katy. Outsmart
the bastard!''

Margot shifted in her chair, straightened her back. Her
lips became a tight line for a moment, then she smiled.
''Thanks. I needed that.''

''Here,'' said Beth, handing Margot the microphone
battery pack. With a wide elastic band, Margot fastened it to
her thigh, then threaded the wire up under her slip and
attached the mike to her blouse collar. She reached for a
loose-fitting blue silk jacket.

Beth pulled a charcoal-gray dress from the rack. ''You
don't think maybe this would be more—'' she hesitated,
then finished, ''appropriate?''

''No. I'm not going on as a talk-show hostess or as an
expert on anything. Today I'm a mother. And I've thought
about this. Beth—'' A glow came into Margot's eyes. But
the expression was not one of joy, but more that of a fever
dream, a look that frightened Beth. ''Beth, do you realize
that Katy—wherever she is—Katy might be watching
today? So don't you see, I can't go on looking like a TV
talk-show host. I've got to look like her mom. I've got

to—'' She stopped, shook her head as if to clear it, then switched gears again. ''Whatever. Let's check your notes on the set. It's only fifteen minutes to air time.''

Margot seemed tough and fragile all at once. Beth couldn't help reflecting that her popularity lay in just that combination. Some snappy journalist had already pegged her ''the phemale Phil,'' but he'd missed something essential. Sure, Margot had the sense of hard-hitting reality that made Donahue compelling, and she had the same kind of genuine compassion that made Phil lovable. But Margot had a vulnerability that made her unique. When guests attacked her, as they occasionally did, the audience often grew surly and defensive.

But her audience today was a different matter. Beth could see that from Margot's point of view she had only two people to speak to today—the man who had taken Katy and Katy herself. As she'd done so many times during the last few horrible days, Beth said a silent prayer for the little girl.

12...

MARGOT CLIMBED THE few stairs to the stage and took her place in the single chair placed there. She noted that there was a water pitcher and tumbler on the small table, as well as a box of Kleenex and a small green plant. The set director must have the same idea as Beth, mused Margot. Usually there were several large, cheerful arrangements of flowers on the stage. Even when the day's topic was a serious one like rape, incest, drug addiction or any of the other subjects that never seemed to lose the viewers' interest—even then there were several large plants. But here she sat next to a single scrawny philodendron. The makeup man came on and patted powder lightly on Margot's nose. "You look marvelous, darling," he said with a wink, rolling the first syllable of "marvelous" around inside his mouth in the manner of Billy Crystal. Gratefulness flooded her. It felt good to be treated like a human being instead of an egg even for just a moment.

But the relief was short-lived. Hurrying toward her, waving his squashed wallet at the security guard, was the police captain. He looked the same as he had each time she'd seen him—pale face with dark circles under his eyes, hair that was neatly combed but too long and his body clothed in wrinkled, nondescript suit parts.

"Mark," called Margot to her producer. "I can't talk to anyone right now. Would you help the captain—"

The police officer cut Mick short and turned to Margot. "I just want a moment, Mrs. DesMarais. It won't take long."

"All right," said Margot. She came down the few stairs

to stand in front of the captain, preventing him from taking a seat. "Please be quick. We go on air in a few minutes."

"I just wanted to try one more time to stop you from doing this." He rubbed his chin, which showed stubble. "Sometimes a mother's plea works, and it's a good way to handle a thing like this. But we don't know what we're dealing with here. We haven't got a clue."

Margot could guess how sincere he was about that statement. But she couldn't read any emotions in his tired face. Was he sorry that he'd botched the investigation, losing all that time hunting for Joseph? Or was he angry that it would look bad on his record? She'd checked around and this was his first big case since being promoted to captain. Margot couldn't understand why he was still in charge, although she knew that it might make the police department look even worse if they handed the case off to someone else. The captain *had* gone by the book, checking out all angles, but he'd been so convinced that Joseph had snatched Katy that Margot knew that only scant attention had been paid to other possibilities.

"Captain, there are no clues because—"

"Jeez, it's freezing in here." The officer was rolling down his shirtsleeves and glancing around as if expecting to find an open refrigerator door.

"It's to compensate for the spotlights. As soon as they go on, the set will warm up by twenty degrees."

He nodded. "Okay, I'm gonna be blunt, ma'am. If the guy is a nut case, and you go on TV all teary-eyed and begging him to let little Katy go, he's gonna be thrilled to pieces. It'll make him even more set on keeping her, hoping he can see you again making him out the big man."

"You may think you're being blunt, Captain, but you're only stating the obvious. I'm not stupid. But I am in trouble. As they say in the movies, the trail is cold, and I've interviewed enough experts on my show to know that it's the first forty-eight hours that count in following clues. If there's anything I can offer to help you," Margot paused and released a huge sigh, "I'll do it in a minute. In the meantime, I'm doing everything on my own that I can."

Margot deliberately turned her back on the captain and stepped over the tangles of cables to where Beth stood talking with Mark. "Look," she said to them, "if the detective is going to be any help at all, you've got to clean him up a little."

Mark glanced over his shoulder at the captain, then shook his head in dismay. Beth let out a puff of air and said, "He looks worse than Columbo warmed over. I'll get Candy to see what she can do."

"Five minutes, Margot," called the director. "Anything I can get you before we start?"

"No, no thanks, Hannah. Just keep your fingers crossed."

"They already are."

Margot settled into her chair and waited quietly while technicians made final light and audio checks. Just as she did before every show, she ran through a mental picture of her audience. Usually she pictured a melange of homemakers, retired people, workers with nontraditional schedules, young people out of school for the day, job hunters. But her imagined audience was never a faceless crowd made up of people her research staff told her to speak to. Her imagined audience was composed of real people, people she'd met with and talked with individually both before and after the show each day. But today she could only see two people in her mind's eye. With a yearning in her heart, she pictured Katy, and with all of her mental faculties tried to call to her young daughter, tried to *cause* her child to watch the television.

Then, as if a storm had risen to obscure her vision, she saw a dark shape—the nightmare shape of a man—someone strong and cruel enough to wrench a child from safety and imprison her in terror. Calling on inner strength she'd never needed before, Margot tried to will that man to watch the television. In all the possible scenarios her brain had dredged up, she gave little room to the notion that this might be a random snatching. She felt certain that the man knew whom he had taken, and Margot was quite sure that he'd be watching TV today—watching to see the results of his actions. And that thought had brought another concrete image: This man had to be physically nearby, either in the Pittsburgh viewing area, which included western Pennsylvania, some of West Virginia and Ohio, or close enough to the fringes of the area that a satellite dish would pull in the signal. Along with her constant sense of guilt that somehow it was her television celebrity that had triggered Katy's kidnapping was the comforting thought that it was her show that—with the invisible ropes of the airwaves—would tie Katy to Margot.

"Thirty seconds, Margot," said the director. "Are you okay?"

"I'm fine." She paused, straightened her back. "I'm ready."

"Good. And five, four, three, two, one."

Margot saw the "Pittsburgh Today" logo appear on the monitor at the back of the studio. The show's theme song played. Hannah had asked Margot if they should forgo the music today, but Margot had replied, "No. It's part of the show. And music can be good. If she's watching, I want Katy to hear it."

For just a moment, when the lights came on, Margot felt lost, unsure of what she was to say. There was no crowd of people, hand-picked by the audience coordinator to be certain to be interested in the topic. She had no guests on her stage to question. Taking a deep breath, she unclenched her hands and faced the camera. "Hello. I'm Margot DesMarais and this is 'Pittsburgh Today.' As many of you may know, last Saturday my five-year-old daughter was abducted by a stranger." Margot hesitated, cleared her throat, then proceeded. "I'm not able to talk about what the police have uncovered in the investigation so far. And I'm obviously not here today in my capacity as a talk-show hostess. Today, my

producer has given me the opportunity to come on and
speak as a mother.''

Margot closed her eyes, shutting out the light, the
cameras, the fear. I can't do it, she thought. Her throat
constricted. She had no voice. But Katy, she thought. She
remembered why she'd come today. With a small, barely
audible moan, she opened her eyes and poured a glass of
water. From the side of the stage, she'd seen Beth approaching, then stop in midstep when Margot picked up the
pitcher.

Beth gave her a brief, tight-lipped smile and a thumbs-up
sign, then backed off.

''Clearly, this is a legal situation where the police are
compelled to search for the person who took my daughter
and bring him to trial. I say 'him' because, as you may have
learned on the news, a man was seen taking Katy away from
the carnival where she was abducted. The police are not
ruling out the possibility that there's more than a single
person involved. But the main message I want to deliver is
this.'' Margot sat forward on the edge of her chair, adjusting
the microphone cord as she did so. ''Please be aware that
my first priority, and the first priority of the police as well,
is the safety of K—'' Margot's voice stuck on Katy's name.
She tried again, ''—the safety of my daughter.''

At that point, Margot rose and turned to greet the captain
as he entered. She shook his hand and nodded toward the
other chair on the stage. ''This is Captain Lewis of the
Pittsburgh Police Department.''

''Hello,'' he said. ''I'm not here to—'' He sounded
nervous. ''Well, why I'm here today is that I want to tell the
perp—uh, the person who took the child that the police
always have two goals in a case like this. First we want to
get the child back. And second we want to apprehend the
individual or individuals who are responsible for taking her.
But the important thing to remember is this: If the child is
returned safely, things are gonna go a lot easier for the
offender.''

Margot listened, aware that the captain's nervousness had vanished now that he was involved in a familiar subject.

"Now it's easier than the party or parties might think to get the little girl safely back to her mother. You don't have to drive her up to a police department. There are lots of places where you can drop her off and she can find someone to help her. The mall or a busy grocery store is a good place. Her mother has told me," he glanced at Margot, then back to the camera, "that Katy knows to go to a clerk in a store for help if she's lost. So if you leave her somewhere, she'll be taken care of. If she was just dropped off out in the country, she might get lost or hurt, so it wouldn't be a good idea to try that. You have any questions, Mrs. DesMarais?"

"No, thank you, Captain, no questions. But I would like to say one more thing. Katy—" Margot shuddered, squinched her eyes shut for a moment, then continued. "Katy, if you can hear me, sweetheart, please be brave. I'm thinking of you every minute, and I'm doing everything I can so that you can come home soon."

With that, Margot rose and walked off the stage, unable to say anything further. She was vaguely aware that Hannah was speaking to the audience, explaining that the remainder of the show's time would be taken up by a rerun of an earlier show.

Beth hurried over to Margot and hugged her tightly.

Margot felt the tears flowing and wiped angrily at them. "I'm sorry, Beth. I couldn't use any of the research. I just couldn't do it that way."

"That's okay. No problem. You did just fine."

"Do you think it did any good? Or did I make things worse?"

"Oh, good. Definitely, you did some good. If whoever took Katy has any thought that he'd like to undo things, the message was clear. The best thing he could do would be to let her go right away. We'll just have to pray it got through to him."

Together, with Beth's arm protectively around Margot's

shoulder, they walked down the hall toward Margot's dressing room. When they were nearly there, they heard a commotion from the direction of the newsroom. Normally, Margot would simply switch on the TV set in her dressing room to see what the news flash was, but today she hurried toward the news studio.

Beth pulled Margot out of the path of a technician as he dragged a mesh of cables toward some video equipment. Writers and the anchorman conferred as they prepared to deliver the newsflash. Snippets of conversation flew:

"—the child been revived?"

"—no others injured."

"Get that tape from eighty-eight."

"What kind of boat?"

"Where'd they take the kid?"

Margot could not stand it any longer. She hurried through the chaos toward Sandy at the news desk. "What child? What's happened?" she demanded.

Sandy, the anchorman, looked surprised to see Margot in his territory. "I'll be with you in a minute, Margot," he said then turned back to the printout he held.

"Okay, Sandy, twenty seconds," said the news director.

Out of habit, Margot quickly backed away from the news desk and went to a corner of the studio. She breathed rapidly as she heard the special bulletin music played.

Sandy began:

"We've just received word that a boat has veered off course at the Three Rivers Boat Regatta and at least one bystander has been injured. A young girl, perhaps four to seven years old, was found floating at the edge of the river. Paramedics began CPR, and the child has been rushed to Allegheny General Hospital. Meanwhile, police are searching for her parents or guardian, but no one has claimed the child. Thus far, no other victims have been found.

"Not since the tragic accident of nineteen eighty-eight, when two bystanders were killed when a speedboat veered off course and plowed into the crowd, has there been any sort of danger to the onlookers at Pittsburgh's annual regatta. New safeguards were instituted following the nineteen eighty-eight tragedy, but once again, something has gone very wrong with the system.''

Margot half-listened to the background information, hoping to hear more about the child soon. She had no reason to think that the child might be Katy, but the fact that they couldn't find the girl's family struck hope into her heart.

Sandy was handed a sheet of paper by an assistant. He glanced at it, then read, ''Because of the chaos, no one is sure how long the girl was in the water. She was pulled out by two teenage boys. Authorities are asking for any information anyone may have on the child's identity. She is Caucasian, of slight build, and appears to be between the ages of four and seven. Her condition is critical. We will bring you further reports as more information becomes available.''

Margot spotted Captain Lewis at the entrance to the studio and ran over to him. ''Please, can you find out more? Can you call someone?''

The captain just stared at her as if she was mad.

''I don't see why you're getting so worked up, ma'am. It's too bad about—''

''It could be Katy. Don't you see. They can't find anyone with the girl. It could be Katy. Maybe he let her go, or maybe she got away. Please—''

''Okay, okay. Chances are they've found her people by now, but I can make a few calls. Where's a phone?''

''Here, right here,'' said Margot, punching a button on a wall phone. ''Dial nine first.''

Just as he was about to dial, the beeper at his waist began to sound. ''Hang on a minute, Miss DesMarais, I got to get this one first.''

''Damn!'' she cried, and paced a few angry steps away from the captain as he dialed the phone.

''Ma'am,'' he called, covering the mouthpiece. ''It's an

officer down at the hospital. It's in my jurisdiction, so I'll be going over there."

"Have they found the girl's parents yet?"

"No, but I'll get back with you if there's anything I—"

"Does she have red hair?"

With a sigh, the captain spoke into the phone. "What color's the kid's hair?"

A pause. "Brown."

"Maybe it's still wet and just looks brown. What color eyes?"

"You got an eye color?" He turned to Margot. "He's checking."

She waited, her teeth clenched, her hands in tight fists.

"Brown. The little girl's eyes are brown."

"Maybe she's wearing colored contacts?" Margot asked weakly, knowing how inane it sounded. She just didn't want to let go of the hope.

"No. I'm sorry. I can't blame you for— Hold on a minute."

The captain listened a moment, then spoke into the phone. "Okay, I'm on my way." He hung up and turned to Margot. "They just found the kid's dad. He'd gone to get some sodas when the accident happened. Then he couldn't get back through the crowd. It wasn't your Katy."

Margot was struck by the kindness in his voice. It wasn't his normal brusque manner of speaking.

"All right. Thank you, Captain. I hope the little girl recovers . . ."

"Well there's some good news there. She woke up right before I hung up the phone. Maybe it's some kind of a sign, an omen for you and your daughter."

Margot reflected that the captain didn't seem like the sort of man to spend much time believing in omens. She just nodded. "Maybe it is," she said quietly. "I'm glad the girl is out of danger."

13...

A LITTLE GIRL whimpered in a woman's arms. When the elevator doors closed, she said, "No, no, no. Mama, no." And when the gentle upward movement began, she screeched. She screamed so hard, it made her body shake. Her skin grew red, and the fat clump of white lace on her socks quivered like leaves in a gale. It was amazing to Billy that she didn't struggle or try to escape. As her terror expanded to fill the moving world of the elevator, she clung even closer to her mother.

Probably never been on an elevator before, thought Billy. He had always liked little kids, so he didn't mind the hurricane atmosphere the girl was creating. In fact, he was grateful for the diversion. He didn't want anyone to take notice of him, and with the girl howling, no one did. With any luck, he would be able to tell the kidnapped child's grampa what he suspected and be out of the hospital in time to get home for "Jeopardy" on TV.

He stepped off at the eighth floor and scanned the Allegheny General Hospital directory. Turning left, he headed for the neurological unit. As he was about to push open the door, a nurse came out. She smiled at him before hurrying on. He felt sweat break out on his back. She had looked directly in his eyes. Long enough to remember him and describe him if asked to do so. To his right he saw a sign that said "Men."

Thank God. The door opened. He entered, closed the door and locked it. Unable to stand the tension any longer, Billy slumped to the restroom floor and watched his hands as they did a stupid dance on the cold tile.

He tried to breathe easily, but could only gasp for a few minutes. His whole system flooded afresh with adrenaline when someone rattled the doorknob. If he could just have a little drink, he'd be stronger. When I'm done, he thought, there's a bottle of bourbon with my name on it. Pulling together all his strength, Billy stood up, turned on the cold water and splashed handfuls onto his face. With a yard-long section of rough brown paper towel, he scrubbed at his face and neck. He felt better.

Before he opened the door, he pulled out a scrap of newspaper that showed a picture of the little girl. It had been four days now since she'd disappeared. All of his hopes that she would be returned had faded. One of "his" children was in danger, and the sense of responsibility that had bloomed when he figured out it was his fault had grown stronger over the last few days. He'd expected it to diminish like every other urge he'd ever had, except the urge to booze it up. But even two quarts of bourbon drunk as smoothly as if it were cool water had not allowed him to get back to his normal life. Oh, he'd fallen asleep, but there had been no rest there.

In his dreams, the children—all of "his" children, the ones he'd worked so hard to give birthrights of health, and smarts, and beauty—those children paraded through his dreams sick, hurt, dirty and calling for help. Some of them dragged sperm tanks along behind them, leaving small, smooth tracks through the dirt. And even the tanks seemed to have voices, that pleaded with him to help.

Squaring his shoulders and calling on some good part of himself that Billy was surprised still existed, he pushed through the door into the hall, then into the neurological unit. The nurses' station was deserted, so he walked slowly down the hall, checking names beside the doors.

There it was. "Gregory Newhouse," it said. That was the name they'd given in the newspaper for the girl's grandfather. "In a tragic, related incident," it had read, "Gregory Newhouse, grandfather of the missing child, suffered an apparent stroke while driving on the Parkway, near the Fort Pitt Bridge.''

Billy pushed lightly on the door. It swung inward, revealing a room dimly lit by light seeping through closed Venetian blinds. A TV screen, installed high overhead, cast a flickering glow on the ceiling, but the sound was not on at the moment. He could see the outlines of a person's feet under a sheet. With his hand in his pocket, he crushed the newspaper photo of the girl into a ball. He walked forward.

Suddenly the room was flooded with light. Billy turned to see a stub of a woman carrying in a breakfast tray. ''Good morning, Mr. Newhouse. How are you today?'' It sounded more like a statement than a question. She moved quickly as she set the tray on the stand and wheeled it toward the bed. ''I see you have company this morning,'' she said, nodding toward Billy.

He nodded back, trying to appear invisible. The man in the bed gazed at both of them with a friendly smile—or maybe it was just a blank grin. Billy couldn't tell.

The woman pressed a button to raise the fellow up and rapidly punched his pillows to give him better support.

Billy was beginning to think maybe the old guy's stroke was bad, the kind that left someone a vegetable. So he was startled when the guy spoke.

''I'm doing better. Hoping to get out of here soon.''

''Good for you. Good for you.'' Everything the woman said sounded like a recording. But at least she made an effort, thought Billy, not like the flying bitches he'd had for nurses at the detox center a few years ago. A smile woulda cracked their faces wide open and spilled out their rotten brains.

A cramp went through Billy's stomach as the aide removed a silver cover to reveal toast.

''See you later,'' she called breezily as she hustled out the door.

Billy began to feel like Boo Radley, some pitiful moron

in a book he'd read in college. Boo used to hide behind doors, trying to be invisible.

It seemed that this grandfather of the little girl wasn't in real bad shape. Billy was just about to tell him what he knew when another fast-moving hospital employee came in. This one had a plastic thing full of tubes of blood. Some of it looked like maybe it had been in the carrier for years.

"One moment please, Mr. Newhouse," said the woman, a Jamaican lilt to her voice. "We've been running behind somethin' terrible this mornin'. If I could just trouble you for a few drops of blood before you begin your breakfast—"

"If there's any left, you're welcome to it," the guy replied.

"Perhaps your friend could lend me a little if you've run out." And with that she smiled a broad, large-toothed smile at Billy.

"Sorry, I'm just checking on the TV," said Billy, and he turned around. With shaking hands, he turned the volume up.

"Must be the wrong room. This volume's fine," he mumbled.

Billy hurried out. His attempts at staying anonymous were a joke. Just like the rest of his life, he thought. He felt dizzy and weak as he hurried out of the ward and down to the elevators.

Déjà vu. As the door slid aside, he was greeted by the wailing of the same little girl who had been on the elevator when he went up. Maybe she was crying because they just did that all day long, he thought. Just rode up and down all day. Maybe they never let the poor kid off the elevator.

As he drove home, he reflected on life and how impossible it was for him to get it right. All he wanted to do was make things right. He just wanted to let somebody know the name of the guy he figured had kidnapped the little girl. At first Billy thought he would tell the kid's father. The newspaper said his name was Joseph DesMarais. But directory assistance said the man's number was unlisted.

Then he had gotten really brave—brave or stupid, he thought—because he had decided to go to the TV station where Margot DesMarais did her show. Billy had figured that maybe he could talk to her privately. But that was a laugh—security was tight, and worse yet, there had been a patrol car parked by the door. She probably had a cop with her day and night. The last person Billy wanted to talk to was a cop, so he thought he'd finally had a good idea when he decided to tell the grandfather.

Now Billy tried to work up the courage to go to the police. But how could he ignore the possibility that they would hold him for questioning. Even one overnight session in jail would kill him, he knew it.

He wouldn't be able to get a drink when he needed one.

And what if they found the sperm bank records out in his garage. His plan to start up a new cryobank when the old one was closed by the parent corporation had never gotten beyond the wishing stage. Still, maybe they'd call it theft—taking the records. Billy was not a lawyer, but he knew he'd screwed up. He wouldn't be so worried if he didn't have those drunk driving charges against him. And the assault charge by the bastard at the bar—the asshole who tried to kill Billy, but somehow the charges were against Billy.

By the time Billy got home, the shakes were so bad he could hardly turn off the ignition of his old Dodge. When at last the tender heat of the bourbon flowed down his throat he felt like that old man in the hospital—he was pretty sure he didn't have any blood left.

Billy pushed some shirts and underwear off the sofa and lay down. He closed his eyes and drank bourbon and breathed deeply. After a while he began to feel better.

14...

JOSEPH WATCHED AS Beth kissed her husband Harry good-bye. Joe grabbed the spoon from the baby just as he was about to fling a blob of oatmeal after his father.

"Well, we should be able to get to work as soon as Frankie is done," said Beth. "I'll take over now," she said, reaching for the spoon.

"No, let me finish. He's a hungry fellow, and I don't think you feed him fast enough." Beth scanned his face. He knew what she was thinking. Was he being serious and critical, or was he kidding? If it was a joke, it was the first he'd made since Katy had disappeared.

Beth busied herself with clearing the breakfast dishes from the end of her kitchen table that was not covered with papers relating to their search for Margot and Katy. She had been working hard along with Joe trying to figure out some way to help find Katy. Beth had been keeping in touch with her replacement at the studio by phone. Joe had to admit that the producer was being incredibly helpful in every way while they made what was probably a futile investigation of their own.

As he fed Frankie, thoughts of Katy as a baby swirled through Joe's head. She had been like her mother even as an infant—impatient to get things done. Maybe it wasn't that she was starving, but she'd always seemed to prefer to eat fast. "Slow down," Margot would say. "She shouldn't eat so fast."

"Why not? It's all gruel. It's not like she has to chew it. She likes to eat fast."

Even then, months after Katy's birth, random thoughts

would float unwelcome through his mind. *Of course she's like her mother. She has her genes. No telling how fast the real father eats.* Always the same thought—the "real father." He'd hated himself for thinking the words then, and he hated himself now. If he'd been a better father, he and Margot wouldn't have broken up. Maybe, somehow, he could have kept Katy safe.

For just a moment, he tried to concentrate his lagging energies on feeding Beth's little son, spooning the room temperature oatmeal into the tiny pink circle of damp mouth. Joe used the spoon like a snow shovel to scrape the excess off his chin and into the maw, the movement well remembered from Katy's babyhood. He was a beautiful boy, he looked like a Gerber baby, except that much of the Gerber was in this baby's wispy hair.

"Do you have any more of this swill?" he asked Beth. "I think he's still hungry."

"Here. Just give him his bone," she said, handing Joe a teething biscuit.

Frankie reached eagerly for the biscuit and began to gnaw at it with a happy slurping sound.

Reluctantly, Joe came to the other end of the table to begin sorting through a stack of papers, putting selected ones into his briefcase. "I'll follow up on these," he said, reflecting that in the last few days he and Beth had had a crash course in criminal investigation. Unfortunately, their amateur work had not turned up anything that would help.

"Wasn't Margot planning to come over this morning?" asked Joe.

"Yes. She should be here pretty soon. Told me she had to pick up a prescription on her way over. Why don't you go ahead. I'll wait till Margot gets here. After we talk, I'll take Frankie down to the newspaper morgue with me and check out the rest of these," she said, holding photocopies of old newspaper articles about child molesters and suspected kidnappers. "Should we meet for lunch somewhere downtown and compare notes?"

"No. I promised Emily that I'd go down and see Margot's dad. She says he's going crazy being in there, threatening to check himself out."

"Can't say I blame him. Maybe what we're doing is a big joke—I know Detective Lewis thinks so—but it's a hell of a lot better than doing nothing."

"And it might be a hell of a lot better than what that bastard is doing." Joe sighed loudly. "If all that time he wasted thinking it was me who took Katy—"

"Don't start that again, huh? It won't help, and it just gets you all worked up."

For a moment, Joe ground his teeth, then he said, "Right. Thanks. And keep pointing that out to me, will you?" He crumpled up some newspaper scraps and tossed them toward the trash can. The scraps missed, but Frankie clapped his hands and laughed.

"Thanks, guy. I needed that."

Beth smiled and handed him the list of phone numbers that Joe planned to try later in the day. She was wiping the gluey mess off Frankie as Joe closed the apartment door behind him.

Because Joe felt more strongly than Beth that the kidnapping might have had something to do with the method of Katy's inception, he'd decided to investigate the sperm bank this morning. A light rain began to fall as he drove out the Parkway to Monroeville. He exited and followed the winding road north that led to the small group of office suites where they'd gone for counseling and to make the arrangements for artificial insemination. The rain poured down heavier in big cold drops as he parked outside the peach-colored brick building. When he strode to the end of the hall and read "Dr. Cocaigne, D.M.D.," on the door, he had to smile. Intriguing name for a dentist, he thought, and turned and went to the other end of the hall, figuring his memory had simply gotten turned around. The door there read "Dentures. Fast, comfortable, affordable." It all felt like a nightmare with a theme. He'd had a college roommate who was obsessed with his teeth and dreamed about losing them on a regular basis. Joe felt as if he'd slipped into one of those bad dreams.

Okay, he thought, *I'm tired, it's raining, visibility is poor. I've just got the wrong office complex.*

He checked through his notes again and stepped outside to read the address. Everything checked out, but when he read the listing of the building's occupants, there was no sperm bank.

As a lover of whodunits, Joe knew that the only way to get at the one useful bit of information in a mystery was to gather hundreds of pieces of wasted data. So, feeling a sad desperation, he set about his search. The building manager was out, and his secretary said she could not give out information on the building's former occupants without his permission. Would he please come back in the afternoon?

Then, one by one, he began speaking to the receptionists in the other offices along the hall. He reflected that the world was moving too fast as he discovered that all of the employees had hired on recently. No one had been there long enough to remember the presence of a sperm bank in the complex. And he cringed at the snickers some people tried to hide at the mention of the term.

Finally, as noon approached and the corridor filled with workers heading out to lunch, he entered the office of Dr. Cocaigne. He was met by a thin young woman with masses of curly auburn hair. She squinted her eyes and thought hard when Joe asked about the sperm bank. "Yeah. I remember something about that. There was some kind a scandal, and the place closed down."

"Please. Anything you can tell me—"

"Sure, but I couldn't tell you much. Wanda's the only one who worked here then. Everybody else is new. But Wanda could probably tell you something, 'cause it seems to me she used to date the guy who owned it. Or maybe he just ran it. Anyway, she said he was kinda weird. He had a

name like a movie—like the Sundance Kid or Billy the Kid,
or something.''

"Good. Is she here today? I'd like to speak with her.''

"Hah! Not hardly. She got married last weekend. She's
laying under the tropical sun on some island, the lucky
dog.''

"When will she be back?''

"Not for another week, can you believe it? That was the
policy when she started here. Two weeks for everybody
after one year. Now you gotta work for five years before
you get two weeks vacation.'' She leaned toward Joe and
winked. "If I was Wanda, I'd make sure I didn't come back
here. At least not for more than nine months, you know
what I mean?''

Joe barely heard the girl's words. To be so close to
finding out something that might help—

"If there was some way I could get hold of Wanda, if you
had a phone number—''

"On her honeymoon! Are you crazy? Excuse me, but
Wanda would kill me.''

"I understand. And I wouldn't ask except—'' Joe hesitated for a moment. He couldn't see any reason for secrecy.
"I imagine you've seen the news reports about the little girl
that was kidnapped.''

"I sure have. The poor thing. I used to watch that Margot
What's-her-name show all the time before I started working
here. She was—''

"Well, I'm the little girl's father.'' Joe waited while the
news sunk in.

"You're kidding! No, I can see you're not. God, I'm
sorry. Have they found out who took her yet?''

"No. And they—'' He had to stop himself from launch-
ing into his list of complaints about the police department.
It would be a foolish and self-indulgent waste of time. "I'm
working along with the police, trying to do what I can to
help.''

"Wow. I'm surprised they let you do that. I watch

'Murder, She Wrote,' all the time—the reruns are on every day when I get home from work—and the police always hate it when that woman tries to help.''

There was something sweet and earnest about this young woman. It was clear to Joe that she wanted to be helpful, but her constant chatter was wearing him down. He remembered another tactic from the mysteries he read. He pulled a twenty-dollar bill from his pocket and handed it to her.

''If you could figure out a way to get in touch with Wanda and find out how I could speak with her—''

''Oh, no,'' she said, holding up her hand, ''I couldn't.''

''Please. I bet you don't get paid a fortune for working here, and I'd be happy to help out with another twenty if I could just speak with Wanda for a few minutes.''

''Well, you're right about the money.'' For the first time since their conversation had begun, she eyed Joe's clothing, as if trying to figure out if he was rich or just desperate. ''I hate to take it,'' she said, taking it, ''but if it'll help find your little girl, I'll do what I can to get you in touch with Wanda.''

Joe wrote down his name and home phone number on a Post-it, and was about to leave when the receptionist spoke again. ''What does this sperm bank guy have to do with it? Do they think he took your daughter?''

''Not exactly,'' Joe answered. ''They just want to question him. You've been a very big help. Thanks.''

''Hey, no problem. I'll be in touch.''

Joe returned to his car and drove downtown to the hospital, the Monongehela River an ugly slate-gray as he crossed the bridge.

When Joe went to the nurses' station to register at intensive care, the nurse glanced down at her records and smiled. ''Mr. Newhouse's condition has improved. He's been moved to the neurological unit. It's just down the hall.'' She pointed the way and told Joe the room number.

As Joe passed the nurses' station in the neurological unit, he hesitated, but the nurse on duty gave him a vacant smile

then returned to her charts, so Joe just followed the numbers
until he reached the right room. An orderly was carrying out
Mr. Newhouse's lunchtray as Joe entered. The tray held
empty plates.

"Looks like you've got your appetite back, Pop. Good
for you."

Margot's father looked toward the door, a weird half-
smile lighting up his face. The stroke had done some
damage to his facial muscles, but not nearly as bad as what
Joe had seen in some of the patients in intensive care. Joe
had continued to call him Pop, even after the divorce. It just
made him feel good to do so, and he knew that Margot's dad
was rooting for them to get back together. Her mom, on the
other hand, would probably draw and quarter Joe if it was
legal and she could find a neat and ladylike way to do it.

"Sure. I've got my appetite back," said Mr. Newhouse.
"I've got everything back except my freedom. There's not
a damn thing wrong with me that a couple of aspirins
wouldn't fix."

Joe pulled a chair close to the old man's bed and sat
down.

"They'll let you out soon, don't worry. Meanwhile I've
got a little progress to report."

"What?"

Joe told him about his efforts to locate the owner or
manager of the defunct sperm bank. "Pop, if I'd known
before what I know now— I did some research in the
periodicals at the library yesterday, and you wouldn't
believe what I found. These damned sperm banks aren't
regulated. I mean not at all. All you have to do to open one
is print up some brochures and buy some storage tanks."

"But surely the doctors—"

"Right. Before the doctors will refer their patients there,
they'll check out the place, but sometimes that's nothing
more than a telephone call. The sperm bank operator, if he's
a good salesman, with a friendly, helpful attitude—"

Joe paused, feeling again the rising of the helpless fury that kept leading him into useless diatribes.

"Take it easy, son." When Mr. Newhouse called him "son," it had an instant calming effect. Joe's own father had died years ago, and he cherished Margot's dad, who had loved Joe as much as any man could love his own son.

"I know how angry you are. So am I." Mr. Newhouse laid his hand on Joe's arm and then, for just an instant, he touched Joe's forehead. It was a loving gesture, the way a parent tests for fever.

"You know, I'm considering having something tattooed on my hand to remind me to stick to the subject," said Joe. "I feel like an idiot, going around playing amateur detective. But if I don't have some direction for all this anger—"

"I know what you mean, Joe. There's nothing worse than not being able to help the people you love when they're in trouble. But don't worry, everything's going to come out all right, son, you wait and see."

Joe got up and walked over to the window. The rain was still falling, but it came down in a gentle mist now, making a sheer curtain between the warm quiet hospital room and the hectic business of downtown Pittsburgh and its working rivers.

He turned back to the old man. There was an IV drip in one arm, and Joe wondered if that was the only thing holding his father-in-law here. Until the stroke, Joe had never considered Margot's father to be vulnerable. Such a childish way to view someone. Joe figured it was because he felt so much like a son to the man. If Pop were to die now—and if maybe he'd lost Katy—what a mess he'd made of everything. If only he could get away and think it all over in a quiet place. But the noise in his head made it impossible to think. The noise of the alarms going off saying, "Do something, do something."

Joe returned to Mr. Newhouse's bedside. "I'll give you a call or stop by if I hear anything more."

"You should go home and get some rest now. It's not going to help Katy if you get sick, too."

"Later, Pop. I have a couple of names of guys that have written letters to Margot that seemed a little off-base."

"Threatening?"

"No, not threatening. But not normal fan mail either. It's probably nothing, but you never know."

"That's right, you never know. So be careful."

"And you take it easy. I'll be in touch."

15...

     MARGOT SAT QUIETLY, observing the other customers. Like her, they were waiting for their prescriptions to be filled. After four nights of no sleep following Katy's abduction, Margot had finally given in to her mother's insistence that she try one of her sleeping pills. Margot reflected that her tiny mother was not as fragile as she appeared if she could take the strong tranquilizer and not be put to sleep for days.

     So Margot had phoned her doctor, and he said he would phone in something more appropriate that wouldn't leave her groggy. If she could just get some decent sleep, Margot thought as she sat waiting, then she would have more energy and clear thinking to bring to her search for Katy.

     While she waited, Margot tried to concentrate on the directions she had brought with her for a built-in desk she planned to construct in Katy's room. They had arrived in the mail the Friday before Katy was kidnapped. Margot decided that she would at least read the instructions so that she'd be ready to build the desk when Katy got back. As she had a hundred times in the last few days, Margot pictured working together with Katy, teaching her woodworking, just as Margot's own father had taught her as a child.

     A tiny baby awoke and waved its arms as it reclined in an infant seat on the bench next to Margot. The weak morning light lay like a soft blanket across the baby's damp face. The infant's mother sat beside the baby's carrier, working a crossword puzzle.

     Margot reflected on the events of the last several days as she waited. Although Margot knew in her rational, logical mind that she was not responsible for Katy's kidnapping, she still felt a primitive and unshakable sense of guilt. If she'd been more watchful, if only she had taken Katy somewhere more educational than the carnival, then maybe none of this would have happened. Beth kept telling her she had a bad case of the ''if only's,'' and she had to learn not to waste her energy on blaming herself. But then who was she to blame? As many times as she'd done shows on forgiving yourself, she still couldn't get rid of the notion that she'd let Katy down. Of course a lot of that had to do with the divorce from Joe. Margot stood up, deliberately shaking off that particular case of the ''if only's.'' Beth was right. There was nothing to be gained from sitting around feeling guilty.

Margot set down her woodworking instructions and wandered restlessly over to look at the magazines, then back to the bench. The baby was trying to stuff one tiny fist into its mouth. ''Would you mind if I held him?'' asked Margot, seeing the mother glancing over toward her. Normally, Margot would never have asked such a thing of a stranger, but she couldn't seem to stop herself.

The young woman eyed her for a moment, then said, ''Sure, go ahead. But it's a girl.''

''Sorry. What's her name?''

''Michelle.''

''She's very sweet.'' Margot picked up the baby, being careful to support its head. ''Hello, Michelle. What a pretty little thing you are.''

''Thanks,'' said the infant's mother. ''I can see why you thought she was a boy. I usually tape a bow to her head or dress her in pink, or something, but it doesn't help much. Most people still think she's a boy.''

''It *is* hard to tell when they're so little,'' answered Margot. ''But she'll get hair soon enough.'' Margot thought about Katy, about how she'd been totally bald for the first eight months of her life. But Margot couldn't bear talking about that now. It was apparent that this woman didn't recognize her, and it was restful to just sit with the mother and her baby, pretending to be normal for a moment. Margot was surprised that she could hold the baby without feeling more pain. But this infant was so different from Katy, so much a part of another world—the warm, insular world she'd left behind when Katy got past being a toddler and when Margot had gone back to full-time work at the TV station.

A tall man came into the pharmacy and wandered slowly over to a soda machine that stood in the corner. He glanced over at Margot and at the woman and her baby, then turned to put his coins into the machine. He looked vaguely familiar, but Margot could not place him. She'd interviewed so many people on her talk show that it had become impossible to remember them all. Because of the way he seemed to be just lurking, sipping at his cola, with no other apparent reason for being in the drugstore, Margot wondered if he might be someone with the police. She wasn't aware of any plainclothesmen having been assigned to follow her.

Margot turned her attention back to the baby, who was beginning to fuss. The little thing was twisting around, trying to suck on Margot's wrist. It was clear what she wanted, so Margot handed the child to the mother, who unabashedly pulled up her Hard Rock Cafe T-shirt and offered her breast to the baby.

Feeling like an intruder, Margot again walked over to the magazines and began leafing through them. The man with the cola came to stand next to her. "Can you tell me the time? My watch is broken," he said.

"It's ten-thirty or so, but my watch is a little fast," she replied.

"I have your daughter. If you'll come with me quietly, she won't be hurt."

"What?" Lights flashed and the room spun for a moment. Margot saw her hand grasping the front of the man's shirt, then she saw his expression. He looked like he was repulsed by her touch. She let go and leaned on the magazine shelf for support.

"If you get hysterical or scream, I'll be gone, and you'll never see Katherine again."

His eyes were so cold, but there was more to her shock than could be accounted for by their coldness or by his words. She looked again directly into his eyes, seeing Katy's eyes at the same time. Margot didn't doubt for a moment that he was telling her the truth. The notion that Katy's biological father might somehow have found and kidnapped Katy suddenly seemed very possible.

"I'm sorry. Oh, God, Katy." She was breathing fast, couldn't catch a breath with enough oxygen in it. "Please, just a minute." With effort, she pulled one long breath, using the time to assess her situation.

"Okay. That's enough time. Leave your things here and come with me. Look like you know me and we're simply going for a ride."

Pulling herself together, she spoke with more force now. "Why should I believe you have my daughter?"

He glared at her for a moment, then slowly reached into his pocket. She half-expected to see a gun, but what he withdrew was worse. There, in his hand, was a torn scrap of cloth with the absurd topknot of a giraffe. Katy's beloved giraffe blouse.

"I'll just get my things and—"

"Forget that." He glanced around the room, showing the first signs of nervousness. "Just come with me, now."

But as Margot began to follow him toward the door, she heard someone call, "Ma'am," and turned to see the young woman with the baby holding Margot's purse up in the air.

Margot looked at the man, who had also turned.

"Get it," he said through gritted teeth.

"Thanks, I don't know what I was thinking of," said

Margot, trying for good eye contact with the young woman. But the mother was concerned with baby Michelle, who had lost hold of her mother's breast and was protesting lustily. Margot began to fold her desk instructions, trying to buy some time, unsure of how she could help herself and Katy once she'd given herself over to this man, yet afraid to chase him away by making a scene.

"Come on, now. You don't want your daughter to get hurt."

At that, both women looked up, Margot's expression one of alarm, the young mother's more of curiosity.

"You know how hurt she gets if you're late picking her up," he said.

"Right," said Margot. But she frowned at the seated woman. "Thanks for letting me hold Michelle. I really love children." The conflicting message of Margot's frown accompanied by the pleasant words seemed to have worked. The woman tilted her head, mild confusion on her face.

"That's okay. Nice talking with you. 'Bye."

"We'll come back for your prescription after we pick her up," said the man. Margot felt him grasp her upper arm. His fingers felt like metal in winter, hard and cold. She turned and followed him outside, where he opened the door of a Volvo for her.

Something about the man told Margot that it would be a mistake to try to run away or call for help. Although he acted cool, there was a desperation and determination in his manner and in those blastedly familiar eyes that told her to simply go along with him. The stakes were too high to let some rash decision ruin everything. She got into the passenger seat and sat quietly as the man climbed in behind the wheel. He started the engine and drove away from the pharmacy. At the first alley, he turned left and parked the car in the shadow of an old brick warehouse. *Is she here? thought Margot. Is my Katy in that building?*

But, no, she was not to be rewarded so soon. The man

turned to her and fixed her with a long stare, then said, "I've been through too much shit lately to put up with any more from you. I can hardly stand to even look at you, but for some reason Katherine wants to see you again. I want her to get well, so I'll take you to her, but—"

"She's sick? Oh please. I'll do whatever you say. Please—"

"Shut up! Now listen. She's not sick; but she's stopped eating. She misses you, that's all. I'd just as soon kill you for what you've done to her, but I'll give you one more chance. If you pull any more crap like you did in the drugstore, I *will* kill you." He paused, apparently to let his words sink in. "But if you do what I tell you, you'll see Katherine tonight."

"I will. I'll do whatever you say."

"Here." He handed her a flowered pillowcase. "Put this over your head, get down on the floor. Be quiet. And don't move."

"I under—"

"Quiet!" he shouted.

Quickly, Margot pulled the cloth over her head and slid down to the carpeted floor of the car.

She heard a rustling, then felt something being thrown over her—a blanket or comforter. In the warm darkness of her prison, Margot tried to think rationally. She quit trying to determine the direction the car was traveling after only a few turns. She fully expected to be hidden on the floor for a long ride, and she was already disoriented. The man had said, "You'll see Katherine tonight." She would wait and—at the very least—try not to anger this man any further. He'd said something about wanting to kill her for "what she'd done to Katherine." What could he mean by that?

She was deep in thought, paying scant attention to the movements and noises of the traffic when she heard what could only be the sound of an automatic garage door operating. For some reason that frightened her more than anything else that had happened on this day. No doubt something would happen now. *Maybe*, she thought in a panic, *maybe now he will kill me. He got me away from the pharmacy and witnesses, and now he can kill me in peace. And no one will know he has Katy. No one will know.*

16...

MARGOT STOOD BEHIND the man and a little to his left as he worked at the combination lock on the door. *If I knew one of those sleeper holds you read about in spy novels*, she thought, *I could end all of this right now.*

In any case, she had to wait for him to finish releasing the Master lock and he seemed to be having trouble with it. The only illumination came from a low-watt bulb in a tarnished brass holder beside the door. "Out of my light!" he snapped. Startled, Margot backed up and bumped up against the railing. She could see that she was still casting a shadow over the numbered circle of the lock, but she was also afraid to go up the stairs. What if she was this close to Katy—she could *feel* Katy's presence behind the gray steel door—what if she was this close and she blew it now?

Margot sat down. The man glanced over his shoulder, his inspection that of a harassed substitute teacher who distrusts everyone in the class. Then he returned to his task, and Margot heard the click of the lock as it gave.

Impatience made Margot careless, and she bumped against him. He raised the back of his hand to her, then paused. A vicious chill traveled down her spine as he stroked his hand against her cheek, then pushed the door slowly open. The gesture was so quick, so catlike, that Margot almost wondered if she'd imagined it.

A table lamp in a corner illuminated a cavernous room, and for a moment, Margot saw no sign of life. Was this just another in a series of sick jokes this monster was playing?

Then she heard a mutter and a muffled cough. Margot peered into the gloom of the far-left corner of the room and saw the outline of a big wing-back chair. There was movement there. Abruptly, two figures stood, a blanket falling to the floor at their feet.

Suddenly, the whole room was flooded with a bright, fluorescent glare. Margot squinted, then sprang forward. There, leaning against a pale, hollow-eyed woman was Katy. At the same instant that Margot moved forward, Katy apparently recognized her mother. They both bolted toward each other, and then, at long last, they were together. They hugged so tightly that they were both panting for breath.

"Mama, Mama," said Katy over and over again. Nothing had ever sounded so beautiful to Margot before in her life. Like orchestra music, it filled her whole body.

"Yes, baby. It's Mama. I'm here." Then she was overcome with tears, unable to speak as she held her child.

But as she cried, gulping back a sick feeling, Margot's hands explored Katy's body. She seemed all bones—not the firm, well-padded bones Margot was used to feeling when she touched her daughter, but delicate, breakable bones.

Warily, Margot glanced behind her at the man, then ahead at the woman, conscious that she held Katy in her arms, but that they were far from safe now. And then Margot became aware that just as she had inspected Katy, her daughter was doing the same thing to her. Katy had pulled back and was frowning at Margot, her small, feverish fingertips exploring the skin on her mother's face.

"Your face looks the same as always," said Katy.

It was Margot's turn to make an assessment. "And you seem a bit warm, sweetheart. How do you feel?"

"Mama, you don't *look* like you were in a accident."

Now Margot felt as confused as Katy looked.

"I wasn't, Katy. Why did you think I was in an accident?"

"But that's why you didn't come. That's why Uncle Rick said you couldn't take care of me."

Sharply, Margot stared at Rick, then at the woman, who had come closer and now hovered over Katy, her hand reaching slightly toward Margot's little girl. Margot shivered all over, not from cold—actually, the room was uncomfortably warm. Still on her knees, facing Katy, she backed away a foot or two. She sensed that she was confronting two nightmarish challenges. One was the obvious difficulty of getting away from this madman. And the other was the question of how to avoid traumatizing Katy any further.

Slowly, unsure of what might happen next, Margot rose and gently guided Katy back toward the big armchair. But just as she sat down and was about to pull her daughter onto her lap, Katy bolted and ran to the other woman. She grabbed the woman around the thighs in the age-old gesture of fear, anchoring herself to someone with whom she apparently felt the most safe. The bottom dropped out. The movement broke what was left of Margot's heart.

"No, Katy! Oh baby, no. You can't—"

"Please," said the woman. She had placed her hands on Katy's back in a protective gesture and now massaged Katy's muscles in little, slow circles. "My name is Sonya. We've been watching over Katy, and somehow she got the idea that you'd been hurt." The woman peeked over at Rick with a look that held fear, but also a veiled resentment. Margot couldn't be sure of her part in Katy's kidnapping. "We *told* her that you had to be in the hospital for a few days, so that must be why she thought you'd been hurt."

So a challenge had been offered. Refute what these people had told Katy and . . . what? Make her realize that she was in a weird world of grown-ups, where she couldn't trust anyone, not even her own mother? Margot knew too well that five-year-old logic was totally incomprehensible to adults and that any discussion about why these people might be "telling fibs" would lead to deeper confusion for her daughter. She wanted to scream out, "Katy, they're kidnappers, crazy people who don't care about anyone but themselves." But then she had only to look across the few feet that separated her from her only child and see the look of fear and betrayal in her daughter's eyes. Katy had believed that Margot was badly hurt. There was no other reason why her mother would have stayed away from her so long. Margot knew that sometimes Katy blamed herself for her parents' breakup. At those sad moments, there was no way to reassure Katy that she was a victim, not a cause. Margot had read all the self-help books and had arranged for Katy to see a counselor, but still Katy sometimes blamed herself. Probably now she thought that if only she'd been a better little girl, her mother would not have sent these people to take her away.

17...

"NO," HE HOLLERED, waking himself from a bad dream. Billy sat up on the sofa where he had passed out. The TV screen's glow hurt his eyes in the predawn light.

"Shit," said Billy. He rubbed at the stubble on his cheeks, then went and punched the TV off.

Billy went into the kitchen and poured a cup of cold coffee from yesterday's pot. He put it in the microwave to heat and went to the bathroom. When he came back, he sat down at the kitchen table with his coffee and stared at the rings on the tabletop. He traced one after another of the interconnecting beer can rings with his finger as he drank the black bitter coffee.

When he was done, Billy stood up as straight as he could, went into the living room and turned on the news. He watched, hoping. But no, the little girl was still missing. The police were following several leads, the newscaster said. It sounded to Billy like they were still in the dark. He wished that he didn't know what he knew.

Billy felt like a victim himself. After all, it wasn't like he invited that guy to come and look at the records. Sure they were supposed to be confidential, but it was the guy with the red hair and green eyes that did something wrong, not Billy.

With a weary sigh, Billy pulled out the photo of the missing girl. He stood up and carried it to the garbage can.

But he couldn't do it.

"Damn it all," he said and went in search of his shoes and car keys. He pushed his feet into a pair of curled up Nikes, got his keys and went out to the Dodge.

It only took ten minutes to drive to the Seven Eleven. He

parked and went inside to the back corner where there was a pay phone. Luckily, there was a phone book there, so Billy looked up the hospital's number. When he got hold of the operator, he asked for Gregory Newhouse's room.

"Hello," came the old man's voice.

Billy almost hung up. His hand shook. "You don't know me, but I have something to tell you." Billy's words tumbled out fast. "I think I know who took your grand-daughter. I think the guy's name is Grader. Richard Grader. It's in the book. Okay?"

"Who is this?"

"It doesn't matter who I am. Just get the police to check it out. I'm pretty sure it's this Grader who has the girl."

"But why? There's been no ransom demand, no commu-nication. Do you know why?"

"It's her father, I think. Her real father. You know what I mean."

"Please, sir. I'm grateful for your help. Even if you don't want to tell me your name, is there some way I could get in touch with you? Or perhaps you would phone me again."

"Gotta go. You sure you got it now?"

"Yes. Richard Graver. Please, I promise to—"

Billy hung up the receiver and clung to it for a minute, needing support. What a moron I am, he thought. Boy, had he really sunk so low that a little conversation on the phone with a sick old man could scare him so much that his body shook?

Still, he felt a certain relief. He had finally done the right thing.

And he deserved a reward. Billy went back out to his car and drove to the Tear Drop Inn. It was early, but he was sure he would find somebody to share a drink or two with.

18...

MARGOT ASKED IF she could have some time alone with Katy, and the man had said she could have a half hour. Katy, still with that hurt look in her eyes, led her mother to the back bedroom. It looked warm and cozy. And it already had the slightly rumpled look that Katy's room always had at home.

Margot thought fast, trying to think how she might repair some of the damage these people had done to her relationship with Katy. "I'm sorry I couldn't come here sooner," she said to Katy. There was no point in telling her daughter the bald truth at the moment. It would frighten her, and who knew what it would do to the madman in the living room who had constructed the lies.

"But why, Mama? I thought you were hurt, so you were in the hospital. Where were you?"

"Honey, Grampa has been sick. He's in the hospital."

"Grampa? Grampa's in the hospital? Not you?"

"I've been there watching over him."

"Is he dead?"

"Oh, no, sweetheart. Grampa's sick, but he's very much alive. The doctors are taking very good care of him."

"Will he get better?"

"I hope so."

"Why didn't you tell me where you were? I was so scared. Rick said I got sick, and I had some bad dreams. But they were just like real. I dreamed he grabbed me and pulled me away from you, at the merry-go-round, Mama. He was mean. It seemed just like real, not like a dream."

Margot held Katy. So it *had* been him she saw that day. Her poor baby.

"Things get mixed up sometimes, Katy. Someone was supposed to tell you that I would come soon. I'm sorry." Margot picked up a book of rhymes and flipped idly through the pages. Then Margot pointed at a picture of a warthog. "Oh look. Just like in our book at home."

Katy smiled and said, "Yes. It's the warthog who wanted to be a big dog. Read it, Mama. Please."

Margot checked her watch. Already five minutes of the time she'd been allotted were gone. She had no idea what would happen when the half hour was over. Margot decided that there were worse ways to spend time than to sit with her arm around her child and read about the warthog who wanted to be a big dog.

All too soon, their time was over. Rick was calling from the living room. "Katherine. Come out on the deck and bring her."

Margot figured "her" must mean herself, so she followed Katy through the house and out onto the deck. The afternoon was too crisp, the area the house was in too shaded for comfort in her shorts and top, but what really made Margot shiver was the look on Rick's face. Moving with exaggerated care, he sat down at the big redwood picnic table and pulled a large, shallow metal box toward him.

Still convinced that quiet observation offered the safest and best chance of getting Katy and herself out of the situation they were in, Margot remained silent. She watched.

Using a small key, Rick unlocked the box. He moved so slowly that the melodrama annoyed Margot almost to the point of speaking as Rick gazed inside the box. Katy, consumed with curiosity, had approached Rick's side of the table and knelt on the bench next to him. "It's a beach ball, but it's not blowed up yet," she said.

Before Margot realized what was happening, Rick took something from the box and clamped it on Katy's arm.

"Wow, a bracelet. Thanks." Katy smiled.

The contents of the box were hidden from view by the lid, but as Katy reached out toward it, saying, "What's the other stuff in the box?" Rick slapped her hand away.

"No!" he roared, and Katy tumbled over backward, landing hard on the deck.

Margot and Sonya both hurried around to pick her up. Katy's face was flushed and tears puddled in her eyes, but she was silent as she stared at Rick.

"What's wrong with you," demanded Sonya. "She was just curious." She brushed at the back of Katy's shorts as if the child had become terribly dusty in her fall. Margot was hyperaware of the gesture, because she found herself doing the same thing on Katy's opposite side. *Like mirror mothers* came the repulsive thought. Margot had read about "mirror twins"—twins who were identical except that all the lefts and rights were reversed. And that's how she felt now—as if she and Sonya were both Katy's mother, tending the child in the same way with only a simple differentiation of polarity to tell them apart.

Shaking her head to dispel the ludicrous notions bounding around in it, Margot led Katy across the deck to sit on a glider. She watched as Rick handed Sonya a deflated beach ball. "Blow it up," he said, his voice cold.

Margot examined the "bracelet" and could see that it was not a simple piece of costume jewelry.

Her eyes on her husband, Sonya began to puff into the ball. Margot could see the interest returning to Katy's eyes as she watched the ball going from a small, limp thing to a large, firm, colorful ball. Sonya's cheeks glowed a hectic pink as she completed inflating the beach ball and pressed the little cap on the hole to seal in the air.

Katy pulled away from Margot and stepped slowly across the deck, glancing sideways at Rick as she went. Margot could tell her daughter was afraid of the man and didn't want to anger him again. But the appeal of the beach ball was strong, probably the first sign of fun she'd seen in days, and she reached for it now.

"Sit down, Katherine," said Rick, and she returned to the glider. "Give me the ball," he said to Sonya.

She handed it to him, then came across the deck to sit down at the other end of the glider. Again the "mirror mothers" thought occurred to Margot as Sonya placed a hand lightly on Katy's shoulder—just like Margot, whose hand rested on Katy's other shoulder. Margot thought of the story of King Solomon and of his solution to the problem of which of two women had a right to keep a child they were arguing over. "Cut the child in half," he told the two women, knowing of course that the real mother would relinquish her claim to save the life of her child.

The two women and the child sat quietly, watching Rick as he worked, most of his movements hidden by the cover of the large metal box. The brightening sun glinted off a pair of chrome scissors. Rick snipped off pieces of duct tape and stuck something to the ball with it.

"Sonya, take Katherine down to the basement and close the door tight. And stay there until I tell you to come out."

"But she wants to see what—"

"Just do it!" he shouted.

Several sparrows took flight at the sudden sound. Sonya led Katy into the house.

"Now, you, come here," said Rick. He walked to the edge of the deck and rested the beach ball carefully on the ledge. Margot could guess what it was that he had taped to the round rubber surface of the beach ball, but hoped she was wrong, merely overdramatizing because of the trouble she was in.

"This," he said, indicating the bright red band taped onto the ball, "is a 'Baby-Come-Back' wristband just like the one that I wear on my wrist. In case you're not familiar with the product, I'll tell you what it does. It is designed to let out a sonic beep if your child wanders more than three hundred feet away from you." He paused, perhaps giving Margot a chance to ask questions. She said nothing.

"I don't know if you understand just how much it means

to me to have my own child with me, but it's important that you try. If I can't have Katherine, I can't have anything. This may sound like the ravings of a lunatic, but I'm just a desperate father. Just a father.'' His voice had fallen from a growl to a whisper, and Margot strained to catch his words. ''I'm also a lawyer, and I know what my chances of getting custody of Katherine would be in the courtroom, so I don't see that I have any choice.''

A cloud had drifted across the sun, and the morning had turned dark, with a smell of approaching rain.

''Ever since I was a kid, I've liked fooling around with electronics. It's something I hope to teach Katherine about when she's a little older.'' He paused again, a vacant look coming into his eyes for a moment.

Then the glazed look passed, and his eyes, dark and sharp, bore into Margot's. ''The wristbands we wear are designed to protect Katherine. If she gets more than three hundred feet from me, we'll get a reminder that something's wrong. Extreme situations call for extreme precautions.'' He cleared his throat. ''Obviously this toy is for demonstration purposes only.''

With that, Rick thrust the ball into the air. The bright colors of the beach toy glowed against the backdrop of dark green pines and firs. It sliced high overhead, then down. When it hit the spongy earth, it bounced lightly, then rolled on down the hill. Suddenly, a blinding flash of yellow-white light lit the whole area, and a shocking concussion of sound crashed in Margot's ears. The beach ball blew up, pitching leaves, broken tree limbs and bits of colored rubber into the air like some giant, deadly tossed salad.

''Oh, my God,'' moaned Margot, understanding full well what it all meant. ''My God, are you crazy?'' she asked, knowing instantly that she'd said the absolutely worst thing she could say.

She heard the impact of his hand on her face before she felt it. Her ears rang as she bounced against the railing of the deck then thudded to the floor. Like a snake striking, he fastened a red band to Margot's wrist.

"Mama," screamed Katy. Margot saw Katy in the doorway, pulling with all her might to get free of a clearly panicked Sonya, who was trying to drag Katy back inside.

"No, Katy, no," called Sonya as Katy broke away and stumbled toward Margot. They fell into each other's arms and embraced on the floor of the deck, even as Sonya plucked and pulled at Katy.

"Never mind, now," came Rick's angry voice. Margot's head swam as she saw Rick push Sonya into the house.

Katy was crying hard, but gulping, trying to gain control. "What happened, Mama?" With small shaking fingers, she touched Margot's lip and stared at the blood there. "What was that noise? I heard a loud noise."

Margot sensed that the right explanation was crucial to survival. How could she reassure Katy and still not say anything that would anger the madman inside the house? She felt confused and frightened.

"It was some old fireworks. Rick was going to make a fireworks display for you, but they blew up in the wrong way." Margot could feel the strength of Katy's grip easing.

"What happened to your face? Did it hurt you when it blew up?"

Margot touched her lip where Rick had hit her. "No," she said, her insides curdling at the lie. "Rick threw the old fireworks over the balcony just in time. But it surprised me so much that I fell and hit the railing of the deck."

Katy looked at her mother for a moment, then glanced over her shoulder at Rick, as if testing the truth of what Margot had just told her. Margot held her breath. She reflected bitterly that it wasn't unusual for mothers to lie to their very young children to protect them. But it was usually about things like where animals had gone when they died or how well they had done at a piano recital when their playing had actually been dreadful. Few mothers felt compelled to lie about the fate of beach balls with plastic explosives taped to them when tossed more than three hundred feet by an insane bastard.

"Mama, you need a bandage for your face. You better come with me." With that, Katy helped her mother up and led her into the bathroom. She'd always enjoyed playing doctor and had gotten into the habit of washing and bandaging any small wounds of her playmates. Margot wanted to cry at the tenderness in Katy's movements. She indicated that Margot should sit on a wooden stool next to the sink. Then, with a clean cloth and warm soapy water, she gently dabbed at the cut on Margot's lip.

"Honey, I can do this myself," said Margot, almost gagging on her emotions.

"No, Mama, I'm almost finished. Don't worry, it will heal soon." They were the exact words that Margot always used when treating Katy's hurts. Children, even at Katy's age, had such difficulty understanding the concept of time—words like "soon" became important. And it was true—with small cuts and scrapes, children did heal "soon." Their young cells grew and replaced old ones so fast it sometimes seemed like a miracle to see how quickly they recovered—and how little they scarred. Margot prayed silently that Katy would come out of this crisis with very little scarring. Some years ago, the news had been full of a story about a toddler who had fallen down a well and been trapped for an incredibly long time. Margot still recalled the comment of one psychologist who had said that an adult would probably not have survived the ordeal, but a toddler—with so little experience of the world—could just accept this bad thing and not fight against it. In doing so, the little girl had lived and recovered from her injuries. Would Katy be like that? Bouncing back from her imprisonment by this stranger, who was her real father?

"Oops," said Katy as she missed her mark. Katy smiled and stifled a soft giggle behind her hand. She had taped Margot's mouth shut. Margot pulled away the end of the bandage and smiled back at her child. She grasped Katy tightly in her arms.

And as she and Katy held each other, Margot could no longer ignore the thought that had been trying to form in her mind. She understood the impact of the demonstration she had just witnessed on the deck. Margot realized that she must give up looking for a way to escape. And finally, she acknowledged the most horrible truth of all: She was still a prisoner, but she had also just become the jailer.

19...

MARGOT'S FATHER PUSHED the control to raise his hospital bed, then sipped at his tea. When his phone rang, he turned down the volume of the TV before answering it.

"Hello."

Gregory could hear a man's voice, but some of his words were drowned out by music and voices. It sounded as if the speaker was in a public building—maybe a store, or an airport.

Gregory had already had several phone calls from friends and acquaintances, all trying to help with theories about the kidnapping. But this call was different. The fellow claimed to know the kidnapper's name. It sounded like "Richard Graver" although the background noise made it hard to be sure.

Gregory's whole body shook with the effort of listening, as he tried to get the guy to stay on the line. The kidnapper was Katy's "real father," the man said. A chill ran down Gregory's spine.

"Gotta go," the man said. "You sure you got it now?"

"Yes. Richard Graver. Please, I promise to—"

The line went dead.

"Richard Graver," he said aloud. Automatically, Gregory sought a pencil to write it down. But then, he remembered, feeling a surge of sadness, that he could no longer write. Or read, really. "Richard Graver," he said, "Richard Graver." Each time he said the name he pressed his call button. He would ask the nurse to write it down for him before he forgot. He wasn't sure if his memory was in working order or not. He wasn't even sure the guy had said "Graver," but that's what it had sounded like. What a stupid damned time for such a thing to happen to his brain, just when Margot and Katy needed him most. "Richard Graver," he continued. Where was the nurse, he wondered. "Richard G—"

Something on the TV caught his attention. There was a photo of Margot and Katy on the screen. He turned up the volume. Gregory listened to the reporter, who stood with her microphone in front of a pharmacy that Gregory recognized. It was not far from Margot's house.

"Police are interviewing a witness who saw Ms. DesMarais leaving the pharmacy with a man. A preliminary description and a police artist's sketch will be released as soon as it is available. Captain Lewis, who is in charge of the investigation of the abduction of five-year-old Katherine DesMarais, Margot DesMarais' daughter, said that—"

Gregory pushed his call button frantically, then suddenly stopped. He was aware that the control had fallen onto his sheet. He could not grasp it. He tried to call for someone, to shout, but his voice seemed to be gone. He could move his lips, but no sound came out. Gregory fought the dizziness knowing full well that he was having another stroke. *Not now, dear God,* he thought, as he felt his consciousness slipping away.

20...

WHEN MARGOT AND Katy came out of the bathroom, Rick was sitting in an overstuffed chair. He looked up and said, "Katherine, press 'Play' on the VCR." Katy glanced up at her mother, a reflex from a more normal time, Margot was sure. At home Katy was not allowed to use the VCR without permission. So different from many five-year-olds, whose parents had given up control and whose children watched what they wanted, when they wanted.

Katy went to the VCR, pressed "Play," then hurried back to her mother's side. Margot held Katy around her shoulders, still frightened by how much weight she'd lost in the short time she'd been out of Margot's care.

"Sit down, Katherine." Again, Katy looked up at her mother. Margot knew that Katy was unaccustomed to hearing her formal name. With a little nod, Margot indicated to Katy that she should do as she was told. To the man, she said, "She's not used to being called Katherine. We've always called her Katy."

The look he shot back was so full of thunder that Margot winced. He rose and stood over her, a tall man, nearly a foot taller than Margot. "I've decided that Katherine is better. You'll call her that, too, from now on."

His tactics of intimidation would have seemed almost ludicrous, especially over such a minor matter, except that he wore on his wrist the trigger that could kill anyone who failed to take him seriously.

Before she had an opportunity to frame a careful reply, or even to decide if it was safe to reply at all, he turned and went into the kitchen. There, he opened a liquor cabinet and poured a tumbler full of whiskey. Then, with one finger, he indicated that Margot should follow him into the room. The arrogance of the gesture was infuriating, but to rebel at this point seemed dangerous, not to mention pointless.

In the kitchen, he handed her an index card and gestured toward the refrigerator. "Can you follow a recipe?" he asked. His tone was full of contempt.

She glanced down at the card and read, in tiny, neat printing, "Chicken Marengo." Margot's ears were still ringing from the noise of the exploding beach ball. But somehow the little card with the colored illustration of an old iron stove with bright red geraniums on it seemed the most bizarre thing she'd yet encountered that day. It represented happy, peaceful sharing of family secrets, usually among women. Certainly, men never printed out their recipes on little cards with pictures.

"I can make this," she said. "But the recipe doesn't sound as good as mine." She waited to see what response her small rebellion would elicit.

The man sat at a bar stool across the expanse of the large orange counter that filled the center of the small kitchen. Slowly, he sipped his drink, keeping his eyes on Margot all the time.

"The baking pans are under the oven," he said at last.

Damn him to hell, she thought. Whatever psychological game he was playing was a subtle one—one that she wouldn't be able to figure out quickly.

If he hadn't been watching her so closely, Margot would almost have welcomed the chance to do something normal again, something as elemental as cooking. For the moment, it was enough to chop the fresh tomatoes and mushrooms and to debone the chicken. After so many endless nights and days of looking for Katy, waiting for Katy, fighting her mind's insistence that she imagine Katy dead—after so many days of hope, it almost seemed enough just to see Katy watching *E.T.* on the TV.

Margot could see Katy nervously glancing over her shoulder from time to time, locking eyes with her. Margot set the burner to a lower setting while she pushed the minced garlic around in oil. Standing by the stove provided a good view of her daughter. Margot gritted her teeth, seething at the control this man seemed to exert on everyone around him with such apparent ease. Her wrist seemed to tingle under the ''bracelet'' he'd locked onto Margot earlier in the day. Something primitive in her wanted to set to work gnawing at the metal clasp, and if that didn't get rid of the hated thing, gnawing her hand off. She had always despised trappers and the whole idea of catching animals in such a monstrous way. When she sensed that the man had turned away for a moment, she stared at him and saw him for what he was—a trapper, coldly going about the business of taking what he wanted no matter the cost in suffering for others.

While Margot worked, and the familiar sounds of the *E.T.* soundtrack wove their eerie mood through the background, she recalled a frightening fantasy she'd had when she was a young child. A book Margot had taken out of the library told the tale of a mother raccoon who had chewed her own leg off in order to free herself and get back to her newborn babies. Margot recalled now the sickness in her stomach as she'd imagined the trapper arriving to find his trap sprung and catching his own arm in its jaw. She'd thought then of how he would feel, imagining how he would try to free his arm from the trap. Even now, as she stripped the yellow skin off a chicken breast, Margot could remember her horror at the violence of that children's story.

As Margot put rice on to steam, she tried to recall how the story had ended. Had some kind person helped the raccoon? Had the mother survived, living out her life with one missing leg? And the babies—what had become of them? Try as she might, all Margot could summon up was the image of the trapper, bloody and weak, gnawing at his own flesh.

''I have to go to the bathroom,'' said Margot, sounding as

strong as she could manage. Then she walked quickly to the bathroom and threw up.

When Margot came out, the music was blaring. Katy, ignoring the movie now, her eyes turned sideways, showed relief when Margot emerged from the bathroom. The man was standing, drink in hand, directly behind where Katy sat.

"Use the white linen tablecloth and napkins," he said, looking at Margot as if he were an employer directing an employee. "They're in the sideboard."

Then he opened the basement door and said, "I'll be back in a minute." Catching Margot's eye, he tapped his forefinger on the band on his own wrist, then raised his eyebrows. With that, he disappeared into the basement, emerging a short time later with a dusty bottle of wine. Margot was already busy cleaning the china. Although it was in a glass-front cabinet, it was vaguely gritty, as if it hadn't been used in a very long time. In fact, the cabin felt like a place abandoned, like a singular ghost town that they'd stumbled on. From everything Margot had ever heard from people who owned small retreats in the woods, there was no place so hidden or so remote that hormone-driven teenagers could not find it and break in to enjoy the privacy. It was then she noticed for the first time that the windows were all barred. The bars were arranged in a diamond pattern, so they looked attractive, but they were sturdy and looked strong enough to keep out an intruder. Margot wondered why she hadn't noticed the bars when she was in the bathroom, her only chance to be alone for a minute and to reflect. Then she realized that the bathroom window was stained glass and must be hiding the fortifications. If she'd felt imprisoned before, now she could hardly breathe. The enormity of the predicament that she and Katy were in came crashing down on her. Margot dropped a serving bowl she'd dug out from the back of the cabinet. With renewed clarity, she saw the need to be careful, to pacify this volatile man until she could figure a route of escape.

Quickly, she bent to pick up the Lenox bowl. It had fallen onto a heavy blue-and-gray oriental rug that filled most of the dining area. The sound of the bowl falling had been cushioned by the rug, and Margot hoped the man hadn't heard. Katy, who was usually horrified when things broke— although Margot had never punished her for accidents—had not moved, apparently engrossed in the movie.

Fortunately, the bowl was unbroken, but a small bit of decorative fillip had cracked off the bottom of one handle. Margot put it into her pocket and set the bowl on the counter. When she looked down at it, the missing piece was not evident.

Rick was back at his position at the bar.

Margot noticed a silver chest on top of the sideboard and opened it. The silverware was beautiful, fine Rogers sterling, but so tarnished that it was nearly black. She searched for and found some everyday stainless in a drawer. She rinsed and dried it before setting the table. All the time she worked, Margot wondered if she was setting the proper number of places. She hadn't seen or heard Sonya since she'd left the room earlier. Margot didn't even know if the other woman was still in the house.

As she worked, stirring the chicken Marengo, Margot tried to center her thoughts on escape, but it was difficult with the man's gaze on her. It was like a lead blanket, weighing her down, making it hard to do even the simplest tasks, let alone plot a brilliant diversion and flight.

With a metallic "bing," the old-fashioned timer announced that the rice should be turned off. The noise made Margot jump. She looked at Rick to see if it had disturbed him, too. Apparently not. He sat like stone, moving only occasionally to bring his glass to his lips. Those lips were straight and cruel, like lines drawn with a straight edge.

"A salad, too," he said. "Just greens and red onion." He barely moved his head, indicating that Margot should go to the refrigerator.

In the crisper she found endive and fresh spinach. There

was a small basket of onions on the counter. Margot took out a giant walnut salad bowl and washed away a fine film of dust before rinsing the greens and setting them to drip on the drainboard.

"What about dressing?" she asked, despising this bastard who'd put Katy and her in this position.

"No dressing."

"I'd like to warm up some corn for Katy."

"Go ahead."

Damn! She had to ask permission to feed her own child vegetables. Margot knew that Katy would not eat the chicken Marengo—she never ate anything with tomatoes in it. And the salad was not the kind a five-year-old would consider edible. But corn was high on the list of her child's favorites, and Margot was determined not to let her own sense of helplessness and rage interfere with Katy's welfare.

There was a plastic bag of ready-made poppy seed rolls on the counter, and Margot put them in the microwave to warm. As she did so, she reflected that the microwave seemed out of place in the otherwise fifties kitchen. It looked unused, and it also lacked the layer of dust that was evident on the other appliances.

Margot worked steadily, doing all the necessary things to get the dinner on the table, all the while hoping for a quiet period after dinner when she could think more clearly about escape. Somehow she knew that cleaning up would be her responsibility. Everything about this situation told her that she was a slave, a necessary—and barely tolerated—presence who was there simply because she was Katy's mother. Maybe just a temporary convenience? Margot wondered.

"What do you and your wife drink with dinner?"

"I'll take care of that. Just set out two wine glasses."

Uh, oh, Margot thought. Three adults, two wine glasses. Was she to be allowed to sit at the table? Was she even to be allowed to eat?

"Katherine, turn that off and wash up," Rick said suddenly.

Margot froze at the coldness of his voice. What if Katy bargained for "just a few more minutes, please," the way she sometimes did at home? Would he punish her?

But to Margot's amazement, Katy quickly turned off the TV and VCR and headed for the bathroom. How had he done that to her? What had he done to make her so obedient—like a little wind-up toy?

"I'd like to eat dinner here in the kitchen with Katy," Margot said.

"We'll all eat together," he replied. "It's a celebration."

"A what? Please, can't we just talk for a minute. I know why you want Katy. I understand your ties to her. Maybe we could work out some sort of custody arrangement. Please—"

"Shut up. No."

He turned away from Margot and hollered down the hall, "Sonya!"

His voice thundered through the quiet house, and Margot saw Katy bolt from the bathroom, terror in her eyes. A second later, Sonya appeared from the hall, her eyes frightened, too.

"Dinner in five minutes," he said, looking significantly at Margot, then at the clock. He disappeared into the bathroom. Margot watched, horrified, as Sonya put her arms protectively around Katy's shoulders and Katy bent toward the woman's body. Something that was not anger, or fear, or jealousy, but a sickening combination of all those emotions coursed through Margot's veins. She swallowed hard to keep from being sick again. Then she did a childish thing. Margot actually pinched the back of her hand to see if she would wake up. It left a red spot on her hand. But the nightmare continued.

Margot was very aware of Sonya glaring at her as she hurried to get the food on the table. When the bathroom door opened, Katy scurried to a chair and sat down. She unfolded her napkin and placed it in her lap.

"Please, sit down, everyone," said Rick, as if this were a happy gathering of friends.

"Oh, Rick. You can't be serious." Sonya pointed to Margot. "You're not going to let *her* sit at the dinner table with us," she said. Her words were strong, but her voice shook.

"We'll discuss it later," said Rick. "Margot, you can serve now."

Katy's eyes followed Margot's every move as she dished out medium-sized portions of the chicken and rice for Sonya and Rick. Sonya kept her eyes downcast.

When Margot began to hand Katy her plate with a large helping of buttered niblets and a portion of cooked rice, Rick touched her arm. His touch seemed polite, gentle. "Please give Katherine some chicken Marengo," he said.

"But she doesn't like tomatoes. I don't—"

"She will eat it!" he whispered.

Fighting off an urge to throw the plate in his face, Margot spooned out a chicken leg and placed it atop the rice.

As she began to hand it across to Katy, he whispered again—a horrible guttural sound—"Sauce. Give my daughter sauce."

An obscene monster, Margot thought desperately, as she scooped out some sauce. To call Katy *his* daughter! How could he even say the word?

Margot put a small helping on her own plate, then waited for Sonya to start. Katy, too, watched Sonya, and Margot tried not to speculate on how this man had bullied these perfect table manners into her lively five-year-old. Then to Margot's horror and surprise, she watched as Katy picked up her knife, carefully sliced off a bite of chicken, placed her knife properly across her plate and put the tomato-covered chicken in her mouth.

There was very little conversation during dinner. And there was no sense of celebration. Margot was relieved when everyone was finished and she could go back to work in the kitchen. Katy started to help clear the table, just as she always did at home, but Rick told her to go to her room and play quietly.

Margot longed for the company of her daughter as she filled the sink with suds and washed the dishes. As she was drying the china bowl that had chipped earlier, Rick came into the kitchen and grabbed it from her hand. He turned it over and inspected the spot where the decoration had been. He ran his finger over the damaged spot, then suddenly he flung the bowl across the room. It crashed against the bars on the window and the pieces rained to the floor.

"That bowl is no longer any good. It was flawed," he said.

"I'm sorry," Margot said, aware that Katy was peeping around the corner, her eyes big with fear. Margot saw that Katy was already in her nightgown. She'd been envisioning some sort of flight into the night and wished that Katy still had shoes and warmer clothing on. Irrelevantly, she noticed that the nightgown was new, unfamiliar. As she bent to clean up the shards of china, Margot had the feeling that this day would never end—that she and Katy had fallen into some terrible time warp, where, no matter what plans they made for the next day, the next day would never come.

"Say goodnight to *her*," said Rick, indicating Margot with a dismissive wave of his hand.

Uncertainly, Katy approached Margot, then flung herself into her mother's arms, squeezing so tightly that Margot could hardly breathe.

"It's okay, baby. Don't worry, I'm here now." And what does *that* mean? Margot wondered. I'm just one more piece in a jigsaw puzzle that is so warped maybe it can never be smoothed out and made right.

"Goodnight, Katherine," said Rick, his voice so cold it seemed to send a shock wave through Katy's body. Margot could sense her child's effort to pull away. The child went over to Rick and stood before him. He placed one brief, silent kiss precisely in the middle of Katy's forehead.

"Goodnight, Father," said Katy.

Father? Katy had called this monster "father"?

She watched helplessly as her little girl walked slowly away to her bedroom.

"Be done with the kitchen in ten minutes," said Rick.

Margot tried to think positively as she hurried to finish washing the dishes and wiping the counters. Katy was okay. Well, whatever psychological game this man had been playing was clearly taking a toll, but Margot sensed that he hadn't physically abused her daughter. At least Katy was better than what Margot had pictured in her worst imaginings.

Another plus was the man's intelligence. He was obviously disturbed, and she'd have to be careful, but Margot believed that if she and Katy weren't able to escape, she would be able to reason with him. Then Margot bumped her "bracelet" against the refrigerator shelf as she was putting away the butter. It scared her to realize that her thinking had become so muddled that she'd forgotten that she and Katy could not merely run away into the night. While it was a distinct possibility that the wrist device was a fake, that it would not do what Rick had promised, it was also too risky to test it out at this point.

At precisely the moment when Margot finished drying and putting away the last dish, Rick strode into the kitchen. His movements were as calm as those of someone getting a spoon to make instant coffee. So Margot looked twice when he pulled the drawer full of stainless steel completely out and calmly dumped its contents into the garbage can.

"I don't like tacky flatware. There is silver polish in the broom closet. Clean the silverware in the chest," he said, pointing to the top of the sideboard.

Could he be any more out of touch with reality? Margot wondered. She was suddenly achingly aware that her only weapons were words and logic. She'd been trying to understand all evening just what weird set of needs would compel a man to act so strangely. And what twisted interdependency would make his wife go along with him— not only go along with him but join in his delusions? Then

she wondered for the first time, was it maybe the wife,
Sonya, who was directing this show? Maybe Rick—although
he seemed to be the leader—maybe he was merely following Sonya's wishes. Margot had no reason to think that they
had children of their own. Maybe Sonya was infertile.
Margot thought about that for a moment as she retrieved
the bottle of silver polish. She'd done several shows on the
problems of infertility and had learned of the deep, even
suicidal depression that some women—and men—could go
into when they learned that they could not have children.
Was something like that involved here?

Margot understood something about the pain of being
infertile. She had watched Joe struggle with it. But when
they'd finally agreed to try artificial insemination, they were
told they were extremely lucky. It "took" on the second try.
She and Joe had been so thrilled to find that they'd have a
baby in less than a year; they had escaped the trauma that
many couples went through.

Or maybe the force here was the sickness of acquisitive-
ness? Had Rick somehow learned Katy's identity and
decided that he would simply take what was his? Were there
other children somewhere in danger of abduction by their
"father"? Had he already snatched them? And if so, where
were they?

Margot felt more and more weary as her bruised mind
circled through the endless possibilities. The fumes from the
silver polish added to the sensation that her head was stuffed
with cotton. One by one, she polished, rinsed and dried each
piece of flatware, cleaning every crevice in the elaborate
design. What kind of people had so much money that they'd
keep what was probably several thousand dollars worth of
sterling silver locked away and forgotten in an unused
vacation hideaway? Maybe the owner was out of the
country, or perhaps sick or dead, or maybe this awful couple
had killed the owners and— "Damn!"

Margot dropped the knife she'd been polishing and
reached for a paper towel to clean her eye. She realized that

she must have fallen into a semidoze and had rubbed her eye with the polish-covered rubber glove. Tears poured from her eyes as she rinsed the affected one with cold water.

"Be done in five minutes," came the cold voice from the living room.

What was this guy's preoccupation with having everything done in so many minutes? Was that part of his apparent need to control his victims' every move? Whatever, Margot realized sadly that she had not come up with any brilliant arguments to offer to the madman in the next room.

Quickly, she finished cleaning the silver and put the box back on the sideboard. When she was done—in three minutes she noted, looking at the wall clock—she entered the living room and sat down in a wing chair across from Rick, who was reading some kind of journal.

"I believe that you care for Katy—Katherine," said Margot, trying to sound reasonable. "If you didn't, you wouldn't have come for me. And I can see that my presence annoys you. Please believe me, if you'll let us go home, I'll instruct my attorney to draw up papers allowing you to have visitation rights with Katy."

He frowned at Margot for a minute, then set his journal aside before speaking. "There's no reason for me to waste my time talking with you. But just for the sake of argument, let me point out a couple of things. One," he said, pounding his fist into the palm of his other hand, "no court would grant me any rights to Katherine because when I made my 'contribution' to the sperm bank, I signed away any rights to any progeny that might result. And, two, if I'd had any rights, I would have ruined my chances by abducting, first, Katherine, and now you."

His voice dripped venom when he said the word "you." "And, yes, your presence does annoy me. And wasting my breath on you annoys me."

With that, he rose, opened a door and flipped a light

switch. He indicated that Margot was to go down the stairs into the basement.

She felt panic. "Please. Why do you hate me so? If I'm Katy's mother, then I'm part of her, so I can't possibly be all bad."

Giving her shoulder a push, he headed Margot toward and down the stairs. "A mother who would beat her own child is always the first to ask why people say she's not a good mother."

"Beat her?" Margot had reached the basement floor and felt the chill from the concrete walls. "I don't beat her. Never! Oh God, if you heard that, it's wrong. Honestly, I—"

"Shut up." He raised his hand as if to strike Margot. She did not cower but continued to stare up at his face with honest astonishment and the horror of the accusation he'd made. They stood frozen like that for a moment.

Then he pushed aside an old metal storage locker to reveal a heavy steel door. He turned a key in the lock and pushed the door open. Striking like a snake, he grasped her wrist. In one quick movement, he shoved Margot into a black space. She screamed, but the door shut in her face, leaving her in total darkness.

21 . . .

"PLEASE, DON'T DO this," cried Margot. She turned and raised her hands in the dark, feeling for the door. With panic growing, she beat her fists against hard, cold metal. But soon she stopped.

Eyes wide in a futile attempt to see something of her prison, Margot forced herself to be quiet. She breathed as deeply as she could, then listened. Nothing. No sound, except her own raspy inhalations.

Slowly, she reached out and placed both of her palms against the door, or what she believed to be the door, that had shut her in only a moment ago.

Then, grimacing in fear as she imagined what she might touch, Margot felt her way to the left of the doorjamb. There, to her relief, her fingertips discovered a light switch. She pushed it up. Nothing.

Margot held still for a moment, holding one hand directly in front of her eyes, hoping that maybe there was some remote source of light that her eyes had adjusted to. Nothing.

Refusing to panic, Margot continued her exploration, moving farther to the left. If she did not lose contact with the wall, she reasoned, she could always return to the door. The thought of that portal to her daughter was a shimmer of mental light, a bit of hope that she held onto as she moved blindly about the room. Now, she felt cold cement, the distinctive texture of cinderblock. Proceeding, with her arms growing heavy, her fingers sensed a warmer material. She decided that it was wood she touched, the side support of shelves. Both sensing and smelling dust, Margot inspected the shelves' contents with her fingers. In neat rows, she felt boxes, bags and cans. In a wicker basket, she felt cold metal and discovered that the basket held kitchen implements, a big spoon, a hand-operated can opener, knives— ''Ow,'' she cried out as something razor-sharp sliced the pad of her thumb. Her voice sounded like an animal's cry in the blackness, and she stuck her thumb into her mouth. Blood and dust curdled on her tongue.

Somehow, the presence of the kitchen implements—even the very sharp paring knife—and the containers that probably held food, seemed comforting, familiar. Perhaps she was simply locked in a storage room or a place for cast-off household items.

Maybe this is a storm shelter, she thought. If so, surely there would be a flashlight or lantern, or at least some candles.

Moving a little more confidently now, Margot explored the lower shelves. More boxes and cans, then a plastic box filled with first-aid supplies. When she opened it, there was a strong odor of disinfectant. On the bottom shelf, her hands moved slowly, but contacted empty space. Then, near the back, she felt what could only be a rifle. It was wrapped in canvas, with metal buckles to close the case.

Margot swallowed hard and went farther to the left. Her mind tried to shut down as it always did when she encountered anything to do with guns. Ever since the day her father had taken her hunting, she had hated guns. He had shot and wounded a rabbit, and before it died it had made a sound like the cry of a human baby. The sound was so pitiful that Margot had wept a long time and would not be comforted until her father promised her that they would never go hunting again. It was years later that he told her that he would have come to that decision on his own. He, too, had never been able to forget that forlorn cry.

Margot heard a sound and realized that it was her own voice. She was so disoriented that she couldn't quite figure if she was humming or moaning. ''Lullaby and goodnight," she croaked, then cleared her throat. She tried again. Softly, she began to sing the old lullaby to herself, comforting herself as she continued to grope in the dark. She had never known all the words, so soon fell to crooning just the tune. When Katy was a baby and had suffered from teething pain, she had been more soothed by the humming than anything else Margot and Joseph tried. Margot sang so off-key that her friends and even Joe gave her a hard time when she tried to join in any impromptu singalongs, but Katy had always gazed at Margot with babyish adoration in her eyes.

Soon Margot encountered a wall at right angles to the one she'd been exploring. Briefly, she considered going on in her counterclockwise direction but changed her mind. If someone was going to put a light source in a room for an emergency, they would probably put it near the door. Feeling her way along, Margot headed back to the door. "Where is it?" she whispered. It seemed to be taking too long to return to her starting point. But finally she encountered the cold, slightly rough surface of the door.

To the right, she located another set of wooden shelves. With amazement, she felt around at eye level and discovered not just one but four lanterns. "Matches, matches," she muttered, moving her hands quickly, eager to see again.

Margot screamed when there was a sudden crash and the sound of shattering glass. She quickly realized that she'd knocked one of the lanterns to the floor. "Damn!" With great effort, she forced herself to stop and calm down. She counted to twenty. That was enough to quiet the thudding of her heart.

She felt about on every shelf in front of her, and while she found other items she could identify, like buckets, dried-out sponges shriveled in their plastic bags, and several three-ring notebooks, she found no matches. Just as she was about to move on to the next post in the dark perimeter, her fingers touched a small, lightweight box. She pried open the top lid, and for a moment was sure she'd discovered a tin of tea, feeling the surface of what she thought was a paper inner liner. But further exploration revealed the rough sandpaper strip that could only mean she now held a box of kitchen matches. She pulled the little drawer open and felt inside. The box was full.

"Please, please light," she said into the air as she struck the match. A flame so bright it hurt filled her vision, then settled down to a softer yellow glow.

Margot squinted into the gloom and could see that she was in a large room. She blinked and made a slow turn, trying to reorient herself. Something told her she should be careful not to waste the matches, even though the box was nearly full. But the small column of flame was so welcome, it provided such relief, she allowed herself to burn just the one with no particular purpose. When its light went out, the darkness swallowed her again, only darker this time.

Clutching the match box firmly in her left hand, Margot again used her tactile senses to inspect the three unbroken lanterns. All three appeared to be like the lamps her dad and she had used when they used to go camping. She lifted them, one by one, and they all felt similar in weight, all giving off the satisfying sloshing sound of fuel.

Still, she hesitated to light the lantern. In her mind's eye she could see that night long ago when their lantern had malfunctioned. One minute she and her father were watching the twin mantles burn cheerily, and the next flames were shooting out for four feet in all directions. "Daddy," she'd screamed. "Hurts!"

He had grabbed her in his arms and sprinted away from the lantern just as the tent caught fire and exploded into a fireball. Her father then had pushed Margot to the ground and rolled her, slapping at her legs with his open palms. Only then did he attend to the flames that marched like will-o-the-wisps across the back of his woolen jacket.

Because he'd moved so quickly and because he had had the forethought to get away from the tent, neither one of them had been badly hurt. Other campers had helped to extinguish the blaze before it grew into a forest fire. Margot would always remember the kindness of those campers as they hurried over with ice and first-aid kits, blankets and clothing. Having lost most of their camping equipment, she and her father had stopped at the local emergency room before driving home that night. The doctor had treated their burns and predicted that they'd heal without scarring. They then had phoned Margot's mother to tell her they'd be returning in the middle of the night and to reassure her that while they looked a bit battered, they were fine. Margot still recalled with amusement and pity the look on her mother's face when she and her father had showed up at the door with ill-fitting, unfamiliar clothes—and no eyebrows at all.

Moving with exaggerated care, Margot set her precious box of matches on the shelf, pushing them safely against the side and toward the back. Then she knelt and felt the floor space for a foot or two in front of her and to her side, finding the space clear except for the fragments of the smashed lantern globe. Still fearful of disaster at any moment, Margot stood and lit another match. She used its light to inspect the area around her. Nothing looked like an explosive.

In the dark, Margot lifted a lantern from the shelf and placed it at her feet. She bent down and pumped the small plunger at the base of the lantern to pump air pressure into the fuel container. Unconsciously gritting her teeth, fearing an explosion, Margot lit a match, lifted the glass globe and held the flame to the mantle. It hissed, smelled briefly of soot then grew bright yellow. Margot adjusted the flame and watched with a flood of relief as the lantern emitted a clean bright white light.

As she lifted the lantern to shoulder level, the room's contours came into focus, like a photo developing in a darkroom. It was a large room with most walls covered with shelves. The floor was tile; there were no windows evident and no other doors.

Margot placed the lamp on a table near the door, checking first and finding it heavy and solid. There were six beds, arranged two by two in different areas of the cavernous room. On the shelves were enough canned and dried foods to last for months.

"A bomb shelter, an honest-to-God bomb shelter!" Margot muttered to herself as she continued her inspection. Under all the beds were bottles—bottle after huge bottle—of drinking water. Lined against the walls, behind the water, were canisters of fuel, the clean-burning kind used in camping lanterns and stoves.

Margot sat down on one of the beds and gazed at the result of what had clearly been a massive effort. But not a recent effort. It wasn't just the layers of dust that covered everything, it was the style of the room and the equipment that told of years passing since it had been assembled.

Margot's tired mind sifted through segments of her TV talk show on which she'd covered survivalists, the groups of wary people that formed in the 1970s after the Vietnam War. This didn't fit into that category. The room she was in felt more like the shelters that people had constructed in the 1950s—the frightening years when many people expected to be incinerated at any moment if they didn't have a safe, underground shelter. She shook her head, amazed at the innocence and naiveté of those days when people believed that they needed only to wait a safe while before resurfacing like gophers to resume their lives.

"We started to make this into a bomb shelter a long time ago," her father had told her once when Margot and he were down in the workshop. She was eight or nine at the time and he'd been teaching her to use the router to decorate a small toy bench they were building together. "Your mother was hysterical half the time, positive there was a bomb that had our specific address on it."

Margot laughed because her father chuckled, but she hadn't quite seen the humor in it. "But I convinced her that we'd make better use of the basement as a workshop. Of course, I had to promise to use it to make the new kitchen cabinets before anything else.'' Margot *did* see the humor in that.

"I don't remember when it was a bomb shelter, Daddy."

"Oh, that was before you were born, Margot.'' Her parents had been married for ten years before she "came along,'' as they put it. When she asked about things, they often told her that: "It was before you were born.'' Margot understood that kind of answer now. How many times had she told Katy the same thing? How many times had she realized that her life ws clearly divided into two distinct segments—the one before and the one after Katy was born?

And now, sitting on the cot in the musty bomb shelter, reliving a conversation from so long ago, Margot understood for the first time that her mother's whole expression of fear and wanting the bomb shelter may have been an elaborate ploy to get the new kitchen. Her mother *was* a bit of a coward, but she was also devious in harmless ways. And Margot's father never seemed to catch on. Or maybe he just pretended not to know.

As Margot considered her desperate situation, she continued to explore the shelter. Everything had a layer of dust on it. Eventually, grinding her teeth together, and thinking of Katy for courage, she returned to the shelves where she'd felt the rifle earlier in her blind inspection. But before she even zipped open the old canvas case, Margot knew that there were no bullets. Next to the case on the shelf, only slightly disturbed by her earlier exploration with her fingers, were two rectangles outlined by gray dust. Margot realized that there had been boxes of bullets sitting there recently and felt sure that Rick had taken the bullets. And left the gun. His idea of humor, she suspected.

Nevertheless, Margot spent a long time exploring the bomb shelter, trying to find a cache of ammunition. Her father had spent many hours teaching Margot gun safety and care before they ever went out into the woods together. She knew how to use a gun, and she *would* use a gun if she had an opportunity. But after a long search, Margot didn't find any bullets.

Finally, like a tired child, Margot lay down and curled up, thinking about her father. She could feel the tears coming and didn't try to stop them. It was so hard to picture her big, strong father there in the hospital, there among the monitors and call lights and shiny high-tech equipment. She wondered how he was doing. Her mind immediately said, call and find out. Her total impotence struck her for the thousandth time that day. Daddy in the hospital, so sick; Katy just one floor above, with a locked metal door between them. Then a worse thought struck her. Maybe Katy was *not* just one floor above her. She sat bolt upright and ran to the door. What if the madman had taken Katy away? Had locked Margot down here to rot and taken Katy far away?

She hammered at the door with her fists, but at last admitted the futility of her actions. Defeated, Margot went back and lay down again on the cot. She fell into a state somewhere between sleep and unconsciousness, in a fetal position in the shelter that provided no shelter.

22...

KATHERINE HAD FINALLY stopped asking for her mother, reluctantly agreeing with Sonya that the sooner she was asleep, the sooner it would be morning and she could see her mother again. Now, Sonya continued to hum softly, stroking the child's downy hair again and again. The room was almost dark, with just a little illumination from the hall light.

If only I could just sit like this forever, Sonya thought. There's nothing I can do about it. Rick has to fix it, so why not just enjoy it?

She ran her fingertips lightly over the back of Katherine's hand, remembering how soft her own little Evan's hands had been, his baby palms like damp moss.

"That's enough." Rick's voice startled her. "Let her sleep now."

Angry at him for breaking into her dream, Sonya rose and left Katherine's room. "She *was* sleeping. I wasn't bothering her."

"She's a sensitive child. You don't know that you weren't bothering her."

"I'm sure I wasn't. You could tell from—"

"Never mind. We have other things to do now," he said, leading the way into the large bedroom next to Katherine's.

Sonya glanced down the long hall, then into the corners of the room. "Where is she?"

"Katherine's moth—her biological mother—is where she can't hurt anyone, at least not for the night."

"I don't like the idea of her wandering around. She makes me nervous."

''She's not 'wandering around,' as you put it. We won't have to look at her again until we're ready. Meanwhile, we have to talk.''

Talking was something that Rick would only do when he wanted to. It seemed to Sonya that she always had a whole laundry basket of issues stored up by the time he was in the mood, but tonight she would try to be a better listener. Maybe if she let him go on, he'd talk himself out of this absurd notion that he could keep Katherine.

Sonya crawled up on the bed behind Rick where he sat perched on the edge. She knelt behind him and began to knead the knotted muscles in his neck and shoulders.

''I need your cooperation for the next few days.'' He brushed her hands away, his movements less intense now. As he removed his shirt, he continued speaking.

''I have to do something right away. Katherine was in real danger from that woman.'' He nodded his head toward the hall, making Sonya wonder again where ''that woman'' was at the moment.

''Rick, I was thinking, if you—''

''Let me talk,'' he said. Sonya began to knead his muscles again. ''I didn't have time to do any significant research on the case. And I don't know if the police will find us here in a few days, or if they'll find us at all.''

He turned to her and kissed her tenderly on the cheek. His lovemaking was always hard and forceful—this was a gentle side of him that she rarely saw. He only used it when he wanted something from her. And that was rare, too. It filled her with an extraordinary and unfamiliar sense of satisfaction—almost as if she had won a prize.

''What I need now is time. I have to go through the law books I have here, and I may need to go back to my office and check out some precedents. I can't leave Katherine here alone, and I don't trust that woman.''

''Maybe you could call Mike and get him to—''

''No. The minute you start bringing in other people, you

ask for trouble. Mike's a fine attorney for routine stuff, but there's nothing routine about the mess we're in now.''

Somehow, Sonya had been thinking of this as Rick's problem. Was she in just as much trouble as he was? It hit her that if the police were to walk through the door at this moment, she could hardly convince them that she was an innocent bystander.

''Do you really think we might have a case?''

''I don't know. That's why I need time.'' He kissed her eyelids. He had *never* done that before. His lips were soft, the sound of his breathing wrapped her senses in a soft cocoon as he moved to nibble lightly on her ear.

Maybe she *did* remember this kind of lovemaking. When she was pregnant with Evan. He'd been so gentle then. And after. After Evan was born, after they'd put him into his crib for the night, after they'd gazed at his sweet face—

With a start, Sonya pushed Rick away from her. What she'd just seen in her mind—

''Please, Rick. Let me talk for a minute.'' She swallowed. ''I'm scared. I can't—''

''Oh, stop it. There's no reason for you to be afraid. I'm taking responsibility for everything that's going on here.''

''No. No. That's not what I mean. It's Evan.''

''What about him?'' There was irritation in his tone again.

''I can't remember his face.''

''You what?''

''I can't remember what his little face looked like.'' She felt her whole body shaking, and she wanted to go into Rick's arms. But he was too annoyed at the moment. He'd misunderstood, thought she was scared about his kidnapping Katherine. What she didn't tell him was that when she tried to think of Evan's face, all she could see was Katherine's. And that scared her the most—that in just a few short hours, Katherine had started to take Evan's place. And she knew that they couldn't keep Katherine. She knew it!

All his talk about researching the case, about precedents. It didn't mean a thing.

Rick got off the bed and went to the bags in the corner. He rummaged through them while Sonya sat on the bed shivering.

"Here," he said, thrusting something into her hands. "Now you don't have to be afraid."

She held a silver-framed photo of Evan. It had to be the exhaustion. The beloved and familiar face of her sweet boy began to flow, to alter, to mix with Katherine's face. She dropped the picture.

Rick hurried to pick it up, to inspect it for damage. "It's okay," he said. "What's the matter with you?"

"I told you, I'm scared." Maybe I'm crazy, she thought. It was not a new fear—it had lived with her since Evan's death. If she was crazy, who would take care of her? Would Rick still be there? Who would take care of a crazy woman?

"Sonya, don't you realize you're always scared. You're *always* scared." He touched his thumb gently to her chin, raising her head so she must look at him. "That's why you have to stay with me. I'll take care of you."

Had she spoken aloud? She leaned against his broad chest. "I'm sorry," she said.

The weariness washed over her. She knew that only one thing would revive her now, let her breathe easily again. Moving slowly, hoping he was as tired of talking, talking, talking, as she was, she began to move her lips over his body. She followed a path from his mouth to his ear, to his neck, to his chest, to all the places she knew made him need *her*. Rick pushed the law book out of the way with his foot and didn't seem to notice when it slid off the edge of the bed and hit the rug with a thud. That's good, she thought. The times when he put Sonya ahead of his law books were few, each one remembered like a pearl to be saved and strung on a silken cord.

23...

    AS MARGOT LAY on the cot, her body and mind more weary than she had ever dreamed possible, she tried to hold on to a positive thought. Katy was alive—and basically okay, although definitely not her normal, energetic self.

    Margot had never felt so powerless in her life. It struck her as funny that she was locked in a bomb shelter, since it was a prison, not a shelter. Margot had found Katy, but what use was she to her daughter?

    As she had done several times during this long day, Margot tried to convince herself that Rick had made some giant mistake—that he was *not* Katy's father. But everything told Margot that he was. It wasn't just the straight red hair and green eyes that matched Katy's that convinced Margot of the truth of Rick's paternity claim. The faces of Katy and Rick were the same—except that Katy's was young and sweet and full of hope—where Rick's was worn, full of pain and had a feverish quality that had more to do with desperation.

    Margot slipped in and out of sleep. Sometimes she dreamed about the day, a little more than six years ago, when she and Joe had sat together and looked over the donor lists, trying to choose one of the sperm donors as the biological father of their baby.

    She recalled their first tentative discussion of the options. It was a chilly, damp morning. When the alarm rang at seven, they were both already half-awake. As Margot rolled over to get up, Joe reached for her.

    "Wait." He turned her face toward his and kissed her gently, then nibbled on the nape of her neck. "Why did you set the alarm? We don't have to be anywhere all day." A crack of thunder made them both jump. They laughed.

Margot reached awkwardly over the nightstand and pulled the shade. With a sound like wet sheets flapping, it flew up and twirled a few times in protest. "I think it's darker in here with the shade *up*," she said.

Joseph ran his hands over her breasts. "Mmm, perfect."

Margot moved closer. Before she gave herself wholly over to the delicious feelings that Joseph was teasing and licking to hot life, Margot gave one last thought to her plan for the day. If she could at least get him to *look at* the list of sperm donors she'd gotten in yesterday's mail, then maybe— "Oh, Joe, yes."

They climaxed to the thunder and lightning that seemed to be stalled directly over their bedroom. "Love you, Margot."

"I love you, too," said Margot as she snuggled closer. "Let's never get up. It's so safe and warm here. We've got a phone—we could order in food and just never leave the bed."

"But the door's locked. How will the delivery boy get in?"

"Person."

"How will the delivery *person* get in?"

"Well, it was a near-perfect plan."

"Speaking of food—" said Joe, stretching.

"It's your turn." They alternated cooking duties on Sundays, fixing huge, fattening, cholesterol-laden breakfasts that they ate in the dining room, using the good china. And no matter what else the menu included, they always had strawberries and champagne. Sometimes, in the dead of winter, it was nothing more than frozen strawberries folded into crepes or—in dire circumstances—merely strawberry jam. In any case, it was a simple tradition that they had both come to enjoy.

While Joe went about preparing the breakfast in his quiet, methodical way, Margot turned on a Hubert Laws album and set the table. The storm continued to thrash and fling fistfuls of water against the dining room windows. Just as Margot placed the old china salt and pepper owls that had been one of her mother's wedding gifts on the table, a painfully bright flash of lightning was followed by a loud crack of thunder. The room blackened, and Joe hollered, "Shit!"

"What?"

"Nothing. Ow! Shit."

Fortunately, there were candles in the holders on the sideboard and matches in the top drawer that were easy to find. Margot lit a taper and carried it into the kitchen. Joe was standing over the stove sucking on an apparently burned thumb. She got ice for him, and the hurt soon went away.

"At least Hurricane Huey's timing wasn't too bad." Joe began spooning the eggs Benedict into a serving dish. "Everything's done."

"I think Hurricane Huey was some other year. Isn't this one Hurricane Louie?"

"Or Dewey?"

Over the strawberries and champagne, and the eggs, blueberry muffins, and fat, juicy sausages, Margot and Joe read the Sunday paper, chuckling over the better parts of the funnies together. Since it was apparent that there was no need to stay particularly sober this Sunday, because neither one intended to brave Hurricane Whoever, they finished the bottle of champagne, laughing as strawberry juice ran down their chins.

By the time they'd cleaned away the dishes and lit a fire in the living room, Margot had almost forgotten her earlier mission. But, as so many times before, she now imagined sharing their love and Sundays with a child.

"I have something I want to show you," she said. She sat on the thick rug next to him and leaned back against the oak sea chest that had been her great uncle's long years ago. She

handed him the manila envelope that sat atop a paper bag on
the table.

Like most people who are handed an envelope that
obviously contains something more important than the
water bill, he checked out the return address first. Margot
knew it would be of no help to him. The sperm bank sent out
its donor list in a modern Tyvek version of the "plain brown
wrapper."

With a fleeting sideways glance at Margot, Joe reached
inside and pulled out some stapled sheets of green paper
with rows of neat type in tiny computer print.

"Heritage Cryobank," he read out loud. He leaned closer
to the fire to get more light on the tiny print. The electricity
was still out. Running his forefinger under the first line, he
continued to read: "Caucasian, Dutch/German, six-foot-
one, two hundred fifteen pounds, medium build, blue eyes,
blond/straight hair, graduate student in health, and get
this—" Joe paused to glare at Margot with one eyebrow
up—the single look of his she could never decipher. "Get
this: His special interests are ichthyology and canoeing."

Joe gazed at Margot for a long, uncomfortable time, then
back at the list. "The sperm bank thing again, huh?"

"Just to consider, Joe. No pressure. I was hoping you'd
keep an open mind about it."

"You know what ichthyology is, right?" he said.

"Sure. It's the study of icks?"

"Very funny. It's the branch of zoology that deals with
fishes. But in the case of this stud, combined with his
ongoing grad student status and his love of canoeing, I'd say
donor number one is a fishing bum."

Margot stared at him. The room was noisy with sleet
slashing sloppily at the windows. Lights from the dining
room and kitchen flickered weakly on, then off again.

She reached out and snatched the list from Joe's hand,
then stuffed it back into its envelope. "You're like everyone
else. You think it's just the stuff of jokes."

Margot jumped up, and holding tightly to the envelope,

she reached down and retrieved the paper bag from the table. Taking her candle from the mantel, she tried to step around Joe so that she could go to the bedroom.

He didn't grab her foot or ankle, but he lightly rubbed her instep with his hand. "Wait. I'm sorry."

She turned, being careful in the small space between the sea chest and the fire. The last thing she needed was for her robe to go up in flames.

"Please. So I'm a jerk," he said. "You're right." He reached up and tugged at the envelope. "Can I have a second chance?"

Margot looked at him, his face clear and open, no signs of mockery there.

Grudgingly, she knelt next to him. As she settled down, the bag slid to the floor between her and Joe and something bright fell partially out. "Wait—" she said, but too late.

Joe held up a tiny mint-green baby sleeper with musical notes embroidered on the collar. "What?" he asked.

"It's all coming out wrong, Joe. I bought that a long time ago, before—"

"Say it. Before we found out I was infertile."

Margot could see the hurt in his eyes when he said the word. She wondered if he'd ever be any easier about it.

"When we first tried to get pregnant, I saw that, and I couldn't resist. Maybe it was like a jinx I put on us by being too pushy—"

"Garbage!" He never would allow an expression of undeserved guilt—except in himself.

"In any case, I brought it out today because I've been thinking really seriously about artificial insemination. It's not a joke. It's a real alternative to a long wait for an infant. And it's a way to have some control over things ourselves. You know I'm not opposed to adoption. And I'd be willing to take an older child. Someday. But first, I'd like to have a baby."

She reached out and took Joe's hands in hers, squeezing hard, trying to press her needs into him.

"It's not just a kneejerk reaction to the fact that we can't have one the easy way. You know that. It's something we've always wanted. Always. And I thought that somehow if I could let you know . . . if I could make you see—" She picked up the sleeper and held it aloft. Then she cradled it like a newborn.

"A baby. We could have a baby. Not just me. We! And the list of donors—that's part of the creative thing. If—" She stopped, worn out, and out of arguments. She was out of breath.

"Oh, honey. I *am* sorry. And I wasn't laughing at you. It's just my own stupid hang-ups about this." He picked up the list and began leafing through the pages. "I mean, out of the blue. You gotta admit it does seem like some kind of 'Saturday Night Live' shopping list."

"I'll admit that. When it came in the mail, I opened it expecting to find some junk mail. It took me a few minutes to figure out it was the information I had phoned for. But then it started to seem kind of wonderful. I mean, when our parents were having their children, all of this technology didn't exist. And now—"

Joe was running his finger down the list as she spoke, and he chuckled. She eyed him suspiciously, thinking maybe he'd gone back into his mocking mood. But it was a happy laugh. He reached for a pencil and lay on his stomach in front of the fire to shed the most light on the small print. He underlined two. "Here. Look at these two," he said. "They both sound great."

She scanned the entries he'd marked.

Donor ID#	Race	Ethnic Origin Mother/Father	Height	Weight	Body Build	Skin Tone	Eye Color	Hair Color/Type	Yrs Coll	Occupation	Special Interests
543	Cauc	French/Engl.	5–10	170	Med	Fair	Blue	Brown/Curly	5	Stu/Eng Lit.	Tennis/Travel/Painting
1744	Cauc	French/Germ.	5–11	168	Med	Fair	Blue	Brown/Curly	2	Stu/Architec.	Music/Photog./Piano

"Why those two?" she asked.

"Because then the baby would be as good-looking as

you. Just look at those characteristics. The baby would have blue eyes and curly brown hair like you. And both of these guys are fairly tall like you. They're not fat, either."

"You forgot to say 'like you.'"

"I never said you were fat."

"You jerk," she said and began to tickle him. They wrestled for a while when suddenly the lights came back on.

"Good," said Margot. "Now we can look at this thing seriously. I've read it pretty carefully, and I think I've found the perfect one."

"Wait, wait," he said, starting to laugh again. "Look at this entry. It says the guy's parents were German and Sicilian. Not Italian, Sicilian. Can you—"

Margot swatted him lightly on the nose. "No ethnic jokes. Now get serious. Look at number one-five-two-two."

"Yes, ma'am," said Joe. "Seriously," he said and read the entry out loud. "Number one-five-two-two. Caucasian, parents French and Irish, he's six-one, a hundred and ninety pounds, medium build, fair skin, green eyes and red straight hair, five years of college, law student, likes electronics, foreign films and running. So?"

"At least in terms of the physical characteristics, who does that sound like?"

"Well, I guess it sounds a lot like a fat version of me."

"Fat! The guy's a runner. It's probably all muscle. He sounds gorgeous."

"Yes, but he likes foreign films. How pretentious."

"I like foreign films," said Margot.

"Yes, but you're not pretentious."

"That doesn't make sense."

"I know. But neither does choosing our baby's father from a Xeroxed list make sense. It's all new to me."

"You know," said Margot. "A thought just occurred to me. When the donors come in to register at the cryobank, they have to put down a lot of information about themselves that's just straightforward fact. Like height and weight and occupation and all that. The one way they can 'communicate'"

—and Margot made quotation marks in the air with her fingers—"is in the special interests section."

"I don't get it."

"Well, the first one you read, for example. He put down that he liked ichthyology and canoeing. It *is* like a joke. And you got it. So maybe he's trying to get people to buy his sperm by letting them know that he has a sense of humor—that if a couple wants a lighthearted, happy baby, they should try him."

"Good theory. But what does that say about one-five-two-two? He sounds like a grump by comparison. Pretty boring interests."

"No. Think about it. He likes electronics. That says he's good with his hands *and* mind. He's a foreign film buff. That says he has an open mind. And running. He takes care of his body's needs. He sounds like a well-rounded person. Just like you."

"It comes back to that, doesn't it?" said Joe. He sighed and stared at the ceiling for an instant. "Maybe he sounds just like me on one line on a piece of paper. But still, it's some other guy. Not me."

"That would be true of an adopted child, too," said Margot. With nervous fingers, she snapped and unsnapped the set of snaps that closed the tiny sleeper.

"Hah," said Joe, a grin forming on his face. He was looking at the list again.

"What?" asked Margot, looking at the bottom of the page where he was pointing.

"Doses," he said, laughing harder. "They call them doses."

Margot read the words next to the asterisk at the bottom of the page.

"The number of doses available on any donor at a particular time is dependent on the number of doses that have been released from quarantine based on current health test data."

"That strikes you as funny?" asked Margot. She didn't get the joke.

"Yeah. Don't know why. It just does."

"So it's still a joke, isn't it?" she asked sadly.

"No," said Joe, sobering. "Maybe it's not so funny. Maybe it's something we could consider."

"Oh, thank you, Joe. That's all I ask. Just think about it." Margot kissed him long and soft on the lips.

"Okay," he said. "But can I think about it later? Maybe it's not the same potency as the ones on this list, but right now I feel another dose coming on."

Margot screwed up her face at the awful joke, but followed him willingly back to the bedroom anyway.

24...

RICK STOOD OUTSIDE the door of the old bomb shelter in the cool basement air. With his right hand, he felt the heavy bulk of the gun. The weight of it pulled at his belt slightly, a sensation he enjoyed.

Another even more enjoyable sensation made Rick shiver in the damp air. Like a favorite old photo, he held to him the knowledge that the bomb shelter, so far underground, was completely soundproof. That woman was locked in there, and she could scream and pound all she wanted, but she would rouse no one. And Rick was the only one with the key to open the door.

Of course, anything bad that happened, she deserved. No punishment was too great for a child abuser. But still, he had promised Katherine that she could see the woman today. He would keep Margot locked away again tonight and then try to wean Katherine from her dependence on the bitch. It wouldn't be long before Katherine would call Sonya ''Mommy'' and mean it. His wife had her faults, but Rick could see that the child was falling in love with Sonya.

Once again he stroked the butt of the pistol, then put the key in the lock and turned it. But right before he pulled the door open, he hesitated. Would she be stupid enough to try to escape, to ambush him somehow? Rick decided to protect himself, just in case. He picked up an empty detergent bottle from the trash can and upended it over the handle of a pushbroom.

He stepped to the side of the door, pulled on the base of the lock and removed it. With something between a snarl and a laugh he shoved the door open with his foot. He was met with total darkness. He didn't hear anything, but he sensed movement.

He thrust the broom handle through the door. He felt, rather than saw, the impact on the end as something smashed into the detergent bottle. A scream came from the darkness as he backed away from the door. He held the gun in front of him. No telling what other plans the woman had.

"Out of there—now!" he ordered.

He heard nothing. "Do you want me to shoot into the darkness? It wouldn't be my fault if I hit you."

Slowly, blinking like a stupid groundhog coming out of hibernation, Margot emerged. She held her hands in front of her, empty and shaking convulsively.

"Very theatrical, bitch." His voice was low and soft. "But I want to ask you something."

Suddenly, he shoved her against the wall, and he pushed the handle of the broom against her throat. Leaning on it with both hands, he glared at her. She struggled, tried to push the handle away. Her eyes showed pain and fear. That was good. He dropped the broom and picked up the detergent bottle.

"Look at this." She held her throat and stared wide-eyed at the empty bottle. "What if this had been Evan's head? Huh? What if I'd sent Evan down to—"

He stopped. His confusion was mirrored in the woman's eyes.

"Please," she said.

"Shut up." His breathing was heavy. "What if it had been Katherine coming through that door? Look at this."

She did as she was told. She reached out and touched the plastic bottle, running her fingers down the edge where it had been split in two, like a rotten watermelon.

"Katy?"

"No," he thundered. "Katherine. What if this had been Katherine?" He watched her. "Of course, it's not like it'd be new to you."

"I never— Oh, God, you gotta believe me. I don't know who told you I abused Katy, but—"

"Katherine." This time his voice was low, like distant thunder. "Her name is Katherine. Why should I believe you when you can't even remember her name?"

"Katherine," she said. "I'm sorry, I meant to say Katherine." She looked him straight in the eyes, then down at the floor.

He tossed the broken bottle into the corner, tired of the whole thing. If Katherine didn't need this biological mother for the moment, Rick would gladly shoot her now and leave her in the shelter to rot. He had fantasized about killing people before. He'd almost actually done it—would have, too, if they hadn't gotten that Dawn out of his house. Now he felt no hesitation at all. He considered what it would mean. He wanted to get on with normal family life. Would it be easier with this woman around or not? He considered the alternatives, holding his pistol in his hand again as he paced the laundry area. Margot continued to cower by the wall.

But then he thought about Katherine and how she'd acted this morning at breakfast. When she asked about her mother, Rick said that she'd be able to see her later. The child had immediately perked up and eaten more in that one meal than she'd eaten since she had arrived at her home.

Katherine simply had to be weaned from this mother. Rick remembered Sonya's worries about weaning Evan from the breast and how pleased she'd been when it went much easier than she'd expected. Rick had secretly thought it was because Sonya's milk had always been weak—he'd hated the smell of it himself—but he never said anything about it to Sonya. People always overestimated the pain of letting go. It was just a human weakness, a paranoia that many people had in common. He couldn't help but feel superior because he didn't suffer that way.

Of course, with Evan, it was different. It wasn't just a matter of losing a child. Rick had lost a part of himself when

Evan died. A part he had never imagined he could replace. Until he discovered Katherine.

For just an instant, Rick considered explaining things to Margot, telling her how much Katherine meant to him. It was natural for her to want to hold onto the child, but she could have more children. And he couldn't. If she'd used a sperm bank, she had to know something about the agony of infertility. She couldn't possibly know it as crushingly as Rick did, or as her poor schmuck of a husband must have. But if she understood the circumstance—if she understood that Rick had been a victim of cancer. Oh, he was cured, but the doctors said the chances of Rick fathering another child were "one in a million." How would Margot like it if someone told her something like that?

He shook his head and laughed. Waste of time thinking that way. This monster wanted the child back. He could see it in her eyes—in her body language. As if being the biological parent gave her the right to possession. Well, it took more than that to make a parent. And every child had a right to live in a family with parents who didn't beat her.

He replaced the gun in his pocket. He would put up with her for a few days, maybe a week . . . but no longer.

From a pile of clean laundry that Sonya had folded and left on the dryer, Rick grabbed a cloth. He pointed to the washtub. "Clean yourself up before you see Katherine." Margot's face was streaked with tears, and her hair was disheveled. He watched as she washed, moving more quickly now. If he didn't know what kind of person she was, he might have felt sorry for her. Her eagerness to see the child was evident. But in the article he'd shown Sonya about child abusers, it had explained that kind of behavior. Even the cruelest, most vicious parents had moments when they felt full of love for their child. It had more to do with possession than with true love, though.

She turned and gazed at him. At least she wasn't jabbering so much anymore.

"You can go and spend some time with Katherine, now.

But don't make any trouble. The more trouble you make, the less you get to see of her.''

"Thank you."

Rick raised his eyebrows. Was she getting cocky? No. She looked genuinely thankful.

"Go on," he said, following her up the steps.

She opened the door, and in a flash Katherine was in her arms. "Mama," she cried. "I've been waiting for you." She gave Margot a noisy kiss, then led her to the couch. "Where were you?"

"Oh, sweetie, I—"

"I told you, Katherine, she was working," said Rick.

The woman looked up, obviously surprised at his answer. But she didn't contradict him. Maybe she was learning. That would make the next few days easier on everyone.

"I'm so glad to see you, Mama. I—" The girl glanced up at him, then stopped talking. Instead, she lay down with her head on the woman's lap, the way a child will do at the end of a long day of play.

The woman stroked the girl's hair. The movement seemed so possessive. It was annoying. "Sonya, have you found the recipe for the soda bread?"

From the kitchen, she answered, "I have it here. And all the ingredients ready. How would you like me to make some extra loaves for—"

"No." The two women and the girl all jumped. Fidgety things. Why couldn't they just relax?

Rick walked over to Sonya and took the recipe card from her hand. He went back to the sitting area and handed the card to Margot. "You make the bread. And, Katherine, Sonya has a present for you. It's in the playroom."

Nobody moved. Rick felt like roaring. They were all trying his patience. "Sonya, go on. Take her into the playroom. And *you* make the bread!"

Sonya practically had to pull the child from the woman's arms. The weaning wasn't going as easily as he'd hoped, but it was still early. Rick sat down to read. Before opening the book's cover, he considered his plan. Maybe a week wouldn't be long enough. If a little more time would make Katherine more secure with her new mother, what could it hurt?

25...

MARGOT COULD HEAR the bright sound of Katy's laughter—no, Katherine, she thought—in the other room. Whatever the "present" was that Sonya had for Katherine, it was clearly something the child enjoyed. Of course, she was such a good kid. By the age of three, she had mastered the art of looking pleased with a present, no matter if it was the biggest dud of the century.

The flour that Margot was measuring made a poof and coated her hands and wrists. She inspected the malevolent wristband she wore for a moment, then carefully wiped the film of flour off of it.

All during her imprisonment in the bomb shelter overnight, she had thought about the device. Did it really contain explosives? If so, how could Rick be so casual about it—telling her she could shower with it, even get it muddy. The only restrictions were that she not allow the device to receive a sharp blow and to stay within three hundred feet of his wristband and Katherine's at all times.

She continued stirring as she watched the back of his head where he sat reading. She felt hot with rage and a sort of helpless shame as she envisioned the pleasure she'd get from giving a "sharp blow" to *his* band. The thought of him being blown to bits gave her an ugly thrill of pleasure, but it was followed by the unendurable thought that his device would trigger Katy's.

Like rats in a maze, Margot's thoughts continued to careen through her tired brain. It suddenly occurred to her that even if she or Katherine got more than three hundred feet away from Rick, *Rick* would not blow up. He must simply have a transmitter in his wrist device. Yes, her observant side said. She *had* noticed that Rick's device was smaller than hers or Katherine's.

Margot tried hard to put it all out of her mind and concentrate on the soda bread for the moment. Bumping her nose up against all the hard, blank mental walls was getting painful. The kitchen, however, was comforting. It was large; yet with the horseshoe counter in the middle, it had the same kind of intimacy that a bar can have in the middle of a cavernous restaurant.

Margot was positive that Rick had had nothing to do with decorating this cottage. It felt like a weekend retreat, but it was probably meant for year-round entertaining, she thought. She vaguely recalled seeing the outlines of a large furnace in the basement.

The furnishings were ample and warm, but the best part was the artwork. The walls were covered with watercolors, some delicate, some bold, filled with deep greens and golds. And everywhere there were pieces of sculpture, mostly small or medium-size, except for a large Madonna and child that sat near the sofa where Rick was still reading. How could he read like that without moving? Margot wondered if he might have fallen asleep, but just then she saw him move to turn a page.

The oven was preheating, and its warmth added to the sleepy feeling of comfort. Maybe this cabin had belonged to Rick's parents. She stood still for a moment, then gave up the effort. She simply could not envision Rick with parents. It was like those cases of psychotic serial killers—the parents on TV saying that their "boy had always been a good boy, quiet, but good."

Margot felt like one of those people now, struggling with the fact that this person who looked so normal was at the very least a criminal—but please God, not a psychopath.

She pounded on the lump of dough so hard that Rick turned around to glare at her. His face told her that she was disturbing him. Bastard! She clenched her fists, but smashed the dough more quietly. It was his game. No amount of pondering, scheming or railing against the fates would change that. But she *could* learn the rules. Even crazies had rules. And when she had them figured out, she would defeat him.

As Margot placed the loaf pan in the oven, Katy came into the kitchen. Margot couldn't help but notice that her daughter walked quietly from room to room here instead of speeding around like the road runner as she did at home. So if she and Katy—Katherine, she remembered—his rules for now— If she and Katherine had to change their ways for this man, what about Sonya? Was Sonya Rick's partner or his victim in this insane mess?

"Can I help make the bread, Mama?"

"I'm sorry, but the bread's already in the oven." Katherine looked disappointed. "But you can help clean up if you like," said Margot.

The child's face brightened. "Boy, what a mess. Did a flock of pigs come through here?" She giggled at the old joke. No one could remember how it had started, but Katy—Katherine—had always been more upset than anyone else if she spilled something. Margot well remembered her tears and how she'd been inconsolable, until, from somewhere, the story of the flock of clumsy pigs had come along. The poor pigs meant no harm, but they'd been born with wings and not much idea of how to use them. So they were always making messes, particularly in the kitchen, their favorite room.

"Oh, yes." Margot shook her head in mock dismay. "Pigs everywhere. And hungry?" Margot handed her daughter a cloth, and the child set to work, smiling as she cleaned the countertop. "They'd have eaten everything if I hadn't chased them out the window." Margot looked at the window and wondered if their imaginary pigs would have fit between the bars.

Would Katherine fit through? Margot wondered. But no, the deadly wristbands. Even if Margot could get Katherine away, the bracelets made all escapes impossible. *If* the bracelets really contained explosives and *if* the man was smart enough to rig them so the proper distance would trigger the explosives, then it would be suicide—and, most unthinkable of all, murder—for Margot to send Katy away. *If* it was all a lie, then it was the most malignant trick every played on Margot in her life.

But at the moment the only way she had to test Rick's truthfulness was impossibly dangerous. Besides, Margot knew that it *was* a possibility. When she'd been a reporter for the TV station, she had covered a case where a bank manager had been forced by a robber to bring out a briefcase of money. The robber had held the manager at gunpoint and placed an explosive collar around his neck, telling him that he would press the button on the transmitter if there was any sign of the police. When Margot interviewed the bank manager later, she asked him if he believed that the robber was bluffing about explosives being in the collar. "I didn't believe or disbelieve him," said the manager. "But it didn't seem like the right time to call his bluff."

Later, the bomb squad leader said that the collar contained enough plastique to have blown the man and anyone near him to smithereens.

Margot came again to the same conclusion she'd reached during the long night in the bomb shelter. Her only hope was to find a safe way to remove the bands from her arm and Katherine's, or to somehow disable the man and for all three of them to leave together.

But what about Sonya? Margot couldn't figure out Sonya's tie to Rick, but Margot didn't think Rick's wife would just stand by while Margot beat him into unconsciousness and dragged him out to the car.

The old-fashioned timer on the stove "binged," and Margot peeked in at the bread. It was a nice golden-brown and gave a pleasant thump when she tapped it with her fingernail. She took the loaves from the oven and set them to cool on racks on the shining countertop.

"That looks good," said Katy. "Can we have some now? With strawberry jam? And butter?"

It broke Margot's heart to think that the answer to such a simple question was not up to her. She was pretty sure that Rick's "Rule Number One" was "Don't do anything without Rick's permission."

"Let's let it cool for a while."

"Then can we go out and play? Will you come outside with me? I can show you Gone Lake. It's really just a little mud puddle now. But Sonya says it used to be a lake, a long long time ago."

"Well, I'm not sure." Margot walked slowly over to where Rick still sat. Like a vulture, she thought. "Do you think the yard is a safe place for me to take Katy—sorry, Katherine—to play?"

It made her sick to have to ask, but damned if she wouldn't put it in her own words, no matter how clumsy. Did Rule Number One allow that sort of tiny rebellion? she wondered.

"Katherine, you can go in the front yard," he answered. "And you, too—" He looked directly into Margot's eyes, then tapped gently at his wrist device.

Margot stepped out the door and breathed deeply, filling her lungs with the slightly damp, earthy air of the dense forest that surrounded the house. There was a small, cleared patch of land in front of the building, about the size of a city yard. It was mostly dirt with some stubbly weeds trying to grow in the dense shade. The "yard" dipped down, then back up again, and Katy gestured toward the lowest point. "See, Mama." She took her mother's hand and led her down to a circular area of mud. "This is where the lake used to be. The water came from over there." Katherine went over and knelt by a trickle of a stream nearby. "Rick said that the people who lived here before dammed it up. Don't yell, I'm not saying a bad word. 'Dammed' means they put sticks and rocks and things so the water couldn't get out. And the water stayed here, and it made a little lake. That's why I call it 'Gone Lake,' because it's gone, but it used to be right here. See?''

"Yes, darling, I see." As always, Margot marveled at how long Katy—Katherine—could talk without seeming to come up for air.

"Rick said maybe we could make a lake here again someday. But not till I learn to swim. I told him I started taking lessons at the Y, but he said *he* would teach me."

The image of Rick teaching her child anything, coupled with the long-term plans and goals he had for the little girl, made Margot feel physically ill. She sat down on the hard earth next to the puddle.

"You want to see the toys Rick and Sonya gave me?"

"Okay."

Margot turned to watch Katherine race up the hill and crawl under the wooden porch. A moment later, she came back out, rear end first, pulling a huge, red laundry basket of toys after her. While Katherine struggled to carry the heavy basket down the hill, Margot inspected the surroundings. No telling how long she'd be allowed outside, and the more information she could gather, the better.

The stony driveway that Margot recalled from her arrival led downhill and out of sight. The trees grew so closely together that she felt as if she were in a solid green-and-brown fishbowl with no sense of what lay beyond. Her watch said that it was eleven o'clock. It was too close to noon, or maybe just too cloudy, to tell exactly where the sun was, although it seemed to be in front of her. That would make sense; people often built houses with the front rooms facing east.

Margot heard a crash, then Katy cry out "Oops, oh no!" She turned to see that Katy had dropped the basket, and the toys were tumbling out in all directions. The child grabbed at a baseball bat and a sand pail. When she reached for a small blue beach ball, she missed. The ball went bouncing away toward the driveway. Katy chased after it.

For a split second, Margot was frozen. Then she leapt to her feet and chased after her daughter, screaming, "Stop! Right now, young lady. Stop! Forget the ball. Oh, please—" She tackled Katy, grabbing the little girl roughly around the knees. They both crashed to the earth in the stones. Katy turned to look at her, confusion in her eyes.

Katherine took a great breath, held it, then let out a wail. "Owwwww," she cried. "Mama, you hurt me."

"I'm sorry, baby. Oh, I'm so sorry. I didn't mean to. I just got going too fast and I tripped." Margot knew from experience that it would be a few minutes before Katherine allowed her to inspect the boo-boos. Katherine held her hands over both knees, and blood trickled between her tiny fingers. But Margot just clung to her child, panic still fresh in her breast.

"But why were you chasing me? I almost caught the ball. Now it's all the way down the hill."

"Don't worry about the ball, sweetheart. I'll get you another one," said Margot, realizing as she said it how powerless she was. She couldn't even replace a lost toy.

"But you don't have to. Let's just go and find it, Mama, please."

"We can't—"

"Please." Katherine hung her head, then said, "I think Rick might be mad if I lose the ball."

"Did he tell you that?" asked Margot gently.

"No."

Margot touched her daughter's chin, making the child look up. "Honey, do you remember what I told you before about grown-ups telling you scary things." Katy nodded yes, but Margot continued anyway. "Even if a grown-up told you bad things, or said he would hurt you, or he would hurt Mama or Daddy, you should *never* let that make you afraid to tell us something. Do you remember?"

Katy gazed at her, a lost expression in her eyes.

"I remember. But Rick didn't tell me scary things. I just saw how mad he got when Sonya broke a mirror. I think he will be mad if I lose the toys he gave me. He told me to put everything away. So please, let's go get the ball. Okay, please?"

"There's another thing that Rick told me that's even more important," said Margot. She tried to smile. "Now Rick knows that we're not used to living in the forest. He knows that we're from the big city. He said that a person can get lost just like that"—she snapped her fingers—"here in the forest. So we have a rule that is the most important rule of all. Now, are you listening?"

"Uh huh." Katherine's eyes were big.

"You and I are never, *never* to go more than three hundred feet away from Rick, or we could be in big trouble."

Katherine looked down at her feet, then up at her mother again. "My feet?"

Margot laughed. "Do you know what three hundred feet means?"

"What?"

"I can't show you for sure without a very long ruler, but it's not very far. I think we should make our own rule, and we should stay so close that with just twenty giant steps we could touch each other."

"But you said twenty hundred three steps."

Margot knew that when she was calm, Katherine could count into the hundreds, but if she was nervous, anything beyond twenty tended to get muddled, as it just had.

"Tell you what. Why don't you take twenty giant steps away from me, and we'll look and see how far that is."

"But I can't walk, Mommy. I got hurt."

"So you did. Okay, you stay there, and I'll take twenty giant steps away from you."

Margot stood, surprised that her legs felt shaky. She looked down to see her own knees and shins scraped and bloody, surprised that she hadn't noticed the injuries earlier.

Ignoring her bleeding legs, Margot made sure that Katy was watching, then slowly paced off twenty steps, counting aloud as she went. Katy counted with her.

"See. I'm not very far away, am I?"

"No." Katherine's voice sounded forlorn. "Could we go inside now and get Band-Aids?"

"Sure."

As Margot hurried over to help Katy up, she was aware of Rick standing on the porch. A prickling of her skin had told her that he'd been there watching them for some time. Must be how a rabbit feels when it realizes a hunter has been watching it, she thought.

"Ooo, ow," said Katherine. Her tears had dried, but she had always been very dramatic when she had a hurt. She would milk it for days, from the initial drops of blood right through the removal of the bandage and the scab. Even the pink and healing skin held fascination for her.

As they walked up the hill, Margot picked up a couple of toys. When they got to the basket, she put the toys in. Then Margot looked up at Rick. "A blue beach ball rolled down the driveway. We couldn't get it. It's still there."

"I'll get it later. It's time to come inside now," he said.

Margot stowed the toy basket under the stairs and went inside. While she washed Katherine's scraped knees and then her own, she thought about Rick's words. If the wrist devices that she and Katherine wore were actually loaded with explosives, then he would either have to turn the transmitter off or remove his device when he went to retrieve the ball. Rick appeared to be deadly clever and watchful, but maybe at some point he would slip. Margot would watch and wait. She was ready to do anything she had to, to get Katherine to safety.

26...

RICK GLANCED UP from his crossword puzzle. Katherine was going into the bathroom wearing the white terrycloth robe he'd bought her. Her legs were so thin and white—like birchwood spindles poking out from under the hem. He heard Katherine's voice in conversation with Margot, then the child's happy exclamation, "Oooo bubbles!"

Rick wrote in "enable" for the six-letter word for "permit" on the puzzle. Something bothered him as he scanned the "Down" column for the next clue. He sniffed the air. Something different, something sweet.

He could hear the woman's voice, then Katherine speaking. "It's too hot, Mama. It's burning my legs."

Suddenly, Rick sprang from the sofa, flinging the crossword book aside. "No," he thundered as he raced toward the bathroom.

Katherine was just about to sit down in the ocean of bubbles when Rick shoved the door open. He grabbed Katherine under her arms and dragged her from the tub. Quickly, he turned on the taps in the sink, and using both hands he scooped up handfuls of water and splashed it onto her legs, washing away the bubbles.

Katherine jumped up and down, then tried to back away, as the cold water sluiced down her legs. It puddled on the bathroom floor. As Rick worked, the woman held the child around the shoulders and tried to pull her away from Rick. But she and the child were trapped between the toilet and the sink.

Rick was almost sobbing as he interrupted his panicked

activity to inspect Katherine's legs. They weren't red. There were no apparent blisters. He had gotten her out in time.

"Does it still hurt, darling?"

Katherine stared at Rick, then down at her legs. "It wasn't *that* hot. I didn't get a burn. Really."

"Let me see the bottom of your feet."

Slowly, solemnly, the child lifted up first one small foot, then the other. They had the pinkness that comes from going barefoot, but no sign of burns. He stroked the sole of her foot with his hand, and she giggled.

"That tickles."

"Good. Tickles is good."

"The water wasn't hot. She always thinks it's too hot at first." Margot's voice shocked him, seemed to come from far away at first.

He stood up and faced her.

"Where'd you get the damned bubble bath?"

"It was under the sink. It's Avon. We use it at home. It won't burn her."

"Pull the plug," he said. She looked at him for a moment. He wanted to hit her. Then she turned and reached into the suds.

"Aw, please. Please let me keep the bubbles."

"Quiet." Rick found the bottle of bath suds and began to pour the liquid into the sink.

"It's all right, Katy," said Margot. "We'll use bubbles another time."

"No. No bubbles, you—" He stopped in midsentence. Then he threw the bottle into the waste can and left the room.

Rick sat down with his puzzle and tried hard to concentrate. The sounds of splashing water from the bathroom joined his crashing heart to deafen him. He closed his eyes and pressed the heels of his hands hard against his temples.

In his mind's eye all he could see was Dawn. That bitch. Dawn in the bathtub, stinking up the air with her bubble bath. Dawn on the boat ruining his life. His parents had taken in every damned mongrel that showed up on the doorstep—kids from broken homes, retarded kids, cripples, even Dawn.

"Only a few weeks," the social worker had said. "Just a few weeks until her mother is released from prison." Dawn had been the worst of all the monstrous foster children they'd brought in. At least the other kids had all been younger, but Dawn was in his grade—even in some of his classes. The slut made it her business from the moment she'd arrived to make his life miserable. He'd never forget the first thing she'd said to him. Well, the first thing was a nice, polite, phony, "Hi. Nice to meetya." But after the social worker had left and his mother had gone into the kitchen, she'd attacked. "Look, creep. There's about a million places I'd rather be right now than here, so you better try to make it nice for me until I can get out."

"Why should I care if you like it here?"

She stared at him for a moment, one hand on her hip, her lower lip hanging. "You gotta be kidding."

"So who the hell are you, anyway? I don't care if you're miserable."

"You don't know nothing about miserable until you cross me," she said.

With that, she turned and went into the kitchen. He could hear her voice as sweet as honey, saying, "Mrs. Grader. I want to tell you thanks for takin' me in. Anything I can do to help, you let me know."

What a phony bitch. Then he heard, "Well, thank *you*, Dawn. As a matter of fact, you could finish feeding Peace Anna her lunch."

"Be glad to," said Dawn. "That's a cute name," said Dawn with a snigger in her voice.

But, as usual, his mother missed it. "Her mother named her that after a love-in at Berkley. When she came to us for foster care, we tried to call her just 'Anna,' but she wouldn't respond to it."

Rick's mother shook her head as she continued to fill the

baby bottles. Peace Anna wasn't the first retarded kid his folks had taken in, but she was the first four-year-old to still need a bottle and diapers. It was disgusting.

"I don't know what's going to happen to her when she gets into her teens with a name like that," said his mom. "Maybe by then we can drop the 'Peace' part."

As Rick walked past the kitchen door, he saw Dawn pinch the little girl under her arm. Peace screwed up her face for a moment, then let out a long wail, like an air raid siren. He wondered what the kid could've done to piss off Dawn already.

Rick considered telling his mother what he'd just seen, but quickly dropped the idea. It had been a long time since she'd sided with him against any of these mutts. Like an endless, sickening parade through his mind, Rick could see them all now. A full dozen of motley, dirty kids that his parents brought into his home, supposedly to be company for him.

They'd been too old and poor to adopt any normal kids by the time they realized that Rick was to be their only offspring. So they'd gone downtown to the child welfare office and come back with these kids—"the dirty dozen" as he'd come to think of them in later years. At first they were to be "playmates for little Rick." That's how his mother put it—"playmates for little Rick."

For a while he'd wondered if the flow of horrible kids would ever stop. He figured his parents got used to the money they got for each of the kids. His mom got real good at buying used clothes at rummage sales and pocketing the clothing allowance the state gave them. And whenever the state paid for an antibiotic for one of the foster kids, his mom saved out a few pills and kept them for Rick when he was sick. His folks called things like that "transfers of funds," and they bragged to their friends that all this foster business was "so good for Ricky."

It had never occurred to Rick that he could do anything

about the situation. At least he'd always had his own room, and he'd lock himself away there as much as he could.

But what he did to Dawn had ended the whole thing. If he'd known it would be so easy, he would have done it long before. Even now, he smiled at the remembered sense of power. He liked just thinking about the look on her face when she'd stepped into the nice, warm tub full of bubbles— the big *O* she had made with her mouth as she screamed. It was one of his favorite memories.

27 . . .

WHEN JOE RETURNED to Beth's house that evening, he felt disgusted with himself. A full day of investigating and what did he have? The owner of the sperm bank "should call in the next few days" and a possible name for the manager of the sperm bank—not even a real name, just a possible nickname. Good thing I'm not a detective, he thought as he climbed the stairs to Beth's apartment.

He knocked, but no one answered. The door was unlocked. "Beth? 'Lo. Anybody home?" He began to feel uneasy—the silence, the unlocked door.

In the kitchen, Joe saw potato salad sitting on the counter with clear plastic wrap covering it. Even he knew you weren't supposed to leave potato salad sitting around. "Beth? Dennis? Harry?" he shouted, feeling panic.

"Here, Joe." Beth's voice sounded like it was coming from a deep well. "Come on out."

"Huh?" Suddenly he felt like an idiot. He looked out the window and saw Beth down in the backyard. And there was Harry at the grill and the baby in his swing, moving slightly like a leaf in a breeze. It looked like a regular Saturday night sitcom.

"Hey, Joe. Bring down the potato salad, will ya," called Beth. "It's on the countertop by the fridge."

"Yeah, I know." Joe carried the bowl down the back steps and set it atop the checkered cloth covering the picnic table.

"You look kind of green," said Beth, holding a handful of plastic forks.

"That's the color of my imagination."

"What?" She looked confused.

"I'll explain later. Maybe." Joe took the forks from her and tried to look useful.

"Shit!"

Beth and Joe turned to see Harry frantically pushing hamburgers away from a two-foot flame. Little Frankie shrieked with laughter and waved his arms in imitation of his father. Joe reflected that it was a good thing the baby was safely buckled into his swing. He had absolutely no defense mechanisms built in yet.

Beth calmly walked over and handed her husband a pitcher of water that sat on a stool nearby. Apparently this was a regular event for them.

Joe wondered why he'd never gotten into the habit of barbecuing. No time, he thought, miserably. Too busy with the damn job. Ever since the moment that he'd learned of Katy's abduction, he'd been endlessly examining his priorities. What a fool he'd been to let a career come between him and his family. And how could he not have been aware of it? It all seemed so clear now. Now that it might be too late.

With the flame under control, Harry tugged a can of beer free of its plastic webbing. He carried it over to Joe. "You do look kind of green," Harry said. "Bad day?"

"Not good," said Joe, popping the tab and gulping at the cold, bitter beer. "But we'll talk later. There it goes again."

"Shit," hollered Harry, returning to the flaming grill. Joe smiled. He'd had Harry's hamburgers before, and they tasted good, but then Margot had always said he'd like anything he didn't have to cook himself.

Joe chugged his beer and got up to get another. The tenor of his thoughts about Margot lately had been those of a new lover. He found himself smiling mentally as he experienced a deluge of sweet memories, recalling all the things that had attracted him to her in the first place. But he did not welcome the memories. They made him feel too guilty: like a hypocrite, the kind of person who would praise the recently dead even if the person was an enemy. And most of all, he couldn't handle the thought that Margot and Katy might be dead. Sweat covered his forehead as he tried for the thousandth time to push the unthinkable possibility from his consciousness.

A laugh from the baby followed by a terrified howl brought everyone's attention to the swing set. With his peripheral vision, Joe had seen something flying by. He looked now and saw a volleyball rolling into the bushes.

Beth dropped everything and ran to the baby, picking him up tenderly and holding him. Joe was surprised to see her reacting so strongly—usually she was calmer about problems.

"What is it, Frankie?" she said.

He was holding his hand up in the air, but there was no sign of injury.

Joe patted the boy awkwardly on the back. "I think the volleyball must have hit his hand."

Frankie tried to agree. "Ba' ba' ba,'" he blubbered.

Joe retrieved the volleyball and tossed it over the fence. A disembodied voice called, "Sorry. Is he hurt?" It sounded like a young girl, maybe a teenager.

"No," said Beth. "He's just getting all the attention he can from it. Right, guy?" She gently prodded Frankie's stomach, and he giggled, grabbing for her fingers with his formerly injured hand. Beth swung him into the playpen and returned to setting the table.

Harry plopped a plate of sizzling hamburgers on the table and sat down. Beth got Frankie and installed him in a travel high chair that hung at the edge of the table. Joe remembered Margot using one with Katy. He had always hated it—Katy looked about as safe in it as she would have looked hanging from a cliff by a piece of dental floss.

"How's the Caddy coming?" asked Joe after the flurry of mustard, salad and beer passing subsided.

"Not bad, not bad at all," answered Harry. "I'm still waiting for a hinge assembly for the rag top. Talked to some guy out in New Mexico about it, and it should be here any day now." He paused to bite into his hamburger. Joseph had heard dozens of horror stories about trying to find original parts for the '63 Coupe deVille.

"Can't put the top down?"

"Can't put it up," said Harry, reflexively glancing up at the sky. "Makes me nervous as hell to have it out like that."

"You mean it's not in the garage?"

"Nope. Dennis has it. Wanted to show it to some girl he met." Harry grinned.

"You know," said Beth, "if you let him take that car whenever he wants it, you're going to spoil him."

"Hey, he's okay with it. Besides, he's done half the work on it."

"I don't care if he did all the work on it. At sixteen, kids just don't understand the value of something like that. They're used to everything being disposable and replaceable."

"I trust him, Bethy."

Joe smiled at the nickname. "Bethy" would have sounded ridiculous coming from anyone else, especially when used to refer to such a strong, capable woman as Beth, but it sounded pleasing when Harry said it. Newlyweds, he thought, then glanced over at Frankie and remembered that they'd been married for at least three years. Yes, Beth had done well when she married Harry after her first husband left her. Harry was becoming a good stepfather for Dennis, and he obviously adored Beth and their new son.

"It's not a matter of trust," said Beth. "But Dennis—" She stopped and looked up toward the sound of the garage door opening. The hum of a powerful car motor filled the air along with a very staticky sound that could have been the voice of Whitney Houston. Then they heard the motor shut off. Dennis came out of the garage door that led into the yard.

"Hey, great," said Dennis, catapulting onto the bench next to Joe.

Joe was amazed at the lightning speed of the kid as he assembled his hamburger and filled his plate with two huge spoonfuls of potato salad.

The volleyball sailed over the fence again and whisked by their heads. In a flash, Dennis was up, had retrieved the ball and with a powerful underhand punch, returned it to the owner. "Watch it, scuzbags," he shouted. "We're trying to eat over here." Joe knew there was nothing unkind or insulting about Dennis's language.

"Sorreee," came the reply.

All five returned to their meals, staying carefully away from the subject of Katy and Margot and where they might be. There had been some kind of unspoken agreement, Joe thought. This was a time out, a chance to recharge batteries, to refuel.

Joe ate heartily. It was the first time he had done more than pick at food since he'd first heard the news about Katy. Something told him that he'd crack if he didn't let go of the mind puzzle for a little while. Then what good could he do?

When they'd all had their fill of burgers, Beth cleared the table and went inside. She came back out carrying a huge glass bowl of fruit salad. The colors of the fruit were bright and sparkled in the sun as she approached. Joe started to yell as yet again the volleyball came rocketing into the yard, but there was no time. Like a guided missile hitting its target, the ball splashed directly into the bowl. A multicolored fountain of cantaloupe, strawberries, blueberries and watermelon gushed up into Beth's face.

For an instant everyone froze. The only sound was that of fruit juice dripping on the patio. Then suddenly, all was motion and noise. Joe and Harry hurried over to Beth, Joe taking the bowl from her arms, Harry removing bits of fruit from Beth's hair.

"What a mess," said Beth calmly.

"Aw, Mom, not the fruit salad." Dennis sounded truly despondent. He fished the ball out of the remaining liquid. "I ought to smash this stupid thing."

"Oh, no, honey. It wasn't—" Beth stopped, hiccuped, then began to cry. She sat down on the bench and put the heel of her hand to her forehead and cried—just cried freely and somewhat loudly.

"Mom?"

"Bethy?"

Joe remained silent. He was as awed as the others. None of them had ever seen Beth cry.

"Bethy, I'll make some more."

She waved her hands in the air.

Joe handed her a paper napkin, and she mopped at her cheeks.

Apparently wondering why their ball hadn't reappeared, two teenage girls entered at the back gate.

"You jerks," shouted Dennis. "Look at this." With a sweeping gesture, he indicated the fruit-strewn patio, ending with his hands aimed at his mother.

"Oh, no! Mrs. Bivins, we're sorry. Hey, we're really sorry."

The two girls helped Beth's family and Joe clean up the fruit salad mess while Beth went inside to change her blouse. The girls went back to their yard, and Dennis, Joe and Harry cleared away the rest of the barbecue leavings.

When Beth came back out, she cleaned up Frankie and set him in his wading pool. With his chubby hands, he swatted at a yellow ball that bounced and floated away from him. He giggled and clapped every time the ball escaped his grasp. Joe sat and watched Frankie, recalling Katy at that age. She, too, had loved to splash and play in the pool. He wondered what Katy was doing now.

Beth spoke from the shaded spot near the back door. "Ready to get to work?" On the picnic table, she had laid out the notes and paperwork they had collected so far in their "investigation." Harry was pouring mugs of coffee.

Joe tickled Frankie under his chin, then reluctantly went to the table. The vacation was over.

28...

     SONYA HAD BEEN reasoning it through all day. If she reconnected the telephone and Rick found out, he would be mad. And maybe he would be right to be mad. After all, Katherine's safety was in their hands now. Figuring out what to do to protect her was going to take a lot of work—and time.

     But it still bothered Sonya to think that they couldn't call for help if there was an emergency. What if there was a fire or one of them choked on something? Until things calmed down and Sonya knew how to drive from the house to a hospital, or at least to a doctor's office, she'd feel safer if there was a phone.

     And she had decided what to do. Rick would go into a rage if she reconnected the phone. But Sonya had looked up at the eaves where the connection from the main phone line was; it looked like he hadn't damaged them, just taken them apart. If she could just inspect them more closely, she'd know if she could reconnect them in a hurry if need be. Rick might even thank her if it came to that.

     Sonya had always enjoyed watching Rick when he tinkered with the computer and the stereo, but they had looked too complicated for her to work herself. But the phone lines were a different matter. With the different colored wires, it seemed possible even for an idiot to connect a phone.

     Sonya remembered the day she added a line in their house so that there would be a jack in Evan's room. When Rick came home and she showed it to him, he said, "I can't

believe you did this yourself.'' At first she thought he was
angry, then he smiled.

"Well,'' she said, embarrassed at so much notice from
her husband, "I've seen you do it. And I just followed the
instructions that came with the jack. Listen." She picked up
the handset and held it out to Rick proudly so he could hear
the dial tone.

"The phone wasn't expensive," she hurried to add. She
didn't usually buy things without talking to Rick first. "And
this switch will turn off the ring, so it won't wake the
baby."

"What about choking?" Rick said, the smile gone, his
eyes stone cold.

"Choking?"

"What's to stop the baby from choking when he gets that
cord wrapped around his neck?"

"Well—" She stopped, tried again. "I mean— He's so
little. It'll be months, maybe a year before he can get out of
the crib by himself. And I thought it'd be safer with a phone
in his room, so—"

Sonya stopped, unsure of how to continue.

Rick slowly and deliberately bent and squeezed the tiny
plastic connector from the wall jack. It had taken Sonya
most of the day to run the wires up from the basement and
to install the jack. He looked around and located the box the
phone had been packaged in. Still moving with that under-
sea slowness, he settled the phone into its styrofoam cutout,
neatly wound up the cord and closed the box.

"If you're so desperate to gab on the phone all day, you
can use the one in our bedroom. There's no reason to bother
the baby with it."

Sonya hung her head. He was right. It was *partly* her own
need to talk to someone once in a while. Her face flamed
with the shame of having tried to make it sound noble. Of
course, if Rick wasn't so insistent that she stay near the baby
all the time, even when he was safely asleep in his crib, then
she wouldn't have felt so locked in. But Rick *was* a good

father, and she figured the overprotectiveness would wear off eventually.

As Rick carefully scrutinized the receipt for the telephone, Sonya began to gather up the tools she had used.

"Don't put those away. Take the jack off and return that, too. Luckily, you didn't ruin the package when you opened it."

Something in Sonya smarted and wanted to yell and hit. She only wanted to talk to her mother. Rick got mad if she called her when he was at home. And when he wasn't home, he insisted that she give her full attention to the baby. She'd tried letting the baby sleep on the big king-sized bed in their room while she phoned her mother one day, but Rick had come home and caught her. He insisted the baby could fall off. Sonya couldn't believe he was serious. The baby was only a month old! How could he possibly roll over to the edge of the huge bed. He looked like the dot for a city on a U.S. map. She'd been about to say that when she saw how angry he was. She knew enough to be quiet then.

Now Sonya was glad for that experience when Evan was a newborn. At least she'd learned something about telephone wiring.

Before she set about her plan, Sonya reassessed her situation. She knew that Rick had told Margot she could spend a half hour outside with Katherine. It had been only five minutes since they'd gone out. Rick was sitting, apparently relaxed, by the front window. He was watching them, his eyes not moving from the window. She was sure there would be enough time.

Sonya went into the kitchen, then out to the deck in back. She'd hung a line of sheets up to dry earlier, hoping for a moment like this when Rick's attention would be diverted. He wouldn't suspect anything strange in her behavior—he liked fresh sheets every day and would only accept "dryer sheets" when it was raining.

With shaking hands, Sonya opened the metal ladder she had brought out earlier and set it under the point where the phone wires dangled by the roof. The earth was soft near the base of the house, and she wiggled the ladder slightly to make sure it wouldn't tip when she stepped up on it.

With her arms stretched as far as possible, she could just touch the wires. They looked familiar, the colors red, green, and black, just like the ones for the jack she'd put in Evan's room. Tentatively, she tried twisting some wires together, trying to remember the instructions she'd read so long ago.

"Bitch!"

Sonya gasped. She gritted her teeth and stifled a cry.

"The hell you think you're doing?"

Quickly she turned, holding tight to one of the wires. But her foot slipped and the ladder tilted in the soft dirt. Sonya felt a pain in her left arm as it brushed against the rough siding of the house. When she landed in the dirt, she picked her head up and saw a foundation stone just below her eye. It filled her vision for a moment, then vanished.

The next thing she knew, she was being pulled up the stairs and into the house, Rick's hand tight on her arm. He seemed to be talking—or yelling—but she couldn't hear any sound. There was only the movement of his lips and the familiar lines of anger between his eyes.

She didn't feel dizzy, just cold and a little nauseous as he led her through the house and down the basement stairs.

"—can't leave—"

"What?" she said.

"—but trust isn't anything—"

"What?" asked Sonya again. She didn't know if Rick was talking funny or if it was her ears. His talk sounded like a staticky radio station, with random bits and pieces of sound coming through.

He pushed her down on a cot. "God's sake—head between your legs and—"

That at least made some sense. Sonya put her head between her legs and felt blood flowing in . When she sat up again, she felt dizzy for a moment, then everything cleared.

She was in the bomb shelter and Rick was standing

before her, legs spread, fists clenched, breathing heavily. He was almost snorting he was so mad.

"I thought I could trust you. Of all the people in the world, you're the *only* one I thought I could trust."

"You can, honey. I was just—"

"Shut up. I thought you gave a shit about Katherine." He began to pace. "I thought I could leave you here with Katherine, and all I'd have to do is put that woman in the shelter. But look at this. You're worse than her."

"I'm sorry, Rick. Honestly, I was just going to—"

"And where is Katherine?"

"What? You mean where—"

"Yeah. Where is she? Right now?"

"In the yard, with—"

"Right. With the woman who beats her every chance she gets."

"But—"

"And who's watching her?"

"Well, you were. But I'm sure—"

"You're sure? You're *sure* she's fine?"

"Please, Rick. I wasn't trying to fix the wires. I was just—"

"Damn you, Sonya. I gotta go. Someone here has to have a sense of responsibility."

Rick turned and switched on an overhead light. He stalked out of the shelter. The door slammed shut. Sonya waited a moment, then got up from the cot. She walked to the door and pushed. It was stuck.

She pushed again. No, it wasn't stuck. It was locked.

Sonya leaned her throbbing head on the cold metal door for a moment. She could hardly believe that he'd locked her in. If he had told her to stay, she would have. He didn't have to lock her in.

She returned to the cot and lay down. She cried, and muttered to herself, "—just wanted to know how it worked. If somebody got sick. While you were gone. Not to really do it. Just to know how." A swirling, high-pitched tone filled her thoughts, and Sonya clawed at the blanket. But her fingertips were numb.

"—hurt. Maybe he hit her."

The sound was not Sonya's own voice. She knew that. She touched her lips. Dry. Things jumping around. Couldn't focus.

"Please. —help her?" Again, the words were jumbled, but now Sonya knew the voice was Katherine's. She tried to sit up. Gentle pressure held her down.

Then she saw the woman and felt the sway of the cot as Margot sat down next to her. "Try to hold still."

"What?" Sonya tried for more words, but they wouldn't form.

"You have a bump on your forehead. Katy found it."

"Katherine?"

"I'm right here, Sonya. Can't you see me?"

"I see you, dear." Sonya touched Katherine's cheek. Still her fingertips did not send back a message. But it gave her pleasure just to look at the little girl's face. So like Evan's. So like Rick's. She let the pleasure wash over her, not struggling, and she heard that rushing, watery sound again, then saw a tunnel of lights before her eyes.

"Sonya! Mama, I'm scared. I think she's dying. Is Sonya gonna die?"

"No, Katy. We'll help her. Go get that pillow."

Sonya could hear the two talking; their voices were clear but somehow far away.

"Now, when I lift up her head, you put the pillow under her head and under her shoulders. Ready?"

"Yes."

"One. Two. Three. Now."

Sonya felt her body rise. It was like floating in water. A coolness came under her head and neck.

"Is she asleep?"

"No, sweetie. She's had a bump on her head. Apparently a bad one."

"Should we put a bandage on it?"

"No. She needs to rest."

Rest. Yes. That sounded good to Sonya. Yet something warned her not to rest. She wanted a drink of water. She tried to rise, and again her hands held her down.

"No. Let go." Sonya pushed against the hands. Her head began to pound.

"Please, Sonya. Try to lie still. You've had a bump on your head. If you—"

Suddenly her vision cleared, and so did her mind. Sonya looked up and saw that woman hovering over her. "Get away from me."

"I won't hurt you," said the woman.

"We'll help you, Sonya." Katherine's voice was sweet, soothing. "You were sleeping."

"Do you know what happened?" asked Margot.

Sonya ignored the question.

"Did Rick hit you?"

"No! He didn't hit me. *We* don't hit. Not in our family."

The woman made a show of looking confused. "What happened to your head?" she said.

"I fell. An accident. A *real* accident."

Again, the woman looked confused. Rotten mother, but a good actress, thought Sonya.

The woman got up and walked out of Sonya's line of vision. She didn't care enough to turn her head to see where she had gone. Katherine sat down and took Sonya's hand. She leaned down and very gently kissed Sonya's cheek. "I thought you were going to die. I was scared."

"Oh, no, sweetheart. I just had a bad bump. It made me feel dizzy for a minute, that's all."

"Do you feel dizzy now?"

"Just a little. But I'm much better."

Sonya felt a new sensation. It took a minute to identify the source. Something wet and heavy on her forehead. She moved her eyes up, and the movement hurt. The woman was smoothing a wet cloth on her forehead.

"Don't touch me," Sonya cried. She pushed the cloth away.

"There's not much I can do for you. You should see a doctor. But I'll help in whatever way I can."

"I don't want your help." Sonya pushed away a blanket and tried to sit up. Again the woman pushed at her shoulders.

"Let go of me, dammit." The pressure came off, and Sonya sat up. She groaned, surprising herself. A sick throbbing began in her temple, and she felt like she'd throw up. She breathed quickly through her nose, with her hand over her mouth. The sensation passed.

"Look, I'm sorry you got hurt. I don't want to be here any more than you do. But your husband has his own ideas. And apparently whatever he says goes."

Sonya didn't like the way the woman had said "your husband." It sounded snotty. Rick would never let her talk like that if he were here.

Then she remembered where they were. Rick had locked them all in. And he'd done it because he felt betrayed. He thought he couldn't trust his own wife. That knowledge hurt more than the bump on her head. If he'd only listened. Just for a minute.

"My husband is only trying to make things right. Things that you've done wrong."

"Your husband—"

"Don't fight." Katherine's voice was a cry of pain. Both women stopped and looked at the child, who'd gone to stand with her back to the door. Her fists were tight little balls, and tears stood in her eyes, ready to spill.

Silence filled the room. Absolute silence. Then the woman bent down and hugged the girl. It looked so possessive to Sonya, the way she held Katherine. A small thrill of triumph coursed through Sonya when she saw what happened next. The woman let go of Katherine, and the child walked over to Sonya. Of her own accord. As if she preferred Sonya. Sonya swiped at the tears on Katherine's cheeks with her thumbs.

"Honey, we're not fighting. We're just making noise. Don't you worry about it."

"Don't you like Mama?"

"I don't really know your mama, Katherine. But I don't like some of the things she's done."

"What things?"

"Never mind now. I think I'd like to rest a while." Sonya didn't want to scare Katherine again. But the blackness was threatening—framing the edge of her vision. It seemed better when she lay down.

Sonya felt a cloth on her forehead and was about to sweep it away when she realized that Katherine had put it there, not the woman.

"How's that?"

"Good, Katherine. That feels good." She felt her consciousness slipping, but Sonya did not fight it this time. It felt like sleep. No threat there.

She dreamed—tedious dreams of trying to leave, but having to crawl, scrabbling with her fingers in the dirt, to pull her body forward. When she woke, she opened her eyes, glad to be out of the dream.

"How are you feeling?"

The woman was sitting on a folding chair close to the cot.

"As if you cared."

"Look—" The woman glanced over her shoulder. Sonya could see Katherine on a cot in the corner, apparently dozing. "We're not going to solve anything by upsetting Katy. I know you don't like me, and—"

Sonya sat up. Her head didn't pound as much this time. "Don't like you? That's not exactly the issue. It's what you've done to Katherine that I don't like. In fact, I hate it. I don't understand how you could—"

"I also know that you're not going to believe anything I tell you. You believe your husband. That's natural. But it's clear that you care about Katy. And that's what we need to talk about. Not you. And not me. Katy.''

"Katherine.''

"All right. Katherine.'' The woman rubbed her eyes, as if she'd been staring into the sun.

"I'm sure your husband cares about Katherine in his own way, but you have to see it's not healthy to simply yank a child out of her life and isolate her like this.''

"He didn't *yank* her out of her life, as you call it. He got her out of a dangerous situation and into a safe place. I think most people would call that a healthy thing to do.''

Margot sighed, and Sonya wanted to slap her. She'd never really felt the urge to hit anyone before, and it surprised her.

"Did your husband tell you that I was beating Katherine? Is that what you've been thinking?''

"He didn't have to tell me. I saw the proof of it myself.''

"Proof?''

"The bruises. The one on her ribs showed *fingerprints*, for God's sake.'' Just the thought of the pain this woman had inflicted left Sonya speechless.

"I saw those bruises, too. But it wasn't me. Oh, God, it wasn't me. I asked Katherine about it, and she said she doesn't remember. But I think when your husband grabbed her, he—''

"Don't. Don't try to blame it on someone else. And least of all on Rick. If you only knew how he loves Katherine—''

"And I think you love her, too. So please, please help us get away from here so we can—''

"Don't ask me that.'' Sonya shook her head. She stood up. The room shifted and swayed, but not for long. She took a deep breath, then walked carefully over to where Katherine still slept. She listened to Katherine's snuffling respirations.

Slowly, Sonya turned back toward Margot. "I think you should know that Rick is going to sue for custody.''

"For custody? For custody of Katherine? You're kidding, right?"

Sonya tightened her fists. "Are you insane? You honestly think I would joke about something as important as his daughter's life?"

"But Rick has no rights. I don't even know how he found out about Katy. It's supposed to be confidential. But even—"

"Confidential? Just because you didn't know for sure who your baby's father was? You think the word 'confidential' makes it sound okay? That makes you less of a slut?"

Sonya headed for the door, but stopped short of trying to open it, remembering that Rick had locked them all in.

"What are you talking about?" Margot's voice had acquired a hysterical edge. "The parents aren't supposed to know the donor's name. And the donor's not supposed to know when, or even if, any of his sperm is used—or if it leads to any live births."

"Sperm? Donor? What are you saying?" Sonya asked. "And *parents*? Rick is Katherine's parent. The fact that you chose not to tell him he had a daughter doesn't take away his rights."

"Oh no." Margot sank onto a chair and dropped her head on her folded arms atop the card table. "I think I understand now. What he told you. Oh, God." She sat and moaned quietly.

Sonya felt the hair rise on the back of her neck. She considered the possibility that she might be locked in with a violent woman who truly was mad. She scanned the room for a weapon, wondering if she'd have to defend Katherine and herself from an attack.

Her body tensed when Margot looked up, but she stood still by the door.

"Let me get this straight," Margot said, lifting her head and watching Sonya. "Your husband told you that we had sex and that I got pregnant, but I didn't know who the father was because I was promiscuous?''

Sonya remained quiet, frightened by the sudden calm monotone of the woman.

"He said he kidnapped Katherine because he wanted to save her? Is that what he said? Because I was beating her? He showed you the bruises and said I'd made them?''

Was the woman confessing? Sonya watched her, ready to fight if necessary. But a movement to the left caught her attention.

"Mama didn't hit me," came Katherine's sleepy voice. The child sat up, then rose and walked over to Margot, rubbing one eye with her fist.

Margot reached out and pulled Katherine into her arms. The child snuggled in, and Sonya felt jealousy. She recognized the feeling and felt its power mixed with rage at all the injustice.

"I know your mama told you to say that, sweetheart. But you don't have to lie anymore. Rick and I will help you so you don't have to get hurt ever again." Sonya swallowed, then continued. "And I know you love your mama. If she loves you enough, then maybe she'll get help, with a special kind of doctor who does counseling. And then you can see her whenever you want to."

"But she doesn't hit me. She really doesn't. And I *don't* tell lies.''

"Katherine—''

"Katy,'' said Margot. "Please go and fold the blanket and straighten up the cot.'' She gave the child a gentle push toward the cot where she'd been napping.

The girl stuck out her lower lip and threw an angry glance Sonya's way before going to do as she'd been told.

Margot got up and walked to the opposite end of the shelter. She sat down on one cot and motioned toward its partner. "Please. Can we talk quietly for a moment, Sonya? Please.''

Sonya took a few steps toward Margot, but did not sit

down. She was prepared to fight. The calmness of the woman could easily be an act. And Sonya's head felt better; she felt completely steady and ready for anything.

"Rick *is* Katherine's father," Margot said, rubbing her palm over the smooth cover of a children's book that had been lying on the pillow of the cot. For the first time Sonya noticed the framed prints hanging on the walls by these two cots—one was the cover of *Goodnight Moon* and one a poster of the cover of *Make Way for Ducklings*. Perhaps this corner of the shelter had been made for a child.

"Rick is Katherine's biological father, Sonya, but only because he was involved with a sperm bank."

"What are you talking about?" Sonya cried. "You're a liar!"

"My husband couldn't father a child," said Margot. "His sperm count was too low. So we used a sperm bank."

"Oh, that's a great story! Did you stay awake all night thinking of that one?" Sonya laughed, her voice cracked and loud to her own ears.

"I don't know how he found out about Katherine. The records are supposed to be confidential. Both to protect the children and the parents. And the donors, too. Just so this kind of thing couldn't happen. If—"

"Confidential! Hah! You'd love this to be confidential. To protect *you*! And your precious career."

"No, not for that reason. It would just get too complicated if everybody knew— I mean they told us some donors have fathered dozens of children. Just think how impossible it would be if everybody knew everybody else's identity."

Sonya paced about the room. She hurried back to Margot, grabbed the children's book from her hands and returned to where Katherine sat staring at the two women.

"Here, Katherine. This looks like a good book."

"You're fighting," the child said, her voice nearly inaudible.

"No. We're just having a serious grown-up talk."

Sonya kissed Katherine on the forehead, then went back

again to the other side of the room. She sat down on the cot opposite the woman and spoke in a low voice. "No more loud talk. Poor Katherine is scared to death."

"You're right, Sonya. Thanks." The woman's conciliatory tone was maddening, but Sonya kept still. "I think I can explain. When we first looked into the options for artificial insemination—"

"No," Sonya whispered. "You're still assuming that I believe your crazy story. You even sound like you've convinced yourself."

"Wait. Wait a minute. Before we go any further, look at Katy."

Sonya turned and looked. The girl hung her head over the book. She turned the pages, but listlessly, not like a child who was interested in the pictures.

Sonya turned back. "So?"

"She's scared, like you said. But she's also tired. She's been having nightmares. Hasn't been sleeping well. And she's losing weight. Maybe these aren't huge troubles at the moment, but they're starting to add up. Your husband is holding us prisoner here, and there's no telling what might happen. It's dangerous. Can't you see? We're in trouble. No matter what he told you, I promise I'll work with you if that's what you want, but we've got to get Katy out of here. Please, please, help us. Help Katy."

"You're getting hysterical and raving about danger. Well, what about the danger Katherine is in when she's alone with you?" Suddenly, Sonya caught her breath and remembered to soft-pedal her anger. The woman had violence in her. Who knew how much.

"Rick isn't trying to hurt anyone," said Sonya. "But we can't just let Katherine walk back into the situation she was living in before. I'm sure you never *meant* to hurt her, but that's where the real danger to Katherine is. Can't you see that? *You're* the danger."

"But he lied about that, too. I swear to you—I swear

it! I never abused Katy. Ask her again. Katy already told
you I never—''

''Look, I've done some reading about child abuse. The
child will deny it to anyone else. That's what they're taught
to do. The only hope is getting help for the parent. But first
you have to get the child out of danger. That's all we're
trying to do right now.''

Margot sat very still and quiet. Then she pinned Sonya
with an intense stare. ''Sonya, do you have any children?''

Like a slap. The question hit and stung exactly like a slap
on the face. Evan flashed before Sonya's eyes, smiling with
his little white baby teeth, reaching for her with his pudgy
hands. ''Not now,'' she replied, unsure of why she felt
compelled to answer.

''You had children?'' Margot's voice was soft, sympathetic. Sonya melted a little at the sound, then hardened
again inside. To have a child, someone as beautiful as Evan,
and to hurt him—Sonya just couldn't imagine such abuse.
She felt like she could kill this woman.

''Yes. We had a son. A beautiful, healthy, happy boy.
Until some crazy, drunk kid ran into him. If only—'' Sonya
stopped, swallowed. ''It's none of your damned business,''
said Sonya. ''And it doesn't have anything to do with
Katherine. Now, I'm sick of talking to you. I'm going to lie
down. My head's pounding.''

''I'm sorry, Sonya.''

''Shut up.''

''All right. But I think you should see a doctor. You
might have a concussion. Even if you feel you have to leave
Katy and me locked in here— We can't do any harm.''

''Now you're a doctor! And I'm supposed to trust you
alone with Katherine?'' She lay down on the cot and pulled
a woolen blanket up to her chin.

''Well at least let me give you some aspirin. Maybe—''

''Will you please shut up. You're giving me a headache.''

''No, she's not,'' said Katherine. She came over to stand

by the cot. "It's not Mama. It's the bump on your head," she said and gently touched the tender lump. "I had a bad bump on my head once, and I had a headache. It was from the bump. Really."

"How did you get the bump, Katherine?"

"I fell at play school, and me and Robert banged heads. He got a big lump, too, and he cried, but I didn't cry. And my teacher took me downstairs and gave me a bag of ice cubes, and him, too, but it still hurt." She touched Sonya's forehead again, then said, "I wish I had a bag of ice cubes for you. It would make you feel better."

"Thank you, sweetie. But a little rest will help the most. Why don't you go read that book with your mother."

With relief, Sonya watched the two head over to the other side of the room and curl up together. Sonya turned her back to them and closed her eyes. She felt shame that she couldn't just unlock the room and leave freely the way the woman thought she could. She would never admit that her own husband had locked her in, too. But worse than the shame was the fear that some of what Katherine's mother said might be true.

In her mind, tired as she was and as much as her head hurt, she listed the differences between what Margot had said and what Rick had told her. Rick said Margot beat Katherine—both Katherine and Margot said no. Rick said he'd had an affair with Margot—she claimed she'd never met him, just picked his sperm from some anonymous "bank." Rick said that Katherine was the result of promiscuous behavior—the woman claimed to have been married when Katherine was conceived.

Sonya had never known anyone who'd actually used a sperm bank. It was a subject that was mentioned in movies-of-the-week or laughed about in semidrunken conversations at cocktail parties. The whole idea seemed ludicrous. Rick was so reserved, so dignified. The notion of her husband, with a little jar—

No. Sonya decided to stop even thinking about the lies.

This Margot was desperate—probably mostly because she didn't want people to find out what kind of a person she really was. That would put an end to her TV career for sure.

Sonya did have to admit that Rick's judgment hadn't been the best lately, but she was sure things would be okay when people found out why he'd acted the way he had. She just wished he'd be a little more open with her, let her in on his plans. Obviously they couldn't stay locked away in this house in the wilderness. He had to work, earn money. Katherine had to go to school. She was kindergarten age now. Sonya moaned quietly as she tried to stop the picture of Evan, tried to stop from thinking about how happy he would have been to start school. He'd always loved other children; loved being with them; not even minding when the others knocked him down. He would just laugh and jump up for more.

Would the memories ever stop hurting? Wasn't there supposed to be a point where she could remember without all this suffering? A point where the memory would bring a smile, no matter how bittersweet?

Well, no matter. Rick was the most practical of men. As soon as he had a chance to think things through, he'd see that he couldn't control things the way he wanted to.

29...

WHEN MARGOT CAME into the kitchen in the morning, she saw a recipe card sitting next to a crepe pan. She read the recipe for strawberry crepes and saw that it was basically the same as her own. In her mind, she clicked off the various possible responses. She had no doubt that the card constituted her breakfast assignment.

She could ignore the order—and risk the consequences of his anger. She knew that Katy was as likely a victim of that irrational anger as she herself was. Or she could make the crepes badly. A childish and pitiful gesture. Or, third, she could make the breakfast and continue to bide her time. It still seemed that her only hope was to wait and watch, to try to be as healthy, alert and strong as possible so that she'd be ready when an opportunity to escape came. Margot had not seen any sign that Sonya might be willing to help. The few hours they spent locked in the bomb shelter had only seemed to make Sonya more angry with Margot, and more possessive of Katherine.

Margot bit into a strawberry as she cooked. She was careful not to stain the case of the wrist device. It was her firm intention to be free of this situation soon, but she'd do her best to stay civilized until the time came. Margot knew something about the psychology in captive situations. Her talk-show audience could not get enough of the subject, and she'd covered it from all angles on her show. So she knew how likely it was for her to lose perspective and to put off the moment of confrontation.

As Margot heated the crepe pan over the flame, Sonya emerged from the bedroom, neatly dressed in khaki pants and a white cotton sweater. She wore hiking boots and had her hair pulled back in a little brush of ponytail. Margot smiled weakly, a plea in her eyes. Sonya merely looked away and began to set the table.

The crepes began to pile up, soft and mellow ivory disks, waiting for the strawberries and cream. Katy—no Katherine, thought Margot—emerged from the bedroom, dressed in stone-washed blue jeans and a new T-shirt. As she appeared, a sound of hammering came from the back of the second floor.

"Guess what, Mama. We're going on a picnic. And Rick has a surprise for me. Well, for you, too, I think. But mostly for me, he said."

Margot hugged her daughter tightly. The child's enthusiasm was genuine. It was eerie and frightening to see Katherine responding so warmly to something when the invitation to the picnic was from a madman. And the very notion of a "surprise" that was arranged by him— Margot breathed deeply and handed Katherine a stack of flowered cloth napkins.

"That's wonderful, honey. Will you put the napkins on the table, please."

"Okay. Mama, the picnic's going to be in the woods, so Rick said you should put on long pants. In case there's any poison iby."

"Ivy, dear."

"Ivy. What's poison iby?"

Margot smiled. "It's a plant that makes some people itch if they touch it. The leaves look like little mittens."

"Can you wear them?"

"Wear what?"

"The mittens."

"No. They're leaves. Not mittens. Leaves shaped like mittens. Oh, darn—"

"Whatsamatter?"

"Burned this one." Margot tossed the blackened crepe into the garbage can.

As she poured another crepe, Margot became aware that the hammering had ceased. Suddenly Rick was there, striding into the dining room and sitting down. As he sat, he buttoned the cuffs on his shirt, a navy plaid wool. She noticed that he, too, wore hiking boots. Something about all this elaborate preparation just for a picnic made Margot nervous. Were they all heading for a more remote cabin? Or a cave? No telling what plans he'd made in his warped mind. With renewed panic, Margot looked around for a weapon, realizing again how hyper-aware Rick was of everything around him.

My chance will come, she thought. She tried to reassure herself while she poured the warmed strawberries and sugar onto the crepes and squirted the whipped cream from a can she'd found in the fridge. She'd been amazed that he'd allowed the canned kind. But, she'd reasoned, perhaps the local stores didn't carry fresh whipping cream. Were they really in such a remote area, or had he just driven in circles to make her think that?

Margot decided to make a test. She would serve him from the rear, staying as close to the kitchen wall as possible and moving quietly so that she'd emerge directly behind his chair. If he didn't sense her there with his hearing or his peripheral vision, maybe she could get behind him and— and what? Hit him on the head? No, she'd already ruled that out. Too much chance that the blow wouldn't have a powerful enough effect.

Could she stab him? That might stop him from retaliating. But could she do it? Margot looked at Katherine, singing tunelessly to herself as she tried to make all the napkins perfectly straight. Yes. For Katherine, she could stab him. But would Sonya just stand there and let Margot do whatever she wanted to? The woman was obviously neurotically dependent on her husband. She was probably smarter and was most certainly kinder than Rick, but there was something in him that Sonya apparently needed in order to exist—or at least she believed she did.

Margot picked up a plate of crepes and walked as soundlessly as she could along the kitchen wall, turning left at the corner that led into the dining room. A shaft of morning sun swept across the table, laying brilliant patterns of color from the stained glass onto the white cotton tablecloth.

"Thank you."

Margot saw him move the fork a quarter of an inch to the left as an indication that she could set the plate down. She did so. The bastard knew she was there. The bastard knew she was weak.

Margot wanted to sink into a hole as she returned to the kitchen to prepare the other plates for breakfast. A silly, demoralizing little test of strength. She felt like a mouse pitted against a lion.

"Katherine. Did you wash your hands?"

"Oops. I'm sorry, Father."

Margot watched her daughter leave the room and go toward the bathroom to wash. That was the second time Katherine had called him "father." Margot figured Rick must have told Katherine to call him that. An urge to scream came over Margot. She grabbed a dish towel and crushed it to her mouth. She wanted to cry. Hit. Throw. Kill.

She squirted whipped cream.

"Will you pour the coffee, please, Sonya."

His voice was like antiseptic on an open wound. It stung Margot into silence. She finished serving the meal and took her place across from Katy's chair. Katherine's chair. In this bastard's presence, she'd try hard to always think of her daughter as Katherine. For Katherine's sake.

Margot glanced to her left. The bathroom door was ajar, and the sound of running water still came from there. Katy—Katherine—always used too much water. No amount of lecturing or reasoning or threatening could change it.

"Why did she call you 'Father'? You're not her father."

"I'm in a good mood now, but it won't last long if you start that. You'll ruin Katherine's day."

Just as Margot was trying to figure how much threat lay in that statement "You'll ruin Katherine's day," Katherine returned and hopped into her seat.

"Oh, boy, pancakes. I love pancakes!" She picked up her fork and was about to dig in when Rick cleared his throat in an exaggerated way. He nodded toward Sonya, who put her napkin on her lap and picked up her fork. Only after watching Sonya take a small bite did Katherine cut into her own food.

"They're crepes, Katherine," said Rick. "They're not pancakes. They're crepes."

"I love crepes," said Katherine softly, her head bowed over her plate.

Again, the image of smashing his head open roared through Margot's imagination. The image was so gory and satisfying that she nearly had to leave the table to be sick. But she would not do that. She'd stay here and continue the game. *How many times will I make and remake the decision to bide my time?* she asked herself. *As many times as necessary*, she thought.

Again, Rick cleared his throat, then he tapped his fork lightly against the rim of his water glass. When all three of the others looked his way, he touched his napkin daintily to the corner of his lips. The gesture was effeminate. It surprised Margot, who'd only seen him acting aloof or macho thus far. Somehow, it was not a reassuring sign.

"I have a surprise for all of you." He paused and glanced benevolently at each one of them in turn. He looked at Katherine last, and he smiled broadly at her. Margot held her breath. "You can see the surprise after our picnic. Do you like picnics, Katherine?"

"Yes! I love picnics. But can I see the surprise first? Can I?"

"No, Katherine. First the picnic, then the surprise."

He laughed, the sound both hearty and macabre to Margot. It was as if a real, normal person was in there with a monster; a normal, loving person trying to assert himself, but losing badly to the monster.

"Can we go home and get my backpack? I always take my backpack when we go on picnics. With me and Mama and Daddy. Daddy always says he's glad I have my backpack because I carry all the hats. And if it gets hot, you need a hat. And I carry—"

"Whoa, slow down. We won't be going that far. And it's very shady where we're going. So don't worry. It's a nice offer, but we won't need your backpack today."

Katherine looked dejected. Her sense of responsibility about carrying the hats and bugspray and other lightweight items was important to her. To have it dismissed so easily was a blow, Margot could see.

"After the breakfast dishes are done—" He looked at Margot, then away— "and when the lunch is packed, we'll head out."

"How far away is it?" asked Katherine. "Is it where the ducks are?"

Margot realized that Katherine was thinking about their favorite park near their house in Pittsburgh. In her mind, she could hardly picture the house. It seemed like a misty, faded dream.

"No. There aren't any ducks." He looked annoyed by the question.

"I hope we're going to have ice cream."

"No!" His tone had changed. It was sharp again. Gone was the smiling normalcy he'd affected only a few minutes earlier. "How could we take ice cream on a hike? It would melt."

"Oh. I didn't know we was taking a hike."

"Were."

"Huh?"

"*Were* taking a hike, not 'we *was*' taking a hike."

"Sorry."

Katherine was confused. She clearly had no idea what she was being lectured about. And Margot was terrified. If he couldn't stay calm for even a few minutes, what might happen next?

Rick rose from the table and went into the kitchen. He returned with a small sheet of paper which he handed to Margot. "The picnic basket is in the cabinet under the oven. Be sure to go lightly with the mustard."

She scanned his notes, written in his now-familiar neat script. He was "ordering" ham sandwiches, carrot sticks, peaches and cans of fruit juice.

Moving quickly so as not to anger him, Margot cleared and washed the breakfast dishes. She found the picnic basket. It was a heavy, old-fashioned wicker affair, lined with stiff cotton gingham fabric. In the lid were niches and holders for silverware, cups and salt and pepper shakers. And there was real silverware—not plastic—tucked neatly into the slots. The silver was tarnished nearly black, and Margot hurried to polish it. No point in starting trouble over something so minor. But while she worked she wondered. The whole place had the feel of quality, of quiet, old grace. A rugged wilderness retreat for people with taste and money. How did Rick fit in? And Sonya?

Rick tried to appear elegant and refined, but Margot sensed something raw and not well-bred in him. Not quite vulgar, but certainly not a match for the dignity of the house. And he didn't seem at home here, any more than Margot *felt* at home. Were they all trespassers? No, that wasn't it either. Rick was familiar with the place, but more like a visitor would be familiar, not like someone who had spent long periods of time here.

Margot finished making the sandwiches and looked for plastic bags. There were none, so she wrapped the sandwiches in waxed paper. She washed the fruit, scraped and sliced the carrots and put everything in the basket along with paper napkins and a package of Oreos.

She glanced into the living room, where Rick was reading and Katherine was working on a dinosaur coloring book Sonya had given her.

"Everything's all ready. Would you like to go now?"

"Yeah. I'm all ready, Mama."

Without a word, Rick set down his book and went to the kitchen. He opened the lid of the picnic basket and surveyed the contents. With thumb and forefinger, he lifted out the small stack of paper napkins and dropped them on the counter. "Cloth," was all he said, and then left the room.

Margot kept her face neutral as she put the paper napkins away and got out four cloth ones.

Just as Margot was about to close the lid, Rick returned to the kitchen and placed a worn, folded cotton blanket on top of the food in the basket.

Sonya appeared from the bedroom. Rick held the back door open while everyone trooped out onto the deck. He glared at Margot and said, "The basket?"

She returned to the kitchen and hoisted the heavy basket off the counter. Margot followed Rick out the door, and they set off along a narrow, little-used path into the woods. A rapid battle took place in her mind: It's heavy, he should carry it; no, that's chauvinistic; but the picnic was his idea and he knows the basket is heavy; we could have used those plastic grocery bags; but they're tacky; well, if he wants quality, let him do the sweating; I hope we're not going far. And finally—this reasoning is sick; it's the kind of reasoning one does in an argument with a friend or acquaintance. What's happening to my mind?

The handles of the loaded basket cut into her palms, and her shoulders began to ache with the strain of the load. She realized that yet again she'd been trying to apply normal, sane logic to a situation that had nothing to do with normalcy or sanity.

Margot tripped on an exposed root and stumbled slightly.

"I'll help you carry it, Mama." Katherine reached up and grasped one side of a handle. If anything, the load felt heavier with the slight tug of the small hands, but love for her daughter filled Margot and made the basket seem much lighter.

A sound caught Margot's attention—a whisper that ran over and through the swishing of their feet along the forest

floor. At the same time, the temperature dropped by at least
ten degrees and the air began to seem moister, misty.

Then suddenly, the foursome stepped off the path, out of
the trees, into a clearing. They stood on a cliff overlooking
a spectacular waterfall. Actually, it was only a very thin
stream of water—almost like that from a water faucet. But
the deep green of the earth, the brilliant blue of the sky and
the satin rainbow that filled their vision was startling.
Almost as one body, the four people drew deep, audible
breaths. Margot sensed something loosening in her chest. A
constriction let go, and she set down the basket and fingered
the wristband. At that moment, Margot knew that she and
Katy would get free. At that moment, she had a vision of
what freedom meant. It was astonishing how quickly it
could be forgotten. Astonishing how quickly one could
adjust to bondage. Not accept it, perhaps, but adjust to it.

On closer inspection, the cliff was not as steep as it had
first appeared. The earth fell away, but stair-stepped down
in terraces to the rocky stream below. The freshness of the
air was invigorating—especially so after being locked away
in a madman's house, thought Margot.

All along the edges of the cliff the land was free of trees
and brush. The sun was warm and clean. Rick moved the
basket from where Margot had set it to a spot that gave a
better view of the little waterfall. "Here," he said. "You
can make the picnic here."

She ground her teeth together, but gave him a small,
acquiescent smile. When she took the blanket out, Katherine
hurried over to help Margot spread it on the ground. She
also helped to lay out the sandwiches and napkins, and to
make each "place" look neat with a napkin and a fat glass
tumbler of juice.

"Mama, after lunch, can I go swimming?"

"Oh no, sweetie. This isn't the kind of water you can
swim in. It's too shallow and rocky. There might even be
rapids farther down, and you know they're dangerous.
Remember when we went to Ohiopyle?"

"I 'member. That was scary."

Actually, Margot and Joseph had taken Katherine on a day when the rapids were gentle. They'd gone on the seven-mile-long river ride in a four-person raft, with several healthy, athletic college students in kayaks guiding the group. The only people who fell into the mild flow of the river were those who wanted to; there was really no threat from the gentle rapids that day. But Margot knew that when the river was very high, the rapids could be killers. Several people died every year trying to escape the freight-train force of the rushing waters. Still, Katy had been properly impressed with what she'd seen. And that had been Margot's and Joseph's goal, in addition to the simple pleasure of the day. They wanted Katy— Oops, Margot thought, she was thinking of her as Katy again. They had wanted Katherine to see that water could be dangerous. Having recently learned to swim, Katherine had begun to believe that she would be safe in *any* kind of water. She'd nearly jumped off a friend's pleasure boat into the swift waters of the Monongehela one day, and it was a day when the water was full of speedboats and idiots renting boats they couldn't necessarily handle. So Margot and Joseph had made the trip to Ohiopyle in southwestern Pennsylvania. They'd had a great time, camping and rafting, and Katherine had learned a new respect for water.

"You did right to ask, Katherine. It's hard to know just by looking which water is safe to swim in."

"Mama. When can you go back to calling me Katy? I keep thinking I'm in trouble."

Margot smiled sadly. Like many parents, she'd gotten into the habit of calling her daughter by her full name only when she was in trouble or when she wanted to make sure she had her full attention.

"That's my fault, baby. We gave you this beautiful name, and then I forget to use it when you're acting good. Which is most of the time. Katherine's a wonderful name for a wonderful girl. Let's get used to using it more often, okay?"

As Katherine nodded, Margot was amazed at the truth in her words. How silly parents were sometimes. "Katherine Diana DesMarais." A lovely name honoring lovely women in their families. And here she'd been using it mainly for discipline. When she got Katy—no Katherine, she thought with love—out of this mess, she'd call her by both names, and *never* yell at her again. At that thought, she laughed out loud.

"What's funny, Mama?"

"Is everything ready?" The sound of Rick's voice cut through the perfect moment like a cold rain.

"I think so."

"Sonya. Come sit down. It's time to eat."

No one spoke as they settled down on the blanket. Margot reflected that if she were operating a movie camera just out of hearing range, this would appear to be an idyllic gathering of friends on a stunningly beautiful day.

"Rick, what is—"

"Don't speak with your mouth full, Katherine."

"I'm sorry," she said, still with her mouth full.

Margot held her breath, never sure what would set this man off. But he just continued eating his lunch.

Katherine swallowed. "Could you tell us now what the surprise is?" asked Katherine. "Can we go to my house? Is that the surprise?"

"No." His forehead furrowed, and he set down his sandwich. He stood and walked a short way down the clearing.

Katherine glanced at Sonya. "Did I make a mistake?"

"I think maybe his feelings are hurt a little. He thinks you don't want to spend time with him."

"Yes I do. He's nice." Margot listened, noting the difference between Katherine's warm words and the insincere tone of voice she used. She was amazed that a five-year-old child would know to play such a complicated mind-game. Was Katherine frightened? Or just trying to be nice to someone who wasn't nice?

In her mind, Margot reviewed all the lessons she'd tried to teach her daughter about being polite and forgiving—and not surprised when some people didn't follow the same rules, when some people acted boorish, cold or mean. Did Katherine sense she was fighting for survival? Or was it merely a question of making the best of a bad situation?

"Look. Mama— Sonya— Look. A ladybug."

Indeed, a ladybug was hiking across the blanket, fading in and out of sight, as it sometimes merged with the nap of the blanket. Sonya reached toward it, but Katherine stopped her. "Let me do it. Please."

"What? Do what?" asked Sonya.

"Put her back in the woods. At home, we always tell ladybugs to fly away, fly away."

"Well, it's not very clean," said Sonya glancing toward Rick, who was returning to the blanket.

"Yes it is. It's clean. Look at how shiny it is." Katherine carefully picked up the tiny beetle and held it out to Sonya.

"Well, go on then, Katherine. But hurry up."

Katherine looked up and saw Rick returning. She got up, carried the ladybug to the edge of the clearing and said, "Ladybug, ladybug, fly away home. Your house is on fire and your children will burn."

Rick stepped to the edge of the blanket and stopped. "I don't want her knowing things like that," he said. "That's a dangerous poem."

"Well, it's not exactly one I'd choose either," said Margot. "I'm not sure where she picked it up, but it's certainly not one of the cozier nursery rhymes."

"A good mother is aware of what her child is learning."

Anger, sick and impotent, surged through Margot's stomach. "I don't want Katherine growing up with an unrealistic view of the world. When she starts kindergarten, she'll be faced with all kinds of unpleasant things. Shielding her from a sad nursery rhyme isn't going to make her life better or easier."

"You're full of wisdom, aren't you?"

"Please, Rick—" Sonya stood up and touched his arm. She gestured toward the abandoned picnic food, then waved her arms toward the clearing. Her movements reminded Margot of a marionette that has been jarred as it hangs on its stand. "Maybe—"

"Maybe you should shut up."

"I'm sorry. It's just that—"

"Let's go. Pick up these things and let's go."

Rick glared at the two women, tapping his foot silently against the grass and moss that covered the earth.

Margot had already begun packing up the leftover sandwiches, and the peach pits. Sonya knelt and began to help. She folded the napkins and stacked them in the basket.

But before everything was put away, Rick walked slowly away from the picnic site toward the path back to the house. Margot saw him pause and look back at the women. Katherine was nearby, squatting down, apparently watching the progress of her ladybug into the woods.

Suddenly, Rick turned and walked quickly down the path. *Has he forgotten about the wristbands?* Margot thought. *Aha! They're fakes. They're not for real.* She was about to breathe a sigh of relief when another thought occurred. *What if it's a test? What if he truly is crazy and he just wants to see if I'll call his bluff? And if he's not bluffing?*

Margot jumped up and hurried after him. As she passed by Katherine, she grabbed her child's arm and tried to speak without panic. "Come on, honey. I think Rick is playing a hiding game."

"But my ladybug. She's not safe yet."

"Never mind that. Come on." Margot tugged on Katherine's arm. "Rick, please wait."

Margot saw him go around a bend in the path. It was a challenge to keep him in sight. The woods were so dense. Thank God there's a path, she thought. She'd never find him without one. "I'm trying, but I don't know how far three hundred feet is," she cried, hoping Rick would hear her.

"What do you mean, Mama?"

"That's how close we have to stay to Rick to win the game."

"One, two, three, four—"

Margot turned to see Katherine painstakingly putting one foot in front of the other, counting as she went.

"Please, oh honey, please. We have to stay close to Rick." Margot reached for Katherine's hand, and for a second their wristbands tangled and tugged at one another. What *was* he thinking? And how far was three hundred feet? She spun, trying to locate Rick, trying to figure how far they'd come from their picnic site.

"Looking for me?" His voice was deep and amused.

Margot shuddered and turned to see Rick just a yard from her, a strange smile on his face. The whites of his eyes showed above his irises. He looked completely deranged.

"Why did you do that? How could you risk it? If this is really rigged with . . . what you said, how could you—" Her knees were weak. Katy's hand was in hers. They clutched each other tightly, and Margot reached out to hold her daughter around the shoulders.

"It was a test. A pretty simple one, you got to admit." A light breeze ruffled the trees, and drops of yellow sunlight seemed to rain on his face. The breeze passed, and all was quiet and dim again, except for the raspy breathing sound that Margot realized was her own.

"What happened? Is Katherine hurt?" Sonya looked from face to face. She held the picnic basket with stray edges of blanket sticking out the top edges.

"Everyone's fine," laughed Rick. Once again, he set off at a good clip down the path toward the house.

Think fast, thought Margot. This "test" may be evidence that the explosive cuffs are fake. We're here in the deep woods. It would be easy to slip sideways.

Sonya was struggling along with the hastily loaded basket some distance behind. Would being lost in the woods be preferable to being held captive by Rick? Yes. Yes. Yes.

Margot glanced behind her three more times before she

saw Sonya drop something and stop to reload her basket.
Margot walked close to Katherine. Just ahead, she saw a
spot that looked as good as any to make their escape. There
was a break in the trees to the left that would let them head
in another direction. She looked down at the murderous
cuffs and froze. If they were fake, why would he leave them
so far behind him, with nothing to bind them to him except
fear? Fear of being killed by an explosion. The horrid
images flowed again, and Margot's resolve foundered. And
now, full-blown, worse than the fear of death for herself
and Katherine came the terror she'd been unable to face so
far. What if the cuffs were real—and what if they worked—
but what if she and Katherine didn't die? Margot continued
walking along, clinging to her child's hand, forced to visualize
the results if Margot made a stupid move and risked the
three-hundred-foot limit of her prison. She looked down at
Katherine, whole, healthy and surprisingly undamaged by
her ordeal so far.

No. This was not the time. And not the way. And just as
Margot made the decision to wait, to continue to bide her
time, Rick reappeared. He was still smiling that demented
grin. "Where's Sonya?"

Just then she appeared. Her face was flushed.

"You. Take the basket."

Margot did as she was told, obedient in defeat.

Just as she'd done before, Katherine grabbed a handle.

"She can do it herself," said Rick to Katherine.

"I want to help her. It's heavy."

Rick glared, but let the small rebellion pass. He strode
forward, again going out of sight around a curve.

Margot knew how much courage Katherine's defiance
had taken. She was normally obedient and only made a
stand when she felt strongly about something. And Margot
also knew that Katherine was afraid of Rick.

They walked on in silence. Suddenly, there was a
thrashing sound from the underbrush to their right. A family
of startled raccoons, a large one and two babies, stopped and

eyed the people. They turned and headed the other direction.

Katherine let go of the basket. "Raccoon puppies," she yelled joyfully and ran after the animals.

"No. Katy. Come back." Margot took chase. She could hear footsteps behind her.

"Stop her," came Sonya's voice. "Rick!"

Margot could not believe that Katy could run so fast. Her small legs pumped. She dodged the outgrowths that stood between her and the fleeing raccoons.

"Stop. Katherine, you come here or you'll be in trouble."

The relief Margot felt at hearing Rick's voice close by, at knowing that no single wristband was anywhere near three hundred feet from another—the relief was like air to a suffocating person. She saw Katy stop. The raccoons ran ahead. They would have been comical as they tumbled and rolled, but the dread in Rick's eyes as he caught up with them was too extreme, too real, to leave any room for amusement.

Margot knew then. The test he'd conducted earlier had been exactly that. A test. A deadly, reckless test that could have left them all dead or maimed. The horror in Rick's eyes was that of a sane man. She guessed that he realized in some remaining rational section of his brain that he'd nearly gone too far.

"Evan, what do you think you were doing?" He knelt in front of Katherine, grasping her upper arms. "Do you realize how dangerous that was?"

Katherine stared at him, confused. "I'm Katy. I mean Katherine."

"Oh . . . yes, of course."

"I just wanted to see the raccoon puppies."

"Puppies?"

For a moment, Margot felt as if she were witnessing the normally delightful scene of two preschoolers trying to explain something to each other—something that neither of them understand at all.

She bent down toward the two. "They're not puppies, Katy. They're raccoon babies. And they're wild animals. Remember what we said about wild animals?"

In one movement, Katy and Rick turned their heads to look at Margot. Like students looking to a teacher for instruction. And Rick said nothing about Margot using the name "Katy." Only a moment ago, he'd called her "Evan." Something clicked in Margot's mind. Rick and Sonya must have had a son named "Evan." Or—worse yet—were these two even sicker than they appeared? Was Evan a figment of their interdependent minds?

"But they looked like puppies." Katy's voice sounded tired. It was almost a whine.

"Lots of wild animal babies are round and fat and furry, like puppies. But they're not puppies." Margot helped her daughter to stand, and she brushed dirt and leaves from the child's pants. "The mother of those baby raccoons was scared. She didn't know that we weren't going to hurt her babies."

"Is that 'stinct?"

"Yes. You remembered. Instinct is something that animals are born with. It helps them to be safe in the wild."

The four people headed back to the path and toward the house.

Katy caught up with Rick and touched his hand lightly. Margot let her go, wondering if the change she'd sensed would hold. "When we get back," she asked him, "can I see the surprise?"

He glanced down at her and kept walking.

Margot answered her daughter's question. "You need a nap before anything else, young lady."

Margot's challenge to Rick's authority, microscopic as it was, went unchecked.

"Okay."

30...

THEY ALL QUICKENED their pace a little as they approached the house. Maybe the picnic hadn't been the best idea, thought Rick. Now they were all sweaty and in need of a change of clothes.

"Can we see the surprise now, Rick?" Katherine caught up with him as he unlocked the door.

"First, take a bath. We all need to get cleaned up before I show it to you."

"Aw, please. I've been waiting all—"

"What?" Rick knew that a sharp tone was the best way to handle a whiny child. He'd spent his childhood surrounded by whiny brats. He would not allow Evan to become one of those horrible monsters. No, he thought, not Evan—Katherine.

"How about some lemonade first?" said Sonya.

"No. After the surprise. If there's much more delay, I'll just wait until tomorrow."

"But you just said—"

"Sonya."

"Sorry." Sonya led Katherine toward the bathroom. In a short time, he could hear the water running in the tub.

Rick went to the small bath off the master bedroom and showered and shaved. As he did so, he thought about the picnic and the mess afterward. Letting that woman get the upper hand—even if just for a split second—was dangerous. It made him feel physically ill to lose control like that. If people knew how it hurt him, they wouldn't do it to him.

He could hear the women discussing something as he put on a fresh shirt. He glanced down and noticed that the front

placket had an ironed-in wrinkle in it. He wondered if
Katherine's biological mother was any better at ironing than
Sonya. Margot certainly was a better cook. He'd never been
able to understand why Sonya couldn't follow simple
instructions. He took the time and made the effort to find
good recipes. All she had to do was follow them. But she
habitually burned things, or undercooked them, or misunderstood the amounts, once substituting a teaspoon of cayenne
pepper for a pinch. He'd had to go out to eat at a restaurant
that night, disgusted not merely at the meal but at her
whining apologies. And it hadn't been more than a couple of
months after Evan's death. How careless and insensitive
could a person be?

"I'm almost done," came Katherine's voice from down
the hall. That was another thing he'd have to work on—that
yelling in the house. This was already the second or third
time she had done that. One more time would bring
punishment. He knew what a houseful of screaming children could do to parents. He'd seen his own parents become
distracted, completely unable at times to concentrate on
the needs of their only "real" child. No, Evan would not be
allowed to run wild like those foster monsters he'd been
forced to live with all those years.

Probably the woman had been too busy with her career to
teach the child proper behavior. Well, it was too late now to
worry about her influence. Katherine was only five, surely
not too old to change. And the woman wouldn't be with
them much longer. No more than a few more days. By then
Katherine would have become so used to Sonya that she'd
soon stop missing the woman.

Moving briskly, he headed out to the hall and stopped at
the base of the circular iron stairway. He'd heard the story
of how the massive iron piece had been salvaged from a
burned-out church and installed in the house when it was
just half the size it was now. Then, the stairs had led to the
only bedroom—the one upstairs that he'd been working to
convert over the last few days. Rick knew that this had been

mainly a "party house," a place for the owners to entertain their quirky friends. He'd pictured someone after a night of drinking trying to come down these winding, narrow stairs to the bathroom in the dark. The image gave him a chuckle.

Rick cleared his throat, then called out, "Okay. It's time for the surprise."

Katherine came over so fast that she slid in her stockinged feet, bumping into Rick. He didn't get angry. "Go put your shoes on, Evan. You can't go to the surprise without shoes."

"I'm Katy."

"You're Katherine." He still didn't get angry. He stood quietly, one hand resting on the cold iron of the banister as he waited.

Soon Katherine returned and the two women came, too, hair combed, faces washed. Everything was ready.

"Now, before we go up, I want to ask Sonya a question."

"What is it?"

"Do you remember when you said that Katherine would be ready for school soon? For kindergarten?"

"Yes."

"Well, you had a good point." He paused, observing the puzzled smile on her face. Fortunately, she kept her mouth shut. That's why he rarely complimented her. She usually got too excited and babbled on in gratitude, taking away the pleasure of offering a simple word of praise.

"Ladies, if you'll follow me," he said. Reaching into his pocket for the key, he led the small procession up the stairs. At the top, there was a small vestibule lit by a hexagonal stained glass window. Golds and reds predominated in the window, so the afternoon sun slanting through gave an impression of a buttery-yellow morning light. Very appropriate, he thought, pausing a moment to appreciate the effect.

The little hallway was just large enough for the four of them to gather. He unlocked the door and pushed it open. "Evan." Rick stopped and shook his head, then started again. "Katherine, kindergarten begins tomorrow morning."

"Really? Wow," she said, her voice hushed and full of wonder.

Rick turned to see the reaction of the women. They surveyed his handiwork. He'd bought a small, sturdy worktable and chair and placed them in the center of the room. Along the length of the one windowless wall he'd installed a huge blackboard—no, he thought—they were green now and they called them chalkboards, as he'd been told by the woman he bought it from. On another wall he'd hung a bulletin board. On shelves along the space under the windows he'd stacked piles of construction paper and workbooks, and boxes of crayons, big, fat pencils and small safety scissors. In the corner there was a larger desk. That was for Sonya, and it held all the materials she'd need to teach their daughter—all the instructions he'd gotten from the state board of education for people who wanted to teach their children at home. Of course, he was supposed to register with the county office, but he knew it would be a mistake to do that now. Maybe later, if things went well—

The women looked at each other. He couldn't read the expression that passed between them. It wasn't amazement. It wasn't appreciation. Whatever it was, it pissed him off.

"Well?"

"Is *this* my school?" asked Katherine. She moved from place to place, examining the materials.

"Yes. What do you think of it?"

"It's great. But how will the other children know to come here? Will the school bus bring them?"

"No, this is your own private school, Katherine. And Sonya will be your teacher. Your very own teacher, and you won't have to share her with anyone else. How about that?"

"But Mama said I would make new friends. I thought there would be other kids to play with at kindergarten. Couldn't I go to the big school we saw before? The one that had all the kids in it?"

Rick looked to Sonya for help, but her face was a mask. It was one of her many faces that he hated.

"Do you have any idea how much work it took to get this ready for you? Do you?"

"No, sir."

Her lip was quivering. Great! She was going to cry. They were determined to ruin things for him. Bitches. Big and little—all bitches.

Rick gritted his teeth and decided to give it one last try.

"Come here, Katherine. There's one more thing you haven't seen." He led her to a tall wooden cabinet. He opened the double doors and revealed a new TV and VCR. He handed her a half dozen of the educational videotapes stacked in the cabinet. She looked at them, then up at Rick.

"Thank you," she said. Her lip was still quivering.

"Now what's wrong?" he yelled.

With a huge plastic clatter, the child dropped the tapes on the hardwood floor and ran to Margot. Her mother picked her up and hugged her tight.

He bent to retrieve the tapes. "You've cracked the cases." He advanced on the trio standing near the door. The child hid her face in Margot's shoulder.

"She's scared," said Sonya. "The classroom is very nice. But—"

"But what?"

"It really *is* a big surprise. You know how it is when a child expects one thing and then you change it. It's very nice, but—"

"Shut up. But! But! But!" He threw a tape across the room. It bounced off of the bulletin board, then fell onto the shelf below.

Rick watched as the woman set Katherine down and led her out the door. He faced Sonya, so angry he could hardly speak.

Sonya looked at the floor when she spoke. "I'm sorry. It's just that—"

"Sorry. That's all you ever are, is sorry. Is this how you give me support? You said you'd try to help. Is this how you help?"

"What did I do?" she asked defiantly. She was doing that modern woman thing again.

"What did you do? Good question. What *did* you do? Anything?" He paced to the teacher's desk and sent the apple-shaped bookends flying off toward the chalkboard. "You didn't do anything. Now you've finally figured out my point. You didn't do a damn thing. You just stood there, like you always do. Like an idiot."

"But if you'd told me," she said. She bent to pick up one of the bookends, trying to fit the broken leaf back onto the apple. "How could I know what to do when I didn't even know—"

"What do you mean you didn't know. It was your idea. Didn't you hear me give you credit for it?"

"But I only said Katherine would have to start school soon. I never thought—"

"Never thought, never thought. You sound like a broken record. 'I'm sorry,' 'I never thought.' Geez, you make me sick."

He sat down on the small student's chair, his knees under his chin and rubbed his eyes.

31 . . .

SONYA LAY IN bed, listening to her husband breathe. His respirations were harsh, like those of someone who was physically exhausted. But it was his emotions causing the problem, Sonya knew. So intense— He'd always been so intense about everything. That was one of the traits she had admired in him when they met. He knew what he wanted, and he went after it in a straightforward way.

But now, as she lay in the dark, in the strange house, in the deep woods of— Sonya was scared, realizing that she still didn't even know where she was.

As she lay next to Rick, tenderly stroking his soft red hair, she knew that it was Rick's intensity that was destroying them. When he was pointed in the right direction, he was a force for good, but she could see now that he was off-track. Sonya had to admit that she'd begun to wonder if he might be lying or at least exaggerating about Margot beating Katherine. Now Sonya was sure. He was lying.

But the schoolroom was what scared her the most. When Evan was only a few days old, Rick had already begun discussing which preschool and private grammar school he should attend. He wanted excellent and exclusive schools with excellent and exclusive friends for his son. But still, he recognized the need for a child to be around children. It simply had to be the "right" children. Rick had often told her about how hard it had been for him growing up with a succession of strange, often violent and dangerous children coming into his house through the foster parent program.

Sonya had met his parents a few times, and although they weren't the classiest people in the world, they seemed good-hearted and not greedy. But Rick insisted that they took the foster children in to get the money the state offered.

Sonya rolled over onto her other side, sick of going over and over things in her mind, wishing sleep would come. She drifted in and out of sleep for a while. Then a shrill scream brought her fully awake. She sat up in the dark, listening, hearing nothing. She was just about to conclude that she had dreamed the scream when a whimper came from Katherine's room. Ah, it was another nightmare.

Quickly, Sonya got out of bed and went to Katherine's room. She found the girl thrashing on the floor, her arms pinned by the comforter into which she had somehow rolled herself like a human burrito.

"It's okay, Katherine. You just fell out of bed." Sonya helped the groggy child to stand up, then unwrapped the comforter. Katherine's eyes were open, but unfocused.

"Do you want to tell me about your dream?"

"It was Mama and my puppy. They were standing by the side and the merry-go-round was going and going and it was too fast. I tried to get off but the horse was too high. And the puppy was wiggling around and Mama dropped it and it ran away and Mama was chasing it and I was trying to get off but I kept going around and around and I couldn't and I was scared."

"Poor Katherine. It was just a dream. Remember, you don't have a puppy?"

"Mama said I could have one. A fat yellow puppy. Where's Mama? I want to see her."

"Of course you do, dear. I'll sing you a song. Go back to sleep now. We'll fix things in the morning, okay?"

"Okay." Katherine hugged Sonya, then lay down on her pillow.

"Rockabye, baby," sang Sonya. She had a beautiful voice—everyone said she did—but she didn't know many lullabyes. She had bought a book and a tape to learn some others when Evan was born, but somehow he always seemed most soothed by the old, familiar tune. Sonya wondered if maybe he sensed that it was the most comfortable one for his mother to sing. In the wee hours of the morning, when poor Evan had suffered the awful pain of colic, she had been able to croon him back to sleep with the old song even when she herself was half-asleep. The words took no thought, the sweet tune came with no effort. It calmed and helped them both. Sonya remembered the scent and feel and weight of Evan's body as he lay in her arms.

Abandoning her memories, Sonya noticed that Katherine had gone back to sleep by the time she got to ''—down will come baby, cradle and all.''

Instead of returning to bed, Sonya went quietly down the hall, through the big living room, where the fire's embers glowed in the darkness, and into the kitchen. She made herself a cup of hot chocolate and went to sit on the floor by the fireplace.

The nightmare that had brought Katherine awake screaming tonight was one of many. And they all involved the merry-go-round in some way. Sonya felt as if her own life had become some kind of nightmare carousel. She tried to avoid the thoughts that revolved endlessly in her head, but now, as she sat with her hot chocolate in the quiet of the nighttime, Sonya let the thoughts form. *Rick was having a breakdown. He had lost touch with reality. Margot was not an abusive mother. Had Margot every really gone to bed with Rick? Probably not. Probably her story about the sperm bank was true.* But the thought that came most often, the thought that hurt the most, was the one about Katherine. *Katherine is in danger.*

Sonya finished her cocoa and took her cup to the kitchen. By the small light from the stove, she washed, rinsed and dried her cup. She placed it back in the cabinet. As she moved, she thought about Katherine. Sonya's heart ached at the thought of not seeing the child anymore. She had come to love her like a daughter. But Katherine was in danger.

Rick had been throwing things—hard, heavy things—with Katherine in the room. Sonya felt sure that he would never deliberately harm Katherine. But his escalating temper couldn't be ignored. Was it an accident when someone got hurt by something thrown in anger? No.

And what about the psychological damage to the child? To think that Rick could seriously suggest that Katherine "go to kindergarten," all by herself, in a made-over bedroom in a house in the woods—

No. Sonya could see that she had no choice. She had to get help somehow. She went back to the living room and put two logs on the fire. She tried to think of a solution, but her mind was spinning.

From a box of Katherine's art supplies, Sonya took a sheet of blue construction paper and a fineline colored marker. She began to list some options.

Phone for help, she wrote.

She thought for a minute. Who would she call? And how? She remembered that she had looked up at the phone wires this morning—the wires she had been studying the day that she fell and hit her head—and had seen that the wires were gone. Rick must have pulled them out completely. No phone.

Drive somewhere and get help. Impossible. Rick had the car locked up and the keys put away. Sonya had looked for them, still hoping for some way out in case of an emergency, but she had never found them.

Go to a neighbor's house for help, she wrote next. "Hah," she said out loud. "What neighbors?" In a civilized place like the city, going to the neighbors was a good option. But she had no idea where she was, or how far from other people. She recalled the drive to the house. When was that? Sonya asked herself. She counted on her fingers and could hardly believe that it had only been four nights ago. On that long drive she recalled seeing nothing but trees. An endless road through the dark with nothing but trees—no driveways, no houses, certainly no stores or hospitals. With her red pen she crossed out "Go to a neighbor's house for help."

Her next entry read, *Write a letter.*

Immediately, she mentally asked herself *To whom?* And before she could think about that answer, she thought, *And how will I mail it?*

Pen in hand, she pondered the problem for a while. Sonya had been born and raised in the city. Her family had rarely gone on vacation, and she had gone to college in the city. To her amazement, she realized that she had never even mailed a letter from the country. But she knew that in the country, people had rural mailboxes, one in front of each house. She knew that you could send a letter just by putting it out in the box and putting up the flag to let the mailman know there was mail ready to go.

Sonya sighed deeply. At least one obstacle had been cleared. That left the question of whom she should send her letter to. A friend? One by one, she had dropped her old friends since she married Rick. He hadn't liked any of them and didn't want her going to meet them without him. "We're a couple now," he would say. "Let's do things as a couple." She agreed, but she realized now, Rick had no friends either, so there was no one to socialize with. And no friend to write a letter to.

Then she had an idea. She could contact the counselor she had visited a couple of months ago. The woman had been kind, sympathetic and reasonable. If only Sonya had been able to convince Rick to go and see the counselor too— But no, this was not the time for "if-only's." But what was the woman's name? And address? Besides, Rick would never forgive her for bringing a stranger into their private lives. No. Forget it. No counselor.

Family then. That left family. But the only family Sonya had was her parents. And her father was so dependent now, with the Alzheimer's making him such a danger to himself and to everyone else. He certainly couldn't help, and her mother couldn't leave him.

The clock bonged three times. Sonya closed her eyes and creased her brows, concentrating hard. No other solutions came to her. Sonya decided that her mother would just have to get someone to watch her father for a short while so that she could help Sonya.

Taking out a clean sheet of construction paper, Sonya began to write.

Dear Mother,

I'm sorry I haven't written yet to thank you for everything when I visited you. It was good to spend time with you. But I was sorry to see Daddy not doing well. I hope he has perked up some since then.

I'm not sure how to say this, but I wonder if you might be able to help us. Probably you've heard on the news about the little girl that was kidnapped. The daughter of the woman who has the morning talk show in Pittsburgh. And her mother, too. Well, this must sound—

Sonya crossed out her last few words and tried again.

Mother, it's a long story, a long, sad story. Rick is the one who took the child. Her name is Katherine, and she's a perfect little girl. Now this is the weirdest part. Rick is her father. That's a long story, too, but he really is her father—biologically, that is. They even look like each other.

Mother, I think something broke inside of Rick when Evan died. He's never been the same since, and I think it's getting worse. I'm not sure what I'm asking you to do, but I know we need help. Rick has us all locked up here in a house in the country. I don't even know where it is. But I thought if you could call the police in Pittsburgh and tell them what happened, that Rick isn't really acting right. I'm sure he wouldn't hurt any of us on purpose, but he gets so angry, I'm afraid for us. Especially for Katherine.

I know you're busy with taking care of Daddy, but maybe all you need to do is make the phone call. You could do that while he's sleeping.

I'm sorry to bother you with this. But I don't know what else to do.

Sonya stopped writing. It was getting close to four A.M. and Rick often woke up at five to go out for a run.

She suddenly realized that she didn't have an envelope or a stamp. There was an old oak roll-topped desk in the corner. Sonya made a hurried search and soon found an envelope in a painted ceramic letter holder, then in the third cubbyhole, a small packet of stamps. The stamps were old, the denomination several postage increases ago, so she licked three and stuck them on, writing "FIRST CLASS" in large capital letters under her mother's name and address on the envelope.

She scribbled "Love, Sonya," on her letter, folded the piece of sunny-yellow construction paper and stuffed it inside. She licked the envelope, closed it and set it on the desk.

For a second her resolve slipped, then she remembered the apple-shaped bookend hurtling across the "schoolroom" last evening toward Katherine's head.

Sonya got a flashlight from a kitchen drawer, then tiptoed down the hall and listened at the bedroom doors. Rick was snoring, Katherine was peaceful, one foot peeking out from under her comforter. And Margot was locked away in the bomb shelter, which Sonya had learned was completely soundproof.

Sonya could hear the steady drumming of rain outside, so she opened the closet door and exchanged her slippers for some hiking boots. She took out her raincoat. When it came free of the metal hanger, there was a tinkling sound as the empty hanger banged into the one next to it. She held her breath. The rhythm of Rick's snoring was broken, but a couple of seconds later had resumed its steady cadence.

I hope I'm doing the right thing, she thought as she got the letter and quietly slipped out of the warm house into the wet, chilly, silver-black night.

Clutching her letter in one hand, with her flashlight beam trained on the driveway, Sonya began her walk toward the road. She stepped with caution, her knees bent. Occasionally her foot slipped on the crushed gravel that covered the driveway.

From the corner of her eye, Sonya sensed movement. She screamed and dropped her flashlight when a huge, glistening snake slithered across the road within a yard of her feet.

"Oh, my God," she muttered to herself as she retrieved her flashlight. "Oh, my dear God."

She continued down the path. It seemed to go on for miles. Her teeth chattered from cold and fear, and the watery circle of her flashlight's beam shook.

Sonya screamed again. Someone had grabbed her arm. She felt pain slice across her shoulder blade and into her neck as someone roughly turned her around.

"Rick. You scared me half to death." When she knelt to retrieve her flashlight, he kicked her hand. Not hard enough to break anything, but it hurt.

"Ow." Sonya stood before him, clutching one hand in the other. "You almost broke my hand."

"Where do you think you're going?"

"Nowhere. I wasn't going anywhere."

"At four in the morning, in the dark, in the rain, you're going nowhere, Sonya? You're just out for a stroll? Is that it, Sonya? Getting a little fresh air?"

He snatched the letter from her hand and tried to read the address. "What's this?" he asked, reaching for her flashlight and turning it on the letter in his hand.

She thought fast. But she couldn't think of any way she could get the letter back from him. How could she explain herself? Sonya took a step toward the cabin and was wrenched back to her position next to Rick. Her eyes had grown more accustomed to the dark, and she could see the trees, dripping what looked like poison mercury onto the soggy earth. She shivered violently, unable to fill her lungs with air.

"You missing your mommy?" he asked. The contempt in his voice was icier than the raindrops rolling down Sonya's neck.

Rick inserted a finger under the flap of the envelope and tore it open. He gripped her upper arm again and tugged her a few feet to the side of the driveway where the trees offered an imperfect umbrella.

"No, Rick. Please don't—"

"Shut up." He smiled as he unfolded the paper.

In a last desperate effort, Sonya swiped at the letter but came away with a small triangular scrap of a corner.

"Don't worry, dear. I just want to see what you have to say to your dear mommy."

Sonya stood still then, her head bowed, thinking about what would happen next. It was ironic. Just a couple of weeks ago, she had been trying to get up the courage to separate from Rick. Now he would certainly insist on a divorce.

"What! You little bitch!"

"No. Rick. Please let me explain. I wasn't—"

"You weren't trying to cut my throat?"

"I thought—"

"You know, if you weren't so pathetic, I'd have to laugh. Were you going to put your little letter in the mailbox?"

Sonya just stared at him.

"They don't have mailboxes out here, you stupid idiot. The people are all part-time residents. They go to the post office. I had no idea you were so stupid."

"Please, Rick. I only wanted to help us. I thought if—"

"And *I* thought you were leaving me. That was bad enough. Why didn't you just get a gun and shoot me while I slept? It would have the same effect. In fact—here." She watched as he threw the letter away and reached into his pocket. He withdrew a small pistol.

Sonya covered her mouth with her hand, felt tears
running down her cheeks.

Rick pulled her hand away from her face and tried to
force the pistol into her hand. The gun was cold and hard.
Rick's fingers were cold and hard too. He hurt her as he
tried to force her fingers open, trying to make her take the
weapon.

"No. That's enough, Rick," she said through sobs. "I
don't want to hurt you. Please, don't. Please, just listen for
a minute. I think we need help. Things have been getting
worse and worse. But there are people who can help. No one
will put you in jail if they can see that you're still so torn up
about Evan's death that you didn't know what you were
doing." She now held the gun in her hand, pointing it at the
ground.

"Maybe everything would have been different if you
hadn't let Evan die," said Rick.

"Rick, he's gone. You have to accept that. Katherine
can't take his place. Margot told me that she would let us
visit with her if—"

"I've tried, Sonya. I *have* tried, believe me. But I think I
never really forgave you for letting Evan die. I wanted to—I
did. But I couldn't."

"Oh, stop it. You've said that so many times, I guess
you've convinced yourself that it was my fault. But I think
you have to stop fooling yourself, Rick. It wasn't my fault.
I let you blame it on me because I knew you'd crack if you
couldn't. But now you've cracked anyway." Sonya sighed.
"I'm sorry. All I can do is hurt you today. But you have to
face facts, Rick. You—not me—*you* were the one watching
Evan when the car hit him. But I never blamed it on you. It
was that drunk kid, trying to impress his friends. I never
blamed you. But I never blamed myself, either."

Rick stood silently, watching Sonya. She had trouble
catching her breath; she felt like she had just climbed a very
long flight of stairs.

"That was a pretty speech. And how is it that you think it's my fault?"

"I didn't say—" She paused. "I was miles away at the counselor's office. You said you would take Evan out and buy him a football. He was in your care when the kid hit him. I don't know how I can say it any more clearly."

"That's right. You were at the counselor's office—the *marriage* counselor's office. Where I told you not to go." Rick began to pace, kicking up stones as he moved at a frenzied pace back and forth across the driveway. "Instead of being with your child, where a mother belongs, you were off spending my good money on a counselor who convinced you that I was a monster. And for this you say it's my fault Evan died."

"I never said you were a monster. The counselor—"

"The counselor again. Fuck the counselor. You still don't understand the significance of what you did, do you? You knew I had cancer. And you knew everything would be fine if I had the surgery right away. But what did you do? You went to a *counselor*. And Evan got run over. And for some reason after that I just wasn't in the mood to go and see the damned doctor for the damned surgery. And I can't make any more little Graders, Sonya. And it's your fault. What you did was the worst thing a wife could do to her husband."

"There's a difference between—"

"Damn right there's a difference. Look at Margot. She spends every waking minute with her daughter. She never goes off and leaves her alone. But the first little sign of trouble in our marriage, you go to a counselor. A fucking *counselor*! Dragging our private lives to a stranger. Going outside the family."

Sonya rubbed her hand. She wondered when Rick would run out of steam. She had seen him in all stages of despair since Evan's death, but he had never acted this way before.

Then Sonya looked down at the gun, still clutched in her hand. A new thought surfaced. What if he tried to kill himself? Sonya was about to toss the gun into the under-brush, gathering her strength to fling the awful thing as far away as she could when Rick slashed at her wrist with the side of his hand. Agony flared through Sonya's arm. She sniffed and stared, trying to comprehend the fact that her husband had just broken her wrist. Sadly she looked up at him.

"Why?"

"You ever hear the word 'betray'?"

"It hurts." Her voice was high and pleading.

"That's right. It hurts. And this?" He pointed to the rain-soaked yellow paper lying on the stones. "The one person in the whole world I thought I could trust, Sonya. You were the one person in the whole world."

Through her own pain, Sonya could see tears flowing from her husband's eyes. He'd said that to her before—that thing about being the one person he could trust—but she couldn't remember when or where.

"Bastard!" she cried. "I meant me. It hurts. It's me this time, not you. My arm hurts." She was keening now, her voice a wail of pain, a pain of the heart as well as the broken bone. "Look. You broke my wrist, you bastard. Don't you care? Don't you care about—"

She stopped. She saw Rick bending down. He was reaching for the gun. At last she understood. With all her strength, ignoring the torture of movement, she tried to kick the gun away. She didn't care if she did harm to Rick. She no longer had a husband. She no longer had anyone to protect her. She swung her leg. And missed. Sonya fell in a heap at his feet.

He picked up the gun. His face was ugly. It was twisted—he didn't even look human any more.

"Sorry, Sonya," he said. He was weeping. "I trusted you," he said. He pointed the gun at her head.

She rolled to the left and felt a sting, then saw the yellow paper, with her words running red across its surface, then an explosion of light, then fire or ice, it felt like both, then—

32...

"OH, SONYA, YOU bitch. Honey, why? How could you?"

Rick knelt on the wet stones, holding Sonya's body in his arms. Her limbs had only twitched weakly for a few seconds, then stopped. The wound had long since stopped bleeding. Rick heard water dripping off the trees. He had no idea how long he had been sitting there holding Sonya's body. Her pretty face was ruined. But she hadn't given him any choice. In his tired mind, Rick tried to figure out where things had gone wrong. He never thought Sonya, of all people in the world, would betray him.

He sat and rocked, almost asleep, until something caught his attention. It wasn't a sound. Then he realized what it was. The sun was coming up. It always seemed different here in the deep woods. Here, the sun didn't burst out full over his neighbor's Tudor house, as it had back in Franklin Park. It sort of snuck up on you, coming through the cracks between tree trunks.

The light made him feel naked and dirty. He saw that his hands were covered with blood and gore and mud.

Rick stood up. He looked down and was surprised to see that he was dressed in his pajamas. He thought hard and remembered that he had followed Sonya out in the night when she left him. He remembered that she was going to tell. The letter. He felt fuzzy, as if he'd had too much to drink.

Stumbling, he wandered about the area where Sonya's body lay. Where was the letter? He couldn't let it go out in the mail. Then he saw it, partly hidden by her hair. He reached down and saw that there was no problem with the letter. Her blood had merged with the words she had written and become one terrible stain.

His mouth was dry. He needed a drink of water. But first, he knew he had to do something with Sonya's body. It was highly unlikely that anyone would come to the house. But if they did, it wouldn't do to have her body lying here in the driveway.

Still, he couldn't stand the awful taste in his mouth. He needed some coffee. And Katherine would be needing breakfast.

Oh, God, thought Rick. She's alone there. Well, not alone. Margot was in the house, but she was still locked up. Sonya had complained so much about how dangerous it was that Rick had left Katherine alone when he came to get her at the airport—when? Rick thought it was maybe four or five days ago. A week at most. She had convinced him that even though Katherine was sound asleep under the influence of the Benadryl, she had been in terrible danger. "What if there had been a short in an electrical wire?" she asked him.

She had convinced him. It was bad to leave a child alone. And he had done it again. Katherine was essentially alone. Panic gripped him as he imagined the house in flames, Katherine beating at the bars on the window, unable to find the door.

He bent over and gripped Sonya by the upper arms. With new strength, born of fear, he dragged her body off the driveway and several yards back into the woods.

He lay her down and started to leave. Then he turned back and arranged her hands over her breastbone and closed her eyes.

Rick hurried through the morning mist back to the house. Everything was silent when he entered the warm living room. He went down the hall and looked into Katherine's room. She was in her bed, sleeping soundly, with one foot sticking out from underneath her comforter.

Unsure of what to do next, Rick backed out of Katherine's bedroom and returned to his own. He walked around to the far side of the bed and lay down on his side, exhausted. When he realized that it didn't matter which side of the bed he lay on, he began to cry. At first, it was a choked, grating sound, like someone having a wound cleaned out by a ruthless doctor. But then a dam broke and he wept, loud and freely, missing Sonya.

"—a Kleenex?"

"Huh?" Rick sat up in bed, scared, unsure of who had spoken. Then he looked to his right and saw Katherine standing there. She held a box of Kleenex in her hand.

She looked frightened, but she stood her ground and spoke again. "I never heard you cry before. What's the matter?"

"Katherine, I—" He couldn't speak yet. The words were choked off his throat.

"I woke up and heard you crying. Your PJs are all dirty. Here," she said, and pulled a Kleenex from the box. "You can blow your nose. I'll go get Sonya."

"Wait." Again, Rick couldn't go on. His throat allowed air and sobs through, but few words.

Katherine looked at him, her head tipped to the side, and waited.

"Go, go," he said then, turning away from her. A few syllables at a time seemed to be all he could manage.

Katherine ran off down the hall, and Rick went into the bathroom. Moving nervously and fast, he stripped off his pajamas and stepped into the shower. He turned the water on as hot as he could stand it and soaped himself vigorously. The familiar motion was soothing. "One, two three," he said out loud. "Four, five, six, seven, eight, nine, ten, testing, testing."

His voice was back. Rick toweled himself dry, then wrapped the towel around his waist and hurried into his room. There he dressed in khaki trousers and a kelly-green knit shirt.

He found Katherine sitting in the living room, watching a videotape of Baby Muppets on the TV. She looked up when he entered. "Are you okay? I couldn't find Sonya."

Rick coughed, then sat down next to Katherine. "I'm fine. Sonya has gone away for now. How would you like to make breakfast?"

"Where?"

"Where what?" Rick asked, annoyed.

"Where did Sonya go?"

"It doesn't matter. Last chance—do you want to make breakfast?"

"Sure," Katherine said with a grin. "What should I make?"

"Scrambled eggs and toast?" he asked.

"I'm not allowed to turn on the stove. And I know how to crack eggs, but I don't know how to scramble them. Mama always does that."

Rick hesitated. "How about cold cereal? Can you make that?"

"I can do everything but cut up bananas. I'm not allowed to use a knife."

"All right. I'll—"

"Wait," she said, smiling proudly. "I can use a soft knife. I know how to carry it so the point is pointing down. So I can cut the bananas, too."

"Good. I'll go get Mar— I'll go get your mother."

Rick forcefully shut out the thought of Sonya that tried to enter his mind. She was no longer a part of his world.

As he did each morning, Rick went to the basement, unlocked the door, then stood back and to the side, pushing it open with the mop handle. He was sure that Margot was no longer foolish enough to think that she could ambush him. Still, until he trusted her further, he would be careful. It struck him as odd that he should care about trusting Margot. Only a few days ago he had been thinking that he would have to get rid of her somehow if he and Sonya and Katherine were to have a normal life.

Margot came out of the room, blinking. She always did that, even though he had put in the fuse that gave light to the shelter.

"Good morning," he said.

She looked at him, evidently surprised at his friendly tone.

"Good morning," she said, and preceded him up the stairs.

As they climbed, he said, "Katherine is making breakfast."

"Katherine?" she answered, puzzlement in her tone.

Rick was rather enjoying Margot's reactions. He was aware that she had perceived him as the enemy.

When they got to the dining room, a happy Katherine ran to her mother and gave her a huge hug.

"I'm making breakfast, Mama. I can't make the coffee, so you can make the coffee, but I filled up the cereal bowls and look—" She dragged her mother over to the table— "Look, I cut up the bananas."

Rick smiled, seeing the chunks of bananas, some as big as ping pong balls, on top of the cereal. But he frowned when he counted the bowls. Katherine had put out four. They were a family of three now, and it was as good a time as any for Katherine to learn that.

"Katherine, you can put one of those bowls in the kitchen. Sonya won't be eating with us anymore."

"Why not?" asked the child.

"It's none of—" He stopped. It would be better to make a clean break of it. "Sonya and I have been having a lot of trouble with our marriage for years now. We've decided to get a divorce. She left last night to go back to live with her parents."

"You mean she's not coming back?"

"Don't whine, Katherine. No. She's not coming back." He spoke more harshly than he had intended, and Katherine's lower lip quivered.

"Now, let's eat this delicious breakfast you made," he said. "Where's the milk?"

"Oops," she said, and hurried off to get it. He noticed when she came back that she had poured it into the crystal pitcher, just the way he preferred. Rick patted her hand as she sat down near him.

They ate breakfast in silence—no words, only the clinking of spoons against their bowls.

When they were done, and Margot began to clear the table, Rick stopped her. "Katherine, you may clear the table," he said. "I want to talk with your mother in the living room."

Margot followed him, and he indicated that she should sit down on the sofa next to him. He turned to her and said, "How are you this morning?"

"I'm fine."

Rick could see that she was trying to remain neutral, but he knew she must be full of questions.

"Now that Sonya has left," he said, "Katherine will need a mother. I've decided to give you a chance to be a better mother."

Margot stared at him. A mix of emotions played across her face, but so subtly that only a very observant person would see it. *She's a cool one*, he thought. *Can't trust her yet.*

Margot cleared her throat, then spoke. "I'm sorry for any hurt I've caused Katherine in the past," she said. "I do want to be a better mother."

Rick was amazed. She was finally admitting that she had been abusive to Katherine. He knew that the admission was the first step to recovery. Maybe there was some hope for Margot and Katherine to have a normal relationship after all.

Just then Katherine came in. "I'm all finished cleaning up. Can I go outside and play now?"

"No," said Rick. "It's too cold and damp outside today."

"Would you like to play Chutes and Ladders?" asked Margot.

"Hurray!" cried Katherine and left the room to get the game.

Rick built up the fire. The flames gave a warm golden glow to the room. He sat and watched as Margot played the game with Katherine. Katherine won three times in a row and was delighted.

The morning passed quickly. Rick spent the time either reading or watching his daughter and her mother enjoying each other's company. He stretched and yawned, aware that he hadn't had such a pleasant, peaceful few hours in a long time.

After lunch was over and the dishes cleared and washed, Katherine asked if she could watch another video. "Not until you've had a nap," said Rick. "Ask me again when you wake up."

When she had gone to her room and everything had been quiet for a while, Rick asked Margot to sit on the sofa with him, just as he had earlier that day. She did so, giving him a shy smile as she sat down.

"It's been a nice day so far, hasn't it?" he asked.

"It *has* been peaceful," she said.

"I'm sure you noticed that things had gone sour between me and S— me and my wife."

"You didn't look very happy."

"The breakup has been brewing for a long time. Ever since Evan died. It was her fault he was killed, you know.

"I'm so sorry about your little boy."

He gritted his teeth. He hated it when people talked about Evan. For a moment he couldn't recall why he'd even brought it up. Then he remembered what he had meant to explain. "He was killed by a drunk teenager. If she had been watching him the way a mother should, Evan would be alive now."

This time Margot was silent, but her face was sympathetic. Rick tried to figure out why he had hated this woman so much. Oh, yes. Margot had been hitting Katherine. But she had just admitted it and had promised to do better.

All at once, he realized what had happened. He was being given a last chance. Here, right here in this house, was the perfect family he had always wanted. No wonder things hadn't been working out before. Sonya was not Katherine's biological mother. How unnatural to think that Sonya could be a mother to Rick's daughter. She had had her chance with Evan and had made a tragic error. Sonya was gone. And right next to him was the mother of his child. A beautiful woman. He reached out and touched her hair, pulling a curl straight, then watching it spring back when he let go.

Suddenly he stood up. "Katherine is asleep. Let's have some brandy."

"All right," she answered.

When he handed her a snifter, their fingers touched. Was it his imagination, or did she hold the touch longer than she had to?

Rick asked Margot to tell him about Katherine when she was a baby.

"She was wonderful. From the moment she was born, you could see the intelligence in her eyes."

"When did she start walking?"

"At ten months. It was something, watching this tiny person speeding all over the house."

They continued talking, hitting on topics like college, hobbies and favorite books. Rick had not been so happy in years. He felt like a much younger man—a young man on a first date with a young woman who adored him.

When Rick went to refill their brandy glasses, he tried to understand what was going on. He decided that it must have been Sonya's influence that had made Margot seem so repugnant. Sonya had poisoned everyone's interactions.

After he put more logs on the fire, he sat down and asked Margot to tell him more about Katherine's babyhood. Margot grew animated when she talked about her daughter. Rick saw the resemblance between Katherine and Margot, not just in features, but in small gestures and in facial expressions. He hadn't been aware of the similarities before.

At one point, Rick asked Margot about her own childhood. She smiled and talked about growing up as the only child in a happy home. Her father, especially, had spent time with her, teaching her woodworking, helping her with homework and doing almost everything together.

When Margot, acting as a good first date should, asked Rick about his childhood, he shook his head sadly and told her the horror his parents had made of his adolescent years with the parade of foster children.

"So you must have been relieved when it was time to leave home for college," she said.

"No, the foster monsters stopped long before that. We only had them in the house for two years—actually, one year and eleven months. There was an accident. One of the girls got hurt, and the social worker came to check the house. She said our house wasn't safe enough for children, and they pulled all the little creeps out. My parents weren't real happy about it, but you better believe I was."

As Rick spoke, he was amazed at how relaxed he felt talking with Margot, how much he had come to trust her in just one day.

But Rick didn't tell Margot the whole sordid story. To this day, it embarrassed him to remember what Dawn did to him. "A joke," she called it. Some joke.

It had taken Rick a long time to figure out that his date was in on the "joke," too. As a pimply-faced, too-tall ninth-grader, he hadn't believed it when Tiffany agreed to go with him to the dance on the *Gateway Clipper*. "Just ask her," Dawn said. "Maybe she'll say yes."

Tiffany was Dawn's best friend, so he was suspicious. But Tiffany was also the sexiest girl in the ninth grade. Rick definitely wanted to go to the dance with her. So he made himself believe that Dawn was finally trying to be friends by helping him get a date.

On the night of the dance, Dawn's date, who was old

enough to drive, stopped by to pick up Dawn and Rick. When they arrived at Tiffany's house, Rick rang the bell. She opened the door; he couldn't believe how good she looked. She had on a tight black dress that just barely covered her butt. Her black hair was on top of her head in a bunch of wild curls, and she had on long, shiny earrings. Like always, she had on sexy eye makeup.

By the time they got to the boat dock and parked, Rick couldn't stand it any longer. He leaned over and boldly kissed Tiffany. He got hot all over when she jammed her tongue into his mouth.

"Come on, jerk-off," Dawn hollered, banging on his window. He hadn't even been aware that she had gotten out of the car.

"Jerk-off" was her favorite of a bunch of pet names she had for him. Normally he would have wanted to kill her, but tonight and with what tonight promised, it didn't faze him. In fact, as all four of them boarded the boat, he smiled at her and said, "Thanks." He'd never imagined he would say that to Dawn.

The evening went better than he had even fantasized. Some of the guys had snuck some beer aboard, and they kept moving the six packs from one hiding place to another, always managing to stay one step ahead of the teachers who were chaperoning the students. Rick took a couple of swigs, but then pretended to be a little drunk. He wanted to be sober for later in the night. If he was reading Tiffany's signals right, he would need to be sober.

He slow-danced with Tiffany as the *Gateway Clipper* floated leisurely down the Monongehela and on into the Ohio. Dusk turned to dark, and white lights twinkled from buildings along the shore. Lights of red, gold, blue and green were strung above the deck, and they cast a magic glow on Tiffany as she pressed her body close against Rick's.

When the three-piece band took a break, Tiffany headed toward the restroom along with Dawn and their other girl friends. Rick drank a little more beer with the guys, then leaned over the rail to wait for Tiffany to return. He watched the dark waves as they reflected the carnival lights on the boat.

At last, Tiffany returned. She was in hysterics, hanging onto Dawn's arm as if she'd fall down without support. Dawn was giggling and so were two or three other girls who came toward Rick. He wondered if maybe they had found a little liquid refreshment while they were gone.

Rick smiled and held out his hand to Tiffany. Instead of her hand, she gave him a photo. It had the bulky feel of a Polaroid shot. Must be the cause of all the laughing, he thought. Rick turned and held the photo so that a green light shone on its surface. For a moment, he couldn't make out the picture. Then he swallowed hard. There, in the middle of a sunlit bedroom, earphones on his ears, eyes squeezed shut in ecstasy, was a photo of himself. A photo of Richard Grader jerking off.

Someone grabbed the picture from his hand. Rick stared at the water. The laughter started up again—and grew and grew until that was all he could hear.

Somehow Rick made it home that night. The next day, all the people in the house came running when they heard Dawn screaming in the bathroom. Her legs were blistered from the knee down. Somehow, they discovered later, lye had gotten into her bubble bath.

"I can't understand it," his mother had said, in tears. "I always keep the lye on the top shelf of a closed cabinet." There was an investigation by the social services agency, and when the social worker decided to "take the children out of the care of the Graders in favor of more suitable homes," he wondered why he hadn't thought of the solution sooner.

33...

JOE AND BETH sorted through the growing stack of papers. They worked quietly, the only sound the tinkle of Frankie's baby music box as he played quietly in the living room. Beth's husband, Harry, had been up early, working along with them that morning until he had to leave for work. Beth saw the grim set of Joe's face, aware that her expression was the same. She knew that they were going over mostly the same ground that the police were covering. But she was convinced that the police were too bound by their new pet theory that Katy and Margot had been taken by the kidnapper who had been at work in Ohio.

"Want some more coffee?" said Beth.

"Thanks, but I think I'll make a few more phone calls first." Joe reached for the phone and jumped when it rang just as his hand touched the receiver.

Beth went to the kitchen.

The conversation was short. When Beth returned, Joe was smiling. He held a slip of paper in the air. "We got it," he said.

"What?"

"The address and directions to Billy the Kid's house."

"The sperm bank guy? Fantastic! Phone number?"

"Disconnected. But apparently he still lives there. How fast can you be ready to roll?"

"Dennis," she called to her older son. "I have to go out. Will you watch Frankie?"

"Sure, Mom."

"I'm ready," Beth said.

As she went to give Frankie a hug, the phone rang again.

When Beth returned to the dining room to get her purse, Joe said, "Bad news. That was the hospital."

"Oh, no. Not Margot's dad!"

"Don't panic. He's not worse. You knew he had another small stroke the other day, didn't you?"

"Yes. When he heard that Margot was missing."

"Right. The nurse said he's okay, but extremely upset about something. Keeps asking for me." Joe looked down at the slip of paper with Billy's address. "Maybe I'd better go and see Mr. Newhouse first."

"Can't Margot's mom go?"

"She's already there, but the nurse says he's asking for me. Keeps pointing to a picture of a headstone in the yellow pages and saying my name. She thought maybe he was worried about my being kidnapped, too. Or could be he's afraid of dying. In any case, the doctor says it would be safer if I came and tried to calm him down."

"Poor guy. It must be so frustrating for him." Beth took the note from Joe's hand. "You go ahead and see Mr. Newhouse. I'll drive out to Billy the Kid's and see if I can find anything useful."

"I think you should wait. You probably shouldn't go out there alone."

"Beg your pardon, why not?"

"Don't get huffy, now. I'm not being sexist. But it *is* in the middle of nowhere, and he is an alcoholic. Not the safest combination for anyone. I probably wouldn't go by myself, either."

"All right, you're right. But I don't want to waste time. I'll get someone else to babysit Frankie and I'll take Dennis. Besides, Harry took the other car, and I hate driving that old Caddy. I don't think it likes me, either."

"All right. I'll call you later."

"Okay," said Beth. "And if I find out anything before that, I'll call you. If you're not at the hospital, I'll leave a message on your machine."

After Joe left, Beth phoned the babysitter, who came right

over. Then Beth kissed Frankie and hurried out to the Caddy
with Dennis. Once they were on the main highway, he
turned on the new stereo he had installed the day before as
a surprise for his stepfather.

"I told you to talk to your dad before you put that stereo
in," Beth said, surprised and angry that Dennis had just
gone ahead on his own and installed the stereo.

"This radio's a million times better than the old one,"
insisted Dennis. "You'd think I'd ripped out his heart, not
some ancient radio. And besides—"

"You're still missing the point," said Beth. "He's trying
to *restore* the car, not improve it."

"Well, he should try to make it better. It's not some kind
of religious relic. I mean, you ever seen a sixty-three Caddy
in the church?"

"Don't get smart," said Beth. She rubbed her eyes and
put her sunglasses back on. The sun had been playing hide
and seek all morning, and it wasn't improving her mood
any. In truth, she was almost glad for the diversion of the
argument. This trip to the sperm bank guy's house—and
that's how she had come to think of this William Kid, the
"sperm bank guy"—could very easily prove to be another
waste of time.

"Okay. But I didn't hurt it any," said Dennis. "The old
stereo's in a box in the garage. Any time he decides he
wants to go back to having two stations full of static, he can
just hook it back up."

"No, *you* can just 'hook it back up,' if that's what he
wants."

"I guess you never even thought that maybe he'd like it.
You never even thought of that, did you?"

Dennis's voice had taken on a definite whine.

"I'm just saying that you should have discussed it with
him first."

"It's pretty hard to make a surprise if you tell a person
what it is first," he said. "You know, if you'd just leave it
alone, maybe Dad and I would get along a lot better."

Beth sighed. She was deeply touched by Dennis's efforts to surprise his stepdad with the new radio. She knew it wasn't just a selfish wish to have a better player for his own rock music. Harry had complained about the quality of the old radio, and Dennis had told her of his plan to replace it. She had to admit that her real fear, the fear that she was expressing so badly in the form of anger, was that Dennis's surprise would be met with something less than joy. It was her son's first major attempt to be friends with his stepdad, and she wanted it to go right. She considered again that maybe she should tell her husband about it; risk ruining the surprise to save the link that Dennis was trying to make.

With an exaggerated movement of his arm, Dennis pushed in a tape and turned up the volume. The hot, spicy wail of Dennis's favorite heavy metal band screamed from the speakers into the summer air. Self-consciously, Beth looked around, but there were no other cars in sight on the small country road. With the top down on the convertible, Beth felt a bit like a component in a massive, moving stereo speaker. A few dairy cows backstepped nervously from their fence as the Cadillac screeched by.

She glanced at the directions Joe had scribbled earlier. "We should be almost there," she shouted.

"What?"

"God!" Beth twisted the dial. "How can you stand it?" It took her a moment to realize that the knob had come off in her hand.

"Geez, you destroyed it," said Dennis.

"I only turned it off. How much did this thing cost, anyway?"

"It wasn't cheap, if that's what you mean."

"I didn't say that, but just—"

Beth twisted around in her seat, then slapped her palm against the side of the car.

"Slow down, slow down. That was it, I think."

With a squeal of brakes, Dennis stopped the car. He shifted into reverse and careened backward down the dusty road. Beth held her breath, fully aware that it was too late to counsel against driving in reverse on a public road.

Miraculously, they stopped safely by the driveway of a small, white clapboard house. Dennis pulled in and turned off the ignition.

Beth and Dennis got out of the car and went to the door. Beth knocked and got no answer. "Hello," she called. Still no answer. "I'll wait a minute and keep trying," she said to Dennis. "Why don't you go around back and see if there's anyone around."

"Okay, Mom," he said and bounded down the steps.

Beth knocked louder and called out again. She tried the doorknob; it was locked. She peered through the side window and saw a messy living room, but nothing unusual. As she headed for the back, she saw Dennis near the door to the garage.

"I checked inside, Mom. Nobody there. But the guy has a BMW in about a thousand pieces in the garage. Boy, would I love a chance to work on that—"

"Never mind that," said Beth impatiently. "I don't want to waste time." Beth tried the back door and found it locked, too. She looked at her son. "Do you think we ought to break in?"

"You kidding?" he asked.

"Yes— No— I don't know. Maybe I *am* serious."

"Why don't we hang around a while and see if this Billy comes home. Look, someone musta been here a while ago."

Dennis pointed to a small pet food dish on the back porch. It had canned food in it that looked fairly fresh.

"A half hour. We'll wait a half hour." Beth wandered toward the Caddy to sit down.

"I'm going back to the garage. I won't touch anything, but I want to look at the car. You wouldn't believe all the stuff he's got out there. And the tanks. Can't see why anybody'd have so many tanks. Let me know when a half—"

"Tanks?" Something clicked in Beth's mind. She rushed

past her son and into the dimly lit garage. There—each one with a numbered tag—were tanks, the kind they use to store frozen sperm in. "Will you look at this?" she said in wonderment.

Dennis pried off the top of one of them and removed a small glass vial. "What's this?" he asked.

"It's probably old sperm," Beth replied.

She looked up quickly at the sound of shattering glass. Dennis had dropped the vial he was holding.

"Yuk! It's like a bunch of dead pets."

"That's enough, now. You can't talk about something that— I mean—" Beth bent down and began gathering the tiny shards of glass. "The hopes and dreams that these represent—"

"Oh, Ma. You gonna get all corny now?"

"If you'd known Margot when she and Joe were trying so hard to have a baby, you'd understand. It seems funny to people sometimes, because they don't know—"

"I know. I know. I'm not saying anything about Margot. I guess that's what I mean. It doesn't seem right to leave all this stuff just sitting out here. Alone." Dennis raised his eyes to the sky in exasperation and turned his back on Beth. "Never mind." Beth watched him as he stalked back to the car and leaped over the side, not bothering to open the door.

Beth was just about to scold him for doing that—the words, "Your father won't like that," were on her lips—when she realized that she'd seen her husband do the very same maneuver a dozen times. Was Dennis right? Was it her efforts to make friends out of these two people she loved so passionately that was hindering the process? The thought was depressing, but somehow it was also liberating. If Dennis was right, if just leaving the two alone would allow them to find their own way, then she could stop her fruitless efforts. And most important of all—Dennis's statement implied that he'd been thinking about the problem, that he *wanted* to be friends with his stepfather.

As she pondered her family's problems, Beth moved

between the scattered BMW parts and discarded tanks. At the back of the garage, she saw some file cabinets. They were dusty and the light was dim, but it didn't take long to discover that the cabinets contained files of sperm donors— old, long-out-of-date files. As she leafed through the first few files in the "A" section, she got a sense of what each contained, in terms of donor profile, characteristics and frequency of donations. And as she read the names, Beth wondered vaguely where they all were now. Had they made it through college? Were they fathers of their own children?

Was there information on the biological father of Katy in these drawers somewhere? Beth wondered. There were so many. She tried to decide whether she should dig in and read each one, hoping for some clue, or phone the police, or Joe, or what? Maybe Billy Kid would come back and throw her out.

Beth decided to try to reach Joe and see if he could drive out and help look. She usually didn't make a habit of breaking laws, but if Billy did come back and want to stop them, surely three adults would be able to subdue him somehow and continue their search.

Dennis was squatting beside the car, petting two fat little kittens while the even fatter mother cat looked on from the shade of the house.

"I think we may be on to something," Beth said. "Hop in and let's go find a phone."

"'Bye, cats," said Dennis. He picked up the kittens and set them down safely by the mother cat, then, literally, hopped into the driver's seat.

34 . . .

AS RICK LOCKED the bomb shelter door, he felt like the richest man alive, safely locking away his most precious possessions. He'd had an extraordinary day with his daughter—and with Margot: the quiet morning by the fire, the brandy with Margot. "Margot"—it was a beautiful name, he decided. Only a few days ago, he had hated the sound of it, thinking that Margot was a burden, a problem he had to eliminate.

He pondered the peculiar way that some things worked out, as he went grimly about his task of finding a shovel and a pickax. Here he had been struggling so hard, against such long odds to keep his family together, when he had simply made a mistake about who his family actually was.

Tools in hand, Rick headed out of the house and down the wet driveway. He felt like kicking himself for not seeing it before. It was the one lesson he had learned from Dawn and Peace Anna and all the other horrible creatures his parents took in. The only family that had a chance of being healthy and normal was a natural family. Two parents with children that belonged to them biologically. No wonder Sonya had become so repulsive to him lately. He had known in his heart that she wasn't Katherine's real mother. It just hadn't been easy to face after all these years together, after he and Sonya had gone through the grief of losing Evan.

Rick stepped off the driveway and into the woods. For a moment, he felt fear. Fear, elemental and cold in his chest. Sonya's body was gone.

Hardly breathing at all, Rick dropped to his hands and

knees and began pushing aside brush and fallen leaves.
"No!" he roared. "It can't be. Not now. Not now. I have
every—"

His hand contacted something— Yes. A sob escaped
from Rick's throat. Her body had been here all along. He sat
still, waiting for his heart to slow before he started digging
Sonya's grave.

By the time Rick had completed his task, it was late
afternoon. While he worked, his mind had gone round and
round, digging away at the same subject. Rick's emotions
were flung back and forth from joy to despair. Of course he
had been given a last chance. No more babies would ever be
born to him. Katherine was his only child in all the world,
in all his life. And he had been playing house here in the
woods, pretending that everything was just fine.

But as he panted and sweated digging Sonya's grave, he
realized that he had two major barriers to overcome before
he could have the life he had always craved—that happy,
secure, *normal* life. Rick knew that Margot was coming
around. He could see it in her eyes. She was beginning to
trust him. It was only a matter of time before she wanted the
same things he wanted. Obviously she had done the best she
could to have a natural family in spite of her husband's
inability to provide her with a child. Now, with Rick she had
the real thing, Katherine's own father. Who could possibly
love Katherine more than her real father and mother?

But the second obstacle was a bigger one. And it would
only become more of a threat with the passage of time.
Apparently the drunk who had the sperm bank records in his
garage—Billy the Kid, Rick remembered with a snort—had
not realized that Rick had gone through the old files out in
his garage and gotten the information he needed to find his
daughter. Either that or he hadn't told anyone yet. If he had,
the police would surely have found Rick by now, he
reasoned. But what was there to guarantee that Billy
wouldn't figure things out at some point. Or maybe he
already had and was just putting off telling the police for
some reason.

The idea that some washed-up drunk could ruin every-thing for him with a few words made Rick so angry that he dug faster.

Rick fought against the emotions that assaulted him when he picked up Sonya's body and laid it in the grave. He considered saying a short prayer, but decided he didn't have time for even that. Shovel flying, Rick covered her body with dirt, ignoring the tears on his face, until the earth was smooth again. He spent a few minutes spreading leaves and brush over the area, then hurried back up the driveway. On his way, he picked up a blue beach ball and carried it to the basket under the porch. After it was stowed away, Rick went inside and put the shovel and pickax away. Then he got two cans of gasoline from the corner of the basement, took them outside and stashed them in the back of his car. He checked to make sure that he had plenty of matches in the glove compartment.

Rick went upstairs again and went into the bathroom. He removed his wristband and set it on the shelf over the bathroom sink, then quickly showered and dressed in clean clothes. As he was about to leave, he debated about going down to speak with his daughter and Margot first. But he decided against it. They had everything they needed to keep them safe and comfortable until he could get back and take care of them.

Rick turned on the ignition and drove as fast as he safely could down the drive, through the deep forest on the two-lane road. Things went well until he saw a coal truck ahead of him. The heavily loaded vehicle crawled at fifteen miles an hour up the steep hills. There was no way to pass safely on the winding, narrow road.

Finally, Rick began to honk, blink his lights and wave his hand in the air. He pulled the steering wheel right and left so that his car careened from side to side within its narrow lane. Before long, on a level spot of the road, the truck pulled over to allow Rick to pass. The driver gave Rick the finger and shouted obscenities, but Rick didn't care.

At last, there it was, in the twilight: the small, rundown house of Billy the Kid. Rick slowed down and pulled into the driveway, but halfway to the house he stopped. He saw an old, powder-blue Cadillac parked by the house. Loud rock music poured from the speakers. Through the fly-specked windows of the garage, Rick could detect movement. There were at least two, maybe three, people in there.

"Shit!" Rick pounded his steering wheel. They must be friends of Billy's. He was probably out there getting drunk with some friends. Showing them the sperm tanks. *What an asshole*, Rick thought. He shows people those tanks like they're babies or something!

He backed out of the drive and headed toward Pittsburgh, unsure of what to do. On the floor, in the back of the car, the gasoline sloshed about.

It occurred to Rick that maybe Billy wasn't out there with friends at all. Maybe the police were there. *In a baby-blue Caddy?* Not likely, but what if Billy already *had* told someone? Of course, it would take the police some time to track Rick down. But what if they were looking for him right now?

Rick made a quick decision. He would take his family and go away for a while. He could find out later if the police were looking for him.

He wasn't far from his Franklin Park neighborhood, he realized; perhaps he should go to his house and get some things that would help him while he was away. He had cash hidden in the attic; Sonya's jewelry was worth quite a bit if he should be short of cash; and there were the silver dollars his father had given him.

Rick turned the steering wheel and headed for Franklin Park.

35...

JOE GOT TO the hospital and up to his father-in-law's room in record time. When he entered, Margot's mother was talking to her husband, trying to calm him down.

"Well, thank God you're here," she said to Joe. "He's been looking at the Yellow Pages all morning, like a crazy man. And now he keeps pointing to a grave marker. Says the marker has Katy and Margot. I told him and the doctor told him that he has to calm down, but he refuses. You see what you can do with him!"

"Joe, Joe," said Mr. Newhouse. "Look."

Joe walked over to the bedside and looked at the picture of a headstone in a monument company's advertisement. He put his arm around Mr. Newhouse's shoulders. "There's something about the headstone you want me to look at?"

"It got Katy. It got Margot."

"Oh, Pop." Joe swallowed hard. "Are you afraid that they might be dead?" asked Joe. He hated to say it, but that seemed to be what Mr. Newhouse was trying to communicate.

"No no no no no!" Mr. Newhouse stabbed at the picture with his finger.

Joe looked at Mrs. Newhouse. "Do you have any idea what brought this on?"

"Well, the nurse said the TV was on when she came in. He had been hitting his call button. But he's been looking constantly through the Yellow Pages ever since the last stroke—"

"When he heard that Margot was missing, too?"

"Yes."

"Did you ever find out who he was on the phone with the day he had the stroke?"

"No. But it was right after that call that he began reading through the Yellow Pages. He fell asleep last night with the book in his lap. I'm surprised he even had the TV on today, he's been so obsessed with that damned directory."

Joe turned back to his father-in-law. "Was it something you saw on the TV today that upset you?" he asked.

"No no."

"It's the picture of the headstone you want me to see?"

"Yes. Got Margot. Got Katy."

"Do you know something about the kidnapping? Something to do with the headstone?"

Mr. Newhouse reached out and grabbed Joe's hand in a surprisingly strong grip. "Yes!"

"Gregory," said Mrs. Newhouse. She began to cry and reached for a tissue."

"Don't fall apart on us now," said Joe with an encouraging smile at Margot's mother. "I don't know how he's heard, but I think your husband has found out something about the kidnapper's name."

With renewed energy, Mr. Newhouse slapped his hand down on the page with the grave marker.

"I'll say some words, and you stop me if something sounds right, okay?" said Joe.

"Go," said Mr. Newhouse.

"Headstone?"

Nothing.

"Monument?"

Nothing.

"Grave marker?"

"Yes yes yes!"

"Good, sir. Is it 'Marker' or 'Mark'?"

"No no no no!"

"Sorry. How about 'Grave'?"

Mr. Newhouse shook his head and made a small sound of frustration.

"Something that sounds similar to 'Grave'?"

"Yes."

"'Gravely'? 'Graves'? 'Graver'?"

"Yes!" Mr. Newhouse pushed the directory off his lap onto the floor, then again grasped Joe's hand.

Joe sat with the Newhouses a while longer until the nurse came in and said that Mr. Newhouse's blood pressure had gone down a bit and he seemed calmer. Joe could see that the old man was fighting sleep. Funny, he had never thought of Margot's dad as an old man before.

Just as Mr. Newhouse gave in and closed his eyes, the phone rang. Joe picked it up.

"Joe, that you?" It was Beth.

"Yes," Joe said. "And Mr. Newhouse may have given us something we can use."

"Wait. You won't believe what we found out there," said Beth. "There wasn't anybody home, so Dennis and I snooped around a little. And we found files. Files, Joe. Four cabinets full of sperm donors. I don't know how we'll ever get through them, but Dennis and I are going—"

"Wait, Beth. Listen. I'm not sure about this, but we may have a name." Joe moved away from the bed. The phone cord was long enough for him to get almost out the door and out of his father-in-law's hearing range.

"It's too complicated to explain right now. In fact, it may be the wild-goose chase of the century, but the kidnapper's name could be Graver or Gravely, or something like that."

"Okay. We'll go back and look right now. It shouldn't take long."

"Why don't you wait, and I'll come out there," said Joe.

"It's too far. It'll be dark soon, and I'm not waiting," said Beth. "I'll call you back soon. Give Mr. Newhouse my love," said Beth. "'Bye."

And it was only when Beth hung up that Joe realized only

she had the directions to Billy the Kid's house. So he waited.

The doctor had told Joe that often stroke patients who are motivated to communicate use all sorts self-devised methods. Apparently the second stroke that Margot's father had suffered in the hospital when he learned that Margot was missing as well as Katy had further affected his speech patterns. The doctor had explained that using a similar or related word was a common method used by stroke patients to compensate for partial loss of language. Joe hoped that Mr. Newhouse's extraordinary effort would pay off.

Joe paced the hall, never going far from Mr. Newhouse's room. When the phone rang, he picked it up on the second ring. "Beth?"

"I got it," she said. "Richard Grader. I checked the phone book and he's in it." Beth gave Joe the address and phone number.

"Thanks. I'll meet you later at your place."

"But what—"

"'Bye." Suddenly Joe felt as if he had more energy than he'd ever had before in his life. He ran out of the hospital to his car. Tires screeching, he sped toward the Franklin Park address Beth had given him.

36...

JOE SLOWED HIS car as he drove by the house of Richard Grader. When Beth phoned the information in to him at the hospital, he had left in a burst of high, but undirected energy.

He drove around the block again, looking at the large, pleasant houses with their perfect landscaping and two- and three-car garages. Not knowing just what he had in mind, Joe parked his car a block and a half away and walked to the Grader house. He went to the front door and rang the bell. A melodic ring echoed inside, but no one came to the door. Joe smelled the scent of the eucalyptus in a vine wreath hanging on the door.

Joe glanced around, thinking he might speak with the neighbors about this Grader, but no one was in sight. He walked around to the backyard and across the patio. Joe knocked on the back door and waited. As he waited, he glanced down at the flagstone steps and noticed a two- or three-inch piece of yarn. Not knowing why, he bent and picked it up. He rolled it between his fingers and tried to translate the strange emotion the yarn gave him. Suddenly he thought he knew what the bit of fluff meant to him.

Joe knocked hard once more. No answer. Then he stepped back and, with the heel of his shoe, kicked in the pane of glass near the door handle. He hesitated, listening. The neighborhood was still, suburban silent.

He reached in, unlocked the door and entered a small laundry room. He scanned the room and noticed a plastic-lined wastebasket with a scrap of cloth hanging over its edge near the washing machine. Holding his breath, Joe

stepped forward and pulled the item from the basket. He
held it up and saw what he suspected. There, torn too badly
for repair, was Katy's favorite blouse—the blouse with the
giraffe with the absurd yarn topknot. He hugged the small
blouse to his chest, fighting a fear greater than he had ever
experienced.

Boldly, Joe walked quickly through the rooms of the house.
He found other signs that Katy had been there, including her
white shoe, the mate to the one they'd found stuck in the
carousel horse's stirrup.

Joe decided to search the den first. He went through a file
cabinet, glancing at each file, hoping for some hint or clue
as to where Margot and Katy might be.

One file contained a recent receipt for a round-trip plane
ticket to Detroit. Joe quickly checked the dates against a
desk calendar. But the dates made no sense—the Pittsburgh-
to-Detroit trip had taken place before Katy was abducted
and the return journey after. Still, Joe set the receipt aside.
He continued searching.

As he riffled through another file, an old-fashioned house
key fell out. He glanced at the file's contents: standard will
and power of attorney documents, and two paid-off mort-
gages for a couple born in the twenties. On a cocktail napkin
there was a Cook's Forest address and a hand-drawn map of
how to get to it. No doubt, a remote location, Joe thought.
A fine location for a kidnapper to hide. Joe had spent a few
summer weekends there with Margot before Katy was born.
He shoved the key and directions in his pocket.

Joe checked the remaining files, but found nothing else
potentially helpful among the orderly folders.

As he walked toward the living room, Joe's foot grazed a
small pile of mail sitting by the front door. He saw a mail
slot and decided there must be a neighbor who carried
Grader's mail in from the curbside mailbox when Grader
was on vacation—or off with his kidnap victims, Joe
thought.

Joe picked up the envelopes and quickly opened a bill
from VISA. There were no recent charges on that one. He

opened a bill from Master Charge and glanced through the month's worth of charges. The final charge on the bill was for last Thursday. It was from Truman's Store. Joe knew the place. They sold gas and groceries. And Truman's Store was in Cook's Forest.

Joe forced his spinning mind to calm down. Margot had disappeared on Wednesday. The Truman's Store charge was for Thursday. Joe reached in his pocket and pulled out the key and tossed it a few times into the air, considering. He felt sure that the key would open a door in the house where Grader had taken his wife—ex-wife, Joe amended miserably—and his daughter.

Joe checked to make sure he had the directions to the house, then with the cocktail napkin in his hand, he headed for the back door. He opened it, turned to close it, then paused to refold the directions paper when *blam*! Something hit him from behind with the force of a steel rod.

37 . . .

AS RICK NEARED his own street, intent on gathering up his valuables, he remembered that he had told the neighbors that he would be away on vacation. No problem there, he thought. He parked a block over and slipped quietly through his neighbor's trees to his own backyard.

Crickets were calling as Rick walked through the damp grass of his backyard. If everything worked out, there would come a time when he could bring Katherine and Margot here to live. It was a good neighborhood for a child to grow up in.

Rick was digging in his pocket for the back door key when he heard a sound from *inside* his house.

He stumbled, then jumped backward off the step and knelt down in the bushes. Rick could see broken glass on the patio.

With a click and a turn, his back screen door opened. It must be the police, he thought. Rick watched as a form hesitated, then stepped down to the patio. There was enough light left to see that the man wore street clothes.

The man turned and closed the door. Rick thought the guy looked familiar. He squinted as the man folded some paper he held in his hand.

Suddenly Rick knew. He had seen the guy on TV and in the newspapers. It was Katherine's father. No! Katherine's phony father. The one who couldn't make a child on his own. It was Joseph DesMarais, sneaking out of Rick's house.

Angry thoughts shrieked through Rick's head like sirens. Long ago, when he had been reduced to selling his sperm to pay his way through law school, he had felt contempt for men like Joe who paid money to buy sperm. Now Rick was like those men himself, unable to create children. And this Joe, this petty thief, sneaking out of another man's house, thought he had a right to Rick's child?

With a primeval sound, teeth bared, Rick leapt from the shadows and flung himself at Joe.

Joe fell to his knees and grunted. "Son of a bitch!"

When the bastard stood up, Rick was ready, adrenaline pumping, rage growing. He caught Joe with a right to the jaw. Joe went down, and Rick put his hand in his pocket. Too late he remembered that he had put the pistol in the glove compartment.

Joe got up into a crouch and threw his whole body's weight into Rick's stomach. Rick stumbled backward. It only took a second to see that Joe was heading to the side of the house. Rick caught up with him as he rounded the corner. He tackled Joe and they both went down.

A grunt of pain and the noise of shattering glass told Rick that he had done some damage. Joe's head must have gone into the basement window. The two grappled with each other, rolling in the grass, but Joe managed to pull free. He rose like a sprinter and again tried to work his way toward the street.

"Bastard," said Rick, rising to his feet. He pulled at the guy's arm and aimed his fist at Joe's jaw again. But this time, Joe blocked it with his right arm, then delivered a brutal uppercut to Rick's chin. He fell, fighting hard to stay conscious. Rick felt two teeth floating in his mouth. In frustration and pain, he spat teeth and blood on the ground.

Rick could see Joe, like someone in a slowed video, going one floating step after another toward the street. As hard as he tried, Rick could not move his body. In desperation, he hit the side of his own head with his palm. Fresh agony exploded in his jaw, but the pain freed his muscles. He pushed himself up, leaning on the brick wall of his house for support. He took two steps forward, keeping his eye on his enemy.

Then a strange thing happened. Joe had reached the curb. Rick watched as he tripped and fell into the road. At the same moment, a Domino's pizza truck screeched to a halt with its left front tire a hair away from Joe's head.

Rick stood still and tried to analyze what he'd just seen. Did the pizza truck hit Joe? Or did Joe hit the truck? Or— Rick fell down again. Everything in him wanted to get up and go over there and kill Joe. But he knew that he no longer had the strength or the opportunity. Maybe, with a few more minutes alone with Joe— But it was too late now. Nothing to do but run away. He would get his family the hell away. No doubt someone would call the cops or an ambulance. Rick didn't want to be anywhere near when they showed up, so he struggled to his feet again, and holding his throbbing jaw, started back to his car.

For an instant, Rick considered getting his pistol from the glove compartment and doing a suburban version of the drive-by shooting. But the chance of being stopped by a cop who'd been summoned by the neighbors was too great.

He reached his car and drove out of Franklin Park. For a moment, he thought about going back to Billy the Kid's house to burn down the damned garage as he had planned. And it would be okay with Rick if Billy was in it. But then he thought of Margot and Katherine, and of how he had been given this one last chance. He pushed down the accelerator harder.

Rick sped through the night to his family. He couldn't stand any more loss, he knew that. If he couldn't have this one simple thing, just a normal family like everyone else had, then he didn't want anything. And if he couldn't have his family, there was no way he'd hand them over to Joe. The bastard had stolen too much from Rick already, he figured.

As he crossed the Allegheny River, Rick decided that his jaw was not broken. But he rolled down his window and spat yet another tooth toward the river's dark water.

38...

"HEY, I'M SORRY, man. I swear I didn't see anyone. Geez, if I'd only seen you. God, I'm sorry. Mr. Anderson's gonna kill me. Unless my dad gets to me first."

"Wait. Never mind. You didn't hit me," said Joe. "I was—"

"Yes I did. I wish I hadn't of. But I did." The kid stopped and swallowed hard. "I hit you all right. You're all bloody. I gotta get you to a hospital. Geez, I'm sorry." The kid stood up and began tugging at Joseph's shirt in an attempt to help him stand up. The shirt was already torn, and the sleeve came off in the boy's hand. If Joseph's face hadn't hurt so much, he would have been tempted to laugh at the look on the young boy's face. A startled scream escaped the boy's lips and he tumbled backward, off-balance against the side of the truck. It was apparent the kid thought he'd torn Joe's arm off.

Joe sat up. The effort caused him pain and the world spun sideways for an instant, but he no longer felt like he would die at any second.

"Hey. Down here." Joe waved both hands in the air. The kid saw two attached hands, two intact arms. He sat down on the night-dewed grass next to Joe.

"I thought—well shit, never mind what I thought."

This time Joe did laugh. Loud and long. The boy joined him. It felt good. Like the way you feel when you put off going to the doctor, and you finally can't stand it anymore, and he gives you a shot, and you actually feel the pain disappearing. But not so good was the sleepiness that overtook Joe suddenly. Idly, he wondered if he might have a concussion.

He concentrated on staying conscious. Two new feet appeared in Joe's line of vision, and he heard an indistinct voice.

"—for Ashers or not. It's been twenty-nine minutes since I phoned and your— Oh my God! What happened to you?"

Joe reached up to rub some dirt from his eye and was surprised to see fresh wet blood on his fist. Something told him that if he didn't think of something fast, one of these guys—either the pizza kid or the impatient neighbor Asher— was going to phone nine-one-one. Because he had just finished his first-ever episode of breaking and entering, nine-one-one was not what Joe wanted. His head was fuzzy. Maybe he could use that to his advantage.

"Look, the boy didn't hit me. I—" Joe struggled to stand. The other two helped him up, and he stepped clumsily off the curb to lean against the truck. It felt warm and smelled of pizza spices.

"I have to admit I been drinking a little."

Neighbor Asher smiled an indulgent smile. But then he said, "I think I better give nine-one-one a call, buddy."

"No, no. No need. The thing I don't wanna admit, you see—not to you guys, you unnerstand, but to my wife—the thing I don't wanna admit is I got in a fight."

Joe made no special effort to slur his words. He was aware that his speech sounded garbled, but that fit his story just fine. "She won't dump me over the drinking. She likes a few herself. But the fighting. Don't know why, but that really pisses her off."

Joe paused, then delivered a zinger—an inspiration of the moment. "It 'specially pisses her off when I been fighting with some other gal's husband."

Asher broke into a loud roar of laughter. The pizza boy glanced at him, then giggled nervously.

"Whatever," said Joe, waving his arm in front of him. The movement almost knocked him back to the ground. "If you guys could give me a hand to get back to my car, I'd 'preciate it. S'not far—around the corner.''

Asher reached into his pocket and pulled out some bills. He handed the boy the money. "Tell you what. You give me my pizzas, then help this guy to his car, okay? I'm sorry as hell for you, buddy, but I got a wife, too. And the thing that pisses *her* off is cold pizza."

Joe nodded. Something about seeing the money seemed to get the kid back to normal. In a flash, he was unzipping the insulated pouch and pulling out three cardboard boxes that gave off warm wet steam. Money was exchanged: Asher took off for his house; and the kid grabbed Joe awkwardly around his chest and propelled him forward.

"Whoa, not so fast. Just make sure I don't tilt too far in any one direction and I'll be fine," said Joe.

"You sure I didn't hit you?" The relief was finally starting to set in. "I mean I didn't feel a bump or anything. I think I would of felt something, don't you? I mean if you hit something, you oughta feel a bump or something?"

They were almost to his car, and Joe was feeling marginally better. "I think I can make it on my own now. Sorry I gave you a scare. Thanks."

"That's all right. Really. I mean I thought my life was over. I'm just glad I didn't hit you. I didn't think I did, ya know?"

To Joe's great relief, they had arrived at his car. The kid opened the door and guided him into the driver's seat. His hand lay gently on Joe's arm, and for a second Joe was truly sorry he had put the boy through such trauma.

"You sure you can drive okay? I mean being dr— I mean, with your head banged up and all?"

"I'm fine. Thanks. And I don't live far."

The kid ran away then like a rabbit that has just wiggled loose from a trap and truly knows how lucky it has been.

Joe reached under the seat and pulled out a box of tissues. He grabbed a wad and mopped his face. The gash at his temple was still oozing bright-red blood. The rest of his face felt sticky and tacky. A quick look in the rearview mirror told Joe that he couldn't drive around in public with that face.

He tried to spit on the tissues, but his mouth was dry. Then he remembered the can of Coke he always carried in the car in case Katy got thirsty while they were on an outing. The thought of his daughter made Joe shake all over. Every once in a while things got so messed up and confused, he lost track of what the hell he was after. He was glad his mind allowed him to go away from it for a few minutes occasionally. Otherwise he would go crazy.

Again, he reached under the seat and fished around. He pulled out an ice scraper, a stuffed penguin and then finally two cans of Coke, still connected by the plastic umbilical cord they'd started out in.

He pulled one can free and popped the tab. Joe drank down half of the fizzy, warm drink, then he poured some on his clump of Kleenex. It hurt, but he mopped away most of the drying blood from his face. Now I can drive around without looking like something from a teenage horror movie, he thought.

Drive where, he wondered. Where had he been headed? Oh yes, to Beth's with the information on where Margot and Katy might be. He burrowed around in his pants pocket until he found the ignition key. He started the car and pulled out.

That's right, he congratulated himself. He figured he was pretty clear-headed considering the beating he had taken.

Suddenly Joe realized why he had found it so hard to bash the hell out of the guy's face. Because it looked so much like Katy's face! But her sweet face all twisted with rage and hatred and fear. Her sweet face ravaged by some malignance that ruined the beauty of the features Joe remembered.

His thoughts were flying all over as Joe drove. He didn't know if it was the fact that all at once he knew they were close to finding Margot and Katy, or if it was the head injury.

Somehow, Joe managed to make the drive to Beth's apartment safely. He climbed the stairs and knocked.

When Beth opened the door, her eyes widened, and she hollered, "Dennis, come here."

She led Joe to the sofa, where he sat down, waiting for the room to stop spinning.

"Honey, get an ice bag," Beth said to her son.

A short time later, Joe felt the shock of something cold on his forehead.

"I got good news," Joe said.

"You better rest for a minute," said Beth.

"No time. I found out—"

"Dennis, get me a bowl of hot water and some paper towels, please."

They weren't listening. For a second, Joe wondered if he was talking. Joe knew he was hurt. Maybe he just *thought* he was talking.

So he yelled. "I know who has them!" he shouted.

"What?"

"I know who has them. It's Katy's biological father. We were right. The bastard— I saw him tonight."

"Where?"

"Never mind. No time to waste." Joe threw the ice bag on the coffee table and stood up. "He's crazy. I could see it. And I think I know where he has them. I gotta go."

Joe headed for the door.

Beth put her hand on his shoulder, and Joe found that he was so weak, he couldn't push it off.

"No way," said Beth. "You're hurt. I'll call the police, then an ambulance for you."

Joe turned, fighting the dizziness. "Beth. Listen to me. The police will take too long. And they'll probably be more interested in the fact that I just broke into someone's house. Beth, this Grader knows I know now. I'm positive that Margot and Katy are okay at the moment. But there's no telling what he'll do next. He's crazy, Beth. I could see it in his eyes."

"But—"

"No buts. I'm going."

"Then so am I. I'll drive." She looked over her shoulder at Dennis. "Watch your brother, honey. Tell your dad where we've gone when he gets home."

"Where *are* you going?" Dennis asked.

"No time," replied Joe and pulled open the door.

"Luck," said Beth's son.

39...

     MARGOT AND KATHERINE had spent the day doing "kindergarten things," as Katherine called them. Margot had helped her to make a felt giraffe puppet, and they had learned two new songs together. Margot's incompetence at reading music notes, coupled with her tone-deaf singing, had led to a half hour of giggling and silly music.

    After many hours had gone by, Margot began to wonder, as she did each time that Rick locked her in the bomb shelter, if he might not come back this time.

    But he did return. Margot heard the door opening, and she and Katherine looked up. Light from the overhead fixture in the shelter illuminated his face, and both Margot and Katherine gasped.

    "What happened to your face?" cried Katherine, running over to him and peering up at his battered features.

    "It's nothing. I tripped and fell. But never mind that. You—"

    "But it looks like a bad hurt. Do you want me to put a Band-Aid on it for you?"

    "No. Thanks. I want you and your mother to come upstairs and pack your clothes as quickly as possible."

    "Why?" asked Margot and Katherine in one voice.

    "We're going to take a trip," replied Rick.

    "Are we going home?" asked Katherine. She seemed excited by the prospect. "Goody. I want to go home. Mama, we're going home."

    As Katherine prattled on, Rick pushed her toward the stairs, then stood back so Margot could follow.

Katherine ran off to her room, her face the happiest Margot had seen it in a long time.

Margot turned to Rick, who was busy rummaging in a cabinet. "Where are we going?" she asked.

He turned to her, and his frown was made more frightening by the red cuts and the swelling of a darkening bruise on his jaw. Margot guessed that his mouth was damaged on the inside, because when he talked, pain showed in his eyes.

"Look. I'll tell you later. There's no time to talk now. If you don't pack and get ready in ten minutes, I'll go without you." He sneered at Margot, misunderstanding the panic on her face. "Oh, don't worry, I'll take off your 'bracelet.' But I'll take Katherine, and leave you here in the shelter."

Margot saw him turn away and begin pulling things out of the storage cabinet that he had unlocked. In a sturdy briefcase, he placed two pistols and various items that Margot remembered seeing when Rick had rigged up his deadly beach ball demonstration.

His whole body shook. Even without seeing his eyes again, she knew that he had gone over the brink. He was completely insane now. And this monster wanted to take Margot and Katherine in his car and drive into the night?

All at once, Margot knew that the chance she was waiting for would never come. No matter how patient and clever and manipulative she was, there would never be a moment when she could safely get Katherine out of this situation. But the danger of going with a madman and his arsenal into the night was greater than the risk of taking a stand. In fact, during the long days since Rick had brought her here, she had been testing various items to decide which had the best handle, the most weight, the most usefulness as a weapon.

Now, as Rick, with cautious movements, packed away the plastic explosives, Margot turned and picked up the tall, heavy sculpture of the mother and child that sat on an end table. She swung it, aiming at the base of Rick's head.

She screamed when it hit, but didn't realize at first what had happened. She had swung so hard. How could Rick be grabbing her with so much strength? Was he superhuman? Then she saw that she had only grazed his ear. The lobe was bright red, but Rick was not fazed. Rick must have heard her, or sensed her movement. The impact Margot had felt must have been from the statue smashing into the wooden cabinet door.

Rick looked at her for a moment, then he slammed his fist into her face. It hit like a steel hammer.

Margot staggered and fell backward, banging her left hip against the coffee table. The pain in her face fought for attention with the pain in her hip. Things got hazy for a time, then Margot opened her eyes.

"Mama, Mama. What happened? Whatsamatter? Mama!"

"I'm all right, Katy. I just fell. You go and finish packing." Her daughter stood still. "Go on now. Go pack!"

The harsh tone brought tears to Katy's eyes, but Margot saw with relief that she was leaving the room.

With a huge effort, Margot managed to stand. "Please," she said to Rick. "Please let Katy go. She's so little. She doesn't understand any of this. But you must see that it's hurting her. You're not her family. She has a mother and father and grandparents who love her. You're not her family. You can make your own family. But please let her go. Please."

"Oh," he said, his tone casual all of a sudden. "I forgot to tell you. I heard some news about Katherine's grandfather on the radio a little while ago. Maybe I'm not her family, but she doesn't have a grandfather any more, either."

"My father? Daddy is—"

"Dead. Yes, your daddy is dead, Sonya."

Margot fought the new pain—the one far greater than the pain in her face and hip. And Rick had just called her "Sonya."

"Katherine," Rick bellowed. "Out here in one minute!"

In far less than that, Katy appeared, her eyes wide. Margot looked at her daughter and knew she had no time to think about anything but getting away.

Rick opened the front door and grabbed Margot's arm. He pushed her out the door, put the briefcase under one arm, then pulled Katherine out with him.

"Don't push," said Katy. "You don't have to push."

But he did just that. Rick shoved Margot, apparently trying to hurry her down the stairs. But the injury to her hip caused her to stumble, and she crashed down the stairs instead.

"Mama!" shouted Katy. "Why did you do that," the little girl cried to Rick as she hurried down and knelt by Margot's side.

Rick set down his briefcase and grabbed Katy under one arm. He had just opened the car door and was trying to force a struggling Katy inside when a shout came from the woods.

"Put her down!" Margot knew the voice—it was Joe, her own Joe. She looked up and tried to see where he was, but everything was dark trees and sky.

Rick released Katy and turned his attention to his briefcase. Apparently Katy saw where Joe was, because with a cry of relief, joy and fear she headed at a run down the hill.

"Daddy," she screamed. "Daddy, you came. Daddy, Daddy."

Like a spectator at a tennis match, Margot lay on the ground, her head going back and forth between Rick and Katy—between Rick as he fumbled among the items in his briefcase for the gun and Katy as she ran as fast as she could toward the trees.

Suddenly it occurred to Margot that Katy was completely exposed as she ran on the driveway. Rick might shoot Katy! Margot pushed herself up, using the strength in her arms to compensate for the weakness in her side. Focusing on his bruised jaw, she lunged for Rick as he raised the gun.

40...

    JOE AND BETH had been watching the brightly
lit house for only a few minutes when they heard a
commotion and saw a man, Grader no doubt, herding
Margot and Katy out the door. When they saw Margot fall
and Katy start to run, calling, "Daddy, Daddy," Joe and
Beth bolted toward the trio by the house.
    Joe raced up the drive, toward Katy. The porch light was
bright enough that Joe could see shapes, but not details.
When he saw the shape of a gun in Grader's hand, Joe
shouted, "Down, Katy. Get down."
    But she kept running, screaming, "Daddy, Daddy!"
    A shot split the air just as Joe reached Katy. He threw her
to the ground and covered her with his body. Joe felt a
white-hot pain slice across the side of his calf. He looked up
the hill and saw Margot lunging toward Grader. She must
have caught him by surprise because he dropped the
gun—and suddenly Margot was pointing it at Grader. When
Rick tried to grab it back from Margot, she fired, but at the
same moment, for no apparent reason, she staggered,
dancing awkwardly to keep from falling. Then Rick dodged
to the side, in front of the car. Margot fired again, but the
bullet hit metal, judging from the sound.
    It all happened in a second or two. Then Joe scooped
Katy up in his arms and ran limping toward Margot. At the
same time, Margot turned and hurried toward Joe and Katy.
His heart was pounding with fear and relief for these two
people he loved. He set Katy down and held out his arms to
Margot. But to his amazement, she picked Katy up in her
arms and ran off in the direction that Grader had fled.

"No," yelled Beth, who stood gasping near Joe. She took off after them, and so did Joe. "Margot, it's us, Joe and Beth. Don't be afraid, we'll help you."

"Help me," cried Margot as she moved through the dark woods.

"Wait. Don't run," yelled Joe. "You're safe now. We'll catch him later. The police will. Margot."

Joe ran after Margot, gritting his teeth and trying to ignore the pain in his leg. It was dark, but his eyes had adjusted enough to see that Margot had set Katy on her feet and was dragging her along a path. It was a fairly straight path, and Joe and Beth followed.

"Please, Rick," called Margot in the night. "Don't. Don't do it."

It made no sense to Joe. He couldn't seem to catch up with Margot and Katy. Tree roots tripped him, and branches slashed at his eyes. One branch grazed his eyeball. He was aware of an electric bolt of pain searing through the side of his head, and his vision became watery, but Joe continued.

Suddenly, ahead of them, he saw a clearing. Compared with the darkness of the trees, the clearing seemed bright. He saw Grader and Margot struggling. Joe could see that they were near the edge of a cliff, or perhaps an embankment of some kind. There was no telling how much danger it added to the fight. Just as Joe got close to them, Margot and Grader fell down. As they fell, Margot put her knee up and Grader landed on it with his chest. Joe plunged into the melee and tried to pull Katy away so that he could get at Grader. Katy was hitting Grader on the arm with a stick. Grader was reaching for Katy.

Joe felt himself growing weaker. He was aware that Beth was rushing over with a stick much larger than Katy's. Joe realized that Grader's fall must have knocked the breath out of him, because he lay in a heap on the ground.

Joe heard Margot shouting, "You son of a bitch. Damn you." As she pushed at his body, Grader finally managed to grab hold of Katy's arm. Just then, Beth joined Margot, jabbing at Grader with her log. Suddenly, Grader's body tilted, then disappeared over the edge of an embankment. He found a handhold, but looked as if he couldn't maintain it for long. But Joe saw that he still had Katy's wrist in his grasp. Joe shook his head and crawled forward. With all his strength, he slammed his fist against the muscle in Grader's forearm. Everything stopped for a second, then Grader let go. He fell, screaming, down into a dark chasm.

It must be a river, thought Joe. Suddenly the dark chasm filled with an explosion. Light and a stomach punch of noise shook Joe out of his near-stupor.

"Mama," sobbed Katy in her mother's arms. Margot held Katy, then reached out to Joe. He joined the embrace, as did Beth. All four of them cried, hugging each other on the grass in the dark. No one spoke, except Katy, who continued to say "Mama" and "Daddy" over and over.

41...

"BUT I DON'T understand why Rick's wristband exploded and not ours," Margot said. "And why didn't he just have a transmitter in his? Surely he didn't intend to blow himself up."

"But that's exactly what he *did* intend to do," said Captain Lewis.

Margot sipped at her coffee. She was grateful that no one else was in the hospital lounge at the moment. It felt so bizarre to sit in the sunny room down the corridor from Joe's room discussing things like explosives and the motivations of a crazy man. Margot knew that it would take time, and probably some counseling, for her and Katy to overcome the mental trauma of their imprisonment. But Joe was recovering from the bullet wound in his leg and the damage done to his eye. He had just been told that morning by the doctor that he would probably be able to see normally when the injury healed. "But I can see *better* than I ever saw before," he had told Margot after the doctor left. "You and Katy—what you mean to me."

It was apparent to Margot that Joe wanted them to have a future together. But she had already decided not to decide anything of import for the time being. Even so, Margot *had* decided to take her daughter during the week left before Katy started kindergarten and go on a quiet, low-key vacation. She and Katy had already spent a happy hour discussing the possible destinations. The one thing they agreed on was that they would go someplace far away from the woods, perhaps to the seashore.

Margot became aware that the captain was explaining

something about Rick. She hadn't been paying attention. Margot knew that she had quickly taken on the habit of shutting out anything to do with Richard Grader. "I'm sorry, Captain. You were saying."

"This is what we've been able to figure out by talking with Grader. He's not too coherent—the doctors still don't know if he's gonna make it. Falling on top of that wristband like he did—the internal injuries alone are severe, not to mention the loss of his hand." Captain Lewis paused and rubbed at his eyes. "Sorry. I'm getting off the subject here. When this Grader saw your husband coming out of his house in Franklin Park, he knew his secret was out. Apparently he didn't want to live if he couldn't have his perfect little family. And he didn't want his perfect little family to live either. What a bastard! Sorry, ma'am."

"That's all right, Captain. He *was* something of a bastard."

The captain laughed, then went on. "Apparently he came back and put on one of those bands himself."

"But why didn't Katy's wristband explode? And mine? He said that they were all rigged to go off at once if any one person got more than three hundred feet away from another. I had suspected he was bluffing or—"

"No, ma'am. He wasn't bluffing. Before he panicked there near the end, he had the bands rigged right. The demolition guys checked them out after they got them off you and your little girl. They said this Grader did a brilliant job. Their words—a 'brilliant job.' I don't mean to scare you, Mrs. DesMarais, but those cuffs would've done some serious harm to you and Katy if they went off. You did the right thing to treat them with respect. But yours didn't go off because when he put the explosives in his own wristband in a big hurry, he goofed. He missed putting back one of the parts—they found it on the floor in the house you were in. That missing part disabled the whole system. His band only exploded because he fell on it with his full body weight. He landed on stones down in the riverbed."

"So you're saying—" Margot stopped as Katy came running into the lounge.

"Hi, baby. Were you visiting Daddy?" asked Margot.

"Uh huh. And then Grandma took me down to Grandpa's room again. He's *still* hungry. Mama, he's just like me, hungry all the time."

Margot laughed and pulled Katy onto her lap. "Remember what I always tell you when you've been sick? When you start feeling hungry again, it's a sign that you're getting better." Margot closed her eyes against the tears. Every time she thought about the lie Rick had told her—that her father had died—

"Too tight, Mama. You're hugging too tight," complained Katy.

"Sorry, Katy. I'm just so happy I get carried away sometimes."

"Me, too," said Katy and squeezed her mother until Margot begged for mercy.

"Katherine Diana DesMarais," said Margot in a stern voice.

"Uh oh," said Katy. "What did I do?"

"I just love you," said Margot.

"And I love you, too, Margot Newhouse DesMarais."

Epilogue...

HIS HANDWRITING WAS still clumsy, the letters large and wobbly. But Richard Grader no longer had to use his whole concentration to form letters using his left hand. Although his right hand was gone, sometimes he could feel the missing fingers. Now, the prison warden kept him in a safe cell, where he couldn't hurt himself. In fact, he was only allowed to use soft crayons, no pens or pencils.

He persisted in his chosen task. The prison shrink had tried to get him interested in the occupational therapy programs, but Rick always gave him the same answer: "When I'm finished."

He was in the thousands now. He would do a count at the end of the day and make a note on his calendar. He wrote:

> One in a million.
> One in a million.
> One in a million.
> One in a million.

Rick had lots of time. Years of prison ahead to finish his task. He would write it one million times, then pack up the pages and send them to the doctor. The one who had told him, "Your chances of fathering another baby are one in a million."

Rick had stopped wasting time wishing that Margot had let him die—wishing that she hadn't stopped his bleeding following the explosion. And he had worked especially hard to stop wasting time wishing that they hadn't told him what they discovered at the autopsy—that Sonya had been pregnant with his child. Very early pregnancy, but pregnant nevertheless. It was only after they told him about Sonya that Rick began to read all the stories about how many people go and adopt a baby and then get pregnant. Didn't doctors realize what harm they were causing when they said things so casually? "One in a million," they had said, not caring how much harm they did. Rick figured the doctors—those quacks who had ruined his life—were the ones who should be in jail.

He shook his head, and went back to his writing.

One in a million.
One in a million. . . .